Destines

The Ark of Power

Destines

The Ark of Power

David Barco

David Barco/Yarborough Press
215 W First St
Van Wert, Ohio/45891

https://www.facebook.com/AuthorDavidBarco

Publisher's Note: This is a work of fiction. Names, characters, places, and incidents are a product of the author's imagination. Locales and public names are sometimes used for atmospheric purposes. Any resemblance to actual people, living or dead, or to businesses, companies, events, institutions, or locales is completely coincidental.

Book design © 2017 BookDesignTemplates.com

Ordering Information: Special discounts are available on quantity purchases by corporations, associations, and others. For details, contact the publisher at the address above.

Destines: The Ark of Power — First Edition

ISBN: 9781072357193

Printed in the United States of America

To my mom, who believed in Harrison's mission since the beginning!

Contents

CHAPTER
1

Tears In The Night

The shower's steam thickens the air while the walls appear as if they are weeping from the heat. Douglas Grady enjoys his showers like this. Stepping right underneath the shower head letting the water massage his aching muscles, it runs right through his short brown hair, dripping off his beard like teardrops. Squinting tightly, blocking his brown eyes from the water, he hears tiny feet hurrying down the hallway. The strong bangs on the door demand his attention.

"Daddy...Daddy!" the excited voice screams through the door.

Douglas slowly opens his eyes, grinning, as he hears his new favorite title squealing continually.

"Harrison, daddy will be there in a second. Go get mommy, and I will be right there."

He could hear the peppy two-year-old scamper down the hallway.

"Mommy...Mommy."

Stepping out of the shower, Douglas grabs his towel and begins to dry his lean biceps off. He put his black shorts on first, pulling his gray shirt over his head that says *Destine Academy Alumni.*

"BABE!" his eyes open instantly, as the voice captures his attention. The sadness in Francis' voice motions him quickly out of the bathroom.

Walking into the living room, blind by the towel covering his eyes as he finishes drying his hair, he hears Harrison unleashing his two-year-old vigorous energy. Uncovering his eyes, he sees Francis sitting on the end of the leather ottoman. Harrison climbs on top of her, pulling himself up by her long mustard blonde hair that travels down to her upper back.

Tears run down her cheeks. Douglas picks Harrison up with one arm. Harrison giggles from the bottom of his belly with batty kicks assaulting the air. Flipping him around, Douglas smiles at Francis.

"It's someone's bedtime," Douglas announces loudly.

Walking down the hallway into the room, he could hear Francis from the kitchen. Douglas cuts the light off and places Harrison in his crib. Springing up, Harrison stands straight up. "Daddy! Power light!"

"How could I forget!" he playfully says back to him.

2

Approaching the crib, Harrison claps with excitement. Douglas lifts his right hand up, fingers relaxed, spread, with his palm facing the ceiling. Tightening his hand slightly, a yellow glow covers his hand. Quickly, he closes his hand and opens it immediately.

Hovering two inches over his right hand is a yellow energy ball the size of a tennis ball. It lights up the whole room, making everything have a yellow radiance. Harrison claps even stronger. Douglas smiles and grabs the yellow energy ball, turning his hand upside down. Darkness invades the room where the light was.

Harrison drops back down into the crib. About to leave, Douglas stops halfway, watching him turning from side to side.

"I love you son."

As he steps into the hallway, Francis is standing there. Frowning, she hands him a note.

"This was just slid underneath the door when you were in the shower."

He stares at the note:

Captain Grady,

The mission is rescheduled to start early. You must leave immediately! No talking to anyone until you arrive at the meeting point. Not even your family!

Sincerely,

Jovan Dirk,

Destine Elder

As Douglas looks down at his wife, he notices the sadness painted all over her face. Leaning against the wall, she gazes up at him.

"I read it. I know I wasn't supposed to, but deep down I knew what it said, I just had to make sure. I packed your bag when you were in the shower. It's by the front door."

Seeing the disappointment on her face, he leans and kisses her forehead. He walks towards the door, grabs his bag, and opens it. Turning back, he stares at Francis still leaning on the wall.

"I love you," she says.

Slowly closing the door, he hears from Harrison's room, "Daddy!"

Squinting, he feels heavy tears rush down, drenching his face. Douglas walks out and closes the front door behind him.

CHAPTER
2

The Silent Mission

13 years later

Glaring up at the ceiling, Harrison does not feel like getting out of the bed. Sitting up, he rubs his face trying to wake himself up. Constantly rubbing his eyes, the repeated motion makes his blue eyes as bright as the sky by all the tears piling up. He grabs the plastic water bottle on his nightstand, gazing at the family picture from when he was two years old.

He sits on his dad's lap in the picture. His toothless smile in the picture saddens him. Picking up the picture, he turns it upside down. Taking a couple of sips of water, he twists the lid on and flings it on the floor. As he begins to run his fingers through his dusky blonde hair, parting it to his right side, he hears his mom walking past his room.

"Do most 15-year-olds take this long to get up? Today is an important day for us and for you!" his mom walks down the hallway. "So, get up. Your friend, JT, will be here in a little bit. Remember?"

"Oh yeah, I forgot," Harrison responds back, stretching his lean arms in the air.

"What do you mean you forgot? You couldn't forget. How could you forget that today is the day when you find out if you and your friends made it in the Destine Academy? Get up and meet me in the kitchen," she says.

Harrison scoots to the side of his bed, dangling his scrawny legs over it.

Yeah, how could I forget this day?

Walking past the TV on his way to the kitchen, Harrison hears the news reporter speaking. He sits down on the old and worn leather couch and starts watching and listening to the female reporter on TV.

"Today makes, and I truly can't believe it, thirteen years since the mysterious vanishing of the Silver Falcons. Led by Captain Grady, the Silver Falcons left on what we all now refer to as the Silent Mission. Most believe that this elite task force made up of four of our finest Destine warriors died on that mission. A small remnant believes they are just missing or were captured by enemy forces. The Destine Elder of our great Destine nation has decreed that the mission was a high rank classified mission that cannot be discussed by anyone. He sends his regards to the four families affected."

Harrison snatches the remote and cuts off the TV.

Sends his regards. You're the Elder and that's all you can give us?

He goes into the kitchen and meets his mom. She is sitting, slowly sipping her hot coffee. Flipping through the Destine nation newspaper, *The Destine Chronicle,* Harrison spots the front page;

Remembering the Silver Falcons.

Underneath, a massive picture of his dad with the other three men behind him covers the entire front page of *The Destine Chronicle.* Stuck in a daze viewing the picture, the hammering on the front door snaps him quickly out of it.

KNOCK! KNOCK! KNOCK!

"Must be JT," his mother says, still reading, and sipping her coffee. "But he usually doesn't knock like that. He must be excited about today."

Suddenly, Harrison catches a glimpse of a slender figure, dashing past the kitchen window with his moppy, straw-colored hair bouncing in unison with each quick stride.

"OPEN THE BACK DOOR! THESE EVIL THINGS ARE CRAZY!" the slender figure screams.

Harrison rushes to the door, instantly. He hurries unlocking it. As soon as he is turning the lock, the door blasts open. Harrison falls swiftly on his back. He stares into JT's light brown eyes that were just slightly darker than honey.

7

"JT, what in the world were you running from?" Francis asks with concern.

At once, two tiny pearl white colored Chihuahuas press their paws against the screen door, growling softly as if they are trying to catch their breath.

"Momma, those things are the definition of evil itself," JT climbs off Harrison and slams the door with disgust. "For years, they chase all the kids in the neighborhood. They live in that house at the bottom of the hill. Their owners must not like kids since their number one mission in life is to devour all the kids that live here."

Still laying on the kitchen floor, he watches intently as JT walks to the cabinet without helping him up. He takes out a bowl, grabs a box of blueberry oats cereal and sits down next to Francis.

"You bust through the door like a lunatic, tackle me, and you can't even help me up? Cereal is really that important to you?" Harrison asks as he stands up, joining them at the table.

"We have been friends since we were seven," JT pours his milk into the bowl of cereal. "You should know by now that cereal pretty much comes number one in my life."

Francis laughs as she puts her cup on the table, placing the paper next to it. "Today is the day you boys find out if you made the Academy. I am just as nervous as I was for Douglas when he was waiting for his acceptance letter from the Academy."

Harrison and JT listen, steadily crunching away at their cereal.

"Letters are dropped off this evening. Did your family plan anything special for it?" Francis asks JT.

Wiping the milk off his chin, JT smiles.

"Actually, I came over this morning because my parents wanted me to ask if Harrison and you wanted to come to my parent's antique shop. They are going to close it and have a watching party for the delivery. If we get accepted, we will continue the party. If we don't, well, I guess we will just cry and continue to eat all the food."

Harrison and his mom shake their heads and giggle.

"What you want to do Harrison? It's your big day. You want to go over there?" Francis asks.

"Yeah, if my friends are going to be there, I will go," he says, slurping the milk out of the bowl.

"Great. I will contact your uncle Adam this morning and let him know to let the delivery person bring it there. He just started working at the Academy this year, so he should be able to do that. He can at least help his sister out like that, right?" Francis says smirking at Harrison as she still drinks her coffee.

"Yeah, I guess," Harrison says.

"Well, thanks for the cereal and for saving me from those wretched beasts that are probably devouring a five-year-old right now, but I got to go help my parents get the shop ready for this evening," JT announces.

"I'll walk you outside to make sure you don't die," Harrison says playfully.

"Bye, momma. I will see you tonight at the shop," JT says.

"Thanks, sweetie, see you then," Francis responds.

Harrison slowly closes the door behind him.

Walking side by side with JT, they stand in the middle of the street as if they own it. His house sits on top of the hill, towering above all the other houses on his street.

"You a little nervous?" JT asks.

"I'm not nervous about tonight and finding out if I get in. I guess I'm just a little nervous about when I actually start there and the whole process," Harrison answers.

"Yeah, I'm sure all the classes for the next four years are going to be tough. But to be an elite warrior of the Destine nation what else would you expect, right?" JT says.

"I'm not as worried about that," Harrison says noticing the interested look on JT's face.

"What else would you be worried about?" JT curiously asks him.

"Well, I am sure you heard that this year, Jovan Dirk, the Destine Elder, is overseeing the Academy. He has brought in some of his officials and people close to him to work there in various spots."

"Yeah, my parents were telling me about that, but what is the big deal?" JT asks, eager to know.

"You can't tell anyone, but when I am there, I will be able to get close to all the people that know about that night my dad went on that mission. I'm going to find out some answers and find out what really happened to him and his team. They're hiding something and I'm going to find out."

"You know how crazy that sounds! That will be about impossible. You are telling me that you are going to the Academy, hoping to find some intel from the people that made the Destine nation vow to silence?" JT asks, slightly laughing at the thought.

Harrison laughs gently under his breath.

"Yeah, but this is my only chance to see what truly happened to my dad. I just know they are hiding something, and I will find out. Whatever it takes."

"I understand, brother. I'm here to help any way I can. Let's just hope we get in," JT responds, putting his hand out, signaling their handshake.

Harrison brings his hand to JT's. He slaps it twice; fist bumps and pretends their hands explode.

Harrison, turning towards his house, hears JT sprint away.

It's time for my silent mission now!

CHAPTER 3

A Mysterious Compass

Stepping through the front door, the dense and muggy air sticks tightly to Harrison's skin as if it was trying to suffocate him. The burnt orange sun sliding down in the sky behind the clouds wasn't taking the heat with it.

Walking to the car, he sees Gavin, an eleven-year old that has been his neighbor since he could remember. Gavin, soaking from sweat, strolls over to Harrison in his driveway, panting like an old dog. His abnormal, thick shadowy brown hair, usually waterproof and immovable, is dripping sweat from his bangs and dangling right above his olive-green eyes, which are at the same level as Harrison's chest.

"Dang, the way you look, it looks like you been outside here for hours. What could you possibly be doing in this heat?" Harrison asks.

"My parents are being lame. I was practicing my forms for our mixed martial arts class for school, and they told me to take that mess outside. They don't understand since they never went to the Academy that I have to take these martial arts classes for the next three years so I can even try to get into the Academy. These classes are a prerequisite and I am struggling in the intro class," Gavin replies.

Harrison chuckles and opens the passenger door of the car. His mom comes rushing to the car, anxiously looking for her keys in her oversized purse.

"You will get it, don't worry," Harrison sits down. "You are only eleven years old and just in the first class. It gets easier, believe me."

"Great! Coming from the one who passed all those classes with straight A's. It must not come as natural to me as it does you. You'll probably go to the Academy and totally impress the instructor who teaches the Power Flow classes. It's not fair. I just wish I was as good as you!" Gavin says.

Shutting the door as his mom cranks the car, Harrison rolls the window down.

Francis smiles at Gavin and lays her hand on Harrison's shoulder. "It won't be a walk in the park. His dad was the only one in the history of the Academy to finish with a 5.0 GPA. No one has ever got higher than 3.9. But if anybody can do it, why not his son?"

Harrison, feeling uncomfortable, tries to make the situation not feel as awkward, gazing steadily at the messy floorboard.

"Tell your parents I said hello and tell your mom we need to do lunch sometime. Have a great evening sweetie," Francis says cheerfully.

"Yes, ma'am," Gavin replies.

Harrison fastens his seat belt as the car pulls out the driveway. He notices Gavin jogging slowly back to his yard, waving to be seen.

"*GOOD LUCK HARRISON!*" Gavin shouts as they drive away.

Peering into the rearview mirror, Harrison sees Gavin shrink in size still waving till he disappears entirely.

Whenever I get down, I need to believe in myself as he does.

Harrison watches people stroll into the shop. Looking up, he spots the sign above the building. *Hall-way of Antiques* lights up the dark sky creeping around it. The letters are all a different color. Harrison remembers JT's dad changing the *q* the other day. Being too cheap to buy new lights, he uses lights people leave at the shop when one of the bulbs quit working.

Harrison steps inside. His nostrils are attacked by the smell of overcooked burgers and stale chips. The normal dusty smell he remembers lingers faintly. The shop looks the same as always, except he has never seen these many people here at once. The walls are cluttered with ancient paintings and giant clocks.

Tables scatter all around with different odd-looking antiques covering them. Harrison, feeling someone grab his shoulder suddenly, turns and sees JT and his other close friends Jaylen and Joseph. Jaylen stuffs his mouth with an overcooked burger. Joseph crams a giant handful of chips into his mouth.

"About time you got here," Jaylen says with pieces of burger shooting out of his mouth.

"Yeah, my mom took a while to get ready, but what's new?" Harrison replies, trying to avoid flying burger pieces.

"What's new is seeing you all dressed up! You finally stepped your game up with this outfit. You might actually get a girl to recognize you now," Joseph says, laughing and wiping the crumbs off his lips.

"Now, hold up! We all know that Victoria Grant is crazy over our guy right here. She has been for the last couple of years in school, and she is supposed to be here tonight. And with you dressed like this, it's going to make her go insane!" JT says.

They all laugh.

"Yeah, yeah laugh it up. We are just friends; she doesn't like me like that. Everyone just likes to mess with me about that," Harrison replies.

Harrison mingles with his group of friends while occasionally talking to other classmates. While he pours some red crème soda into his plastic cup, someone places their hand on his neck. He turns around and sees JT's dad, Braxton Hall, who is the owner of the shop. Even he is dressed nicer than normal, Harrison notices. His peppered colored hair combed but still not styled like usual. His beard, the same color as his hair, is neatly trimmed close to his face.

"Harrison, my boy, how are you doing?" Mr. Hall asks him.

"I am doing well, Mr. Hall. Thank you for inviting me and my mom to your party. It looks like she is enjoying herself," Harrison responds.

"You know you would be the first people we would ask. To be honest, I am just glad your mom decided to come knowing what today is. I was a little worried you wouldn't," Mr. Hall replies.

"Yeah, me too," Harrison says, wiping the crème from his soda off his lip.

"Come with me to my office before the delivery agent gets here," Braxton says quietly.

"Yes, sir."

Harrison follows him.

Closing the door behind them, Braxton hurries to his desk, opening it. Harrison sees him pull something about the size of his hand out with a long chain dangling from it. Walking to him, Harrison wonders what it could be.

"What is it, Mr. Hall?"

Harrison stares at it.

"This right here, I found in Niro, one of the smallest cities in the Golic nation. They are another nation like the Destine nation we live in. The person who owned it didn't know the history of it since it has such a rich history amongst the Destine people. It is a compass that is said to be the Supreme Elder's. He gave it to the very first Destine Elder, one of the legendary five disciples of the Supreme Elder who went and created the great five nations. I want to give it to you."

Harrison examines the compass in his hand. The aged golden color on it makes it look old and worn. The inside looks like a normal compass except it has words from a different language he has never seen before.

"Wow, that's pretty neat, but why would you want to give me something so special?" Harrison asks.

"Days before your dad disappeared, he came to my shop and asked if I had ever come across this compass, or if I have ever seen it at any other antique shops around the nation. I told him I had never seen it and asked the importance of it. He said that he needed it on his next mission. That it would lead him to what he was looking for. The next mission he was referring to was the mission we know as the Silent Mission."

Harrison's heart sinks.

"What is it supposed to lead to then? A certain place or something?" Harrison asks.

"I don't know. Everybody I ask says the same thing, that they aren't too familiar with the story of the compass. I met one individual who says it is called The Compass of Destiny, but that's all he knew. I just figured it was fitting to give to you, being the anniversary of the disappearance of your dad and the day you find out if you made the Academy."

Harrison, holding the compass, does not know how to feel.

"Come on, let's get back in there," Braxton says.

Harrison nods while putting the compass in his pocket. Going back to the party, everybody eagerly waits for them to get back. Near the entrance, Harrison spots JT's mom next to the delivery agent from the Academy. Lifting up the letters, she signals for Mr. Hall to come up there.

Harrison could barely see her since she was shorter than most. Getting closer, he sees her cheeky smile and curly gray hair. The man from the Academy towers over her. Harrison marvels at his dark gray robe that extends down to his knees with two black stripes racing down his side from his armpits to his knees.

"Amber, are those the letters for everyone?" Mr. Hall asks his wife.

"YES! Hurry let's give them out to everybody. The wait is killing us!" Mrs. Hall responds with excitement.

Braxton shakes the agent's hand. Grabbing the letters from his wife, he stands on a table, towering above everyone. Harrison, watching with his friends, listens carefully.

"I just want to say something really quick before we hand these out. I am truly excited for all of you. I never had the opportunity to make it into the Academy. I was rejected twice, which is the limit. Some of you will make it and some won't. I want to say though, seeing a lot of you grow up and get to this point has been amazing, and no matter what your letter says, I am proud of you. Being part of the Destine nation, we all believe we all are destined for something, so if you get rejected, know that you are still a Destine and be proud of whatever destiny is in front of you, even if it is a little antique shop," Mr. Hall announces.

Harrison senses the sincerity in his voice.

Jumping down, he hands half of the letters to his wife. They immediately hand them out. Harrison watches Jaylen, Joseph, and JT get their envelopes. Opening them at once, one by one, they yank the letters out.

"I'M IN!" Jaylen screams!

"I'M IN TOO!" Joseph announces loudly.

"I AM GOING TO THE ACADEMY!" JT hollers.

Harrison spots his mom walk over with an envelope.

"I got yours for you. Open it!" Francis tells him.

"I will but let me go to the front of the shop, so I am not in the way of everyone else," Harrison responds.

Harrison, moving to the front with his mom, sees the agent. The agent sees Francis and smiles. He stops to talk to her. Harrison walks to the corner of the room by himself. He rips open the envelope slowly lifting the letter out. The letter feels like paper he has never touched before.

Opening it up, Harrison loses his breath.

YOUNG GRADY,

YOU ARE NOT READY FOR THE TRUTH. I HATE TO DO THIS BUT IT'S THE ONLY WAY TO KEEP YOU FROM THE TRUTH. YOU SHOULD THANK ME FOR THIS. THIS WILL NOT FEEL NEARLY AS BAD AS THE TRUTH IF YOU FOUND IT OUT.

Harrison's heart sinks to his stomach as the words gradually vanish off the page. Suddenly, feeling his hands get warm, the letter turns red and a red energy ball forms. Harrison immediately feels the energy ball explode.

BOOM!

Harrison, slamming through the front glass window, watches everything go black.

CHAPTER 4

Red Hawks in the Rose Garden

Harrison's head pounds all over. Slowly, opening his eyes, he wonders where he is. Glaring around the room, he observes a woman at his side checking the monitor next to the bed he is laying in.

"Where am I, and where is everyone else at?" Harrison asks, confused.

Turning around, Harrison sees her smiling, checking the IV in his arm. Wearing all white, he notices she is a nurse.

"How did I end up here? Where is my mom, is she okay, and everyone else, are they alright?" Harrison asks eagerly.

Turning around messing with his monitor, her bright red hair, pulled back in a ponytail, illuminates the dark and gloomy room. Her hazel eyes compliment her smile, which comforts Harrison.

"Your mom is outside your room, finally sleeping. She just fell asleep about two hours ago. I never have seen a person stay up for two straight days. Just shows how worried she was about you," the nurse says.

She fixes the blankets on him.

"Wait, did you say two days? How long have I been in here?" Harrison asks.

"You were brought in two days ago after the explosion at *Hall-Way Antiques*. But I will tell your mom you are finally awake. She'll be relieved and can answer your questions. If you need anything, just let me know," his nurse replies.

Harrison lays there, while the nurse wakes his mom. Immediately, Francis rushes in, kissing his forehead as if she has not seen him in months.

"Thank goodness, you are alright. I was so worried I lost you!" Francis says.

Tears of joy fall down her face.

"Mom, is everybody okay?" Harrison asks.

"Some people had minor injuries from the explosion, nothing fatal though. The shop was damaged pretty badly but Mr. Hall was worried about you more than the shop," she replies, sniveling.

"Really, that's great. But if the explosion was powerful to damage the shop and blast me through the window, then how did it not cause more injuries?"

24

"Well that's the thing the doctors and everybody else doesn't understand. For some reason, your body absorbed the energy. They have never seen an energy attack that is designed to target someone like that."

"Really?"

Harrison tries to understand what she said.

Whoever sent that letter wasn't playing around!

"You feel alright, honey?" Francis asks, rubbing his face.

A light knocking on the door stops him from answering. Harrison sees Victoria Grant standing there as he glares at the open door. She runs her fingers through her soft and glossy brown hair, that has sunny yellow streaks like butter. She walks over to his bedside. The unique color of her eyes makes his knees weak. Smiling and blinking slowly, her blueish lime eyes makes Harrison forget to breath.

Harrison's heart races. Victoria hugs Francis closely.

"Ms. Grady, it is good to see you again," Victoria says.

"It's so good to see you too, sweetie. Looking prettier than ever," Francis responds.

"Hey, Harrison, I didn't get to see what happened since I got there late. When I arrived, you were laying in the street. We have all been worried about you," Victoria says.

"I just hate that the party ended that way. Guess I can say I left with a bang, huh?" Harrison giggles softly.

At that moment, his nurse walks by the door and pokes her head in.

"Ms. Grady, if you want to see the Elder's conference about the attack on your son and the antique shop it's being broadcasted live on channel two and it's starting now," the nurse says.

Francis grabs the remote and cuts on the tv.

"Wait, why is the Destine Elder commenting on what happened to me. That doesn't make sense?" Harrison asks, shocked.

"Honey, the letter that had a hidden energy ball set to explode when opened, was in the letters that were from the Academy's registration department. There is a lot of confusion right now. Some people are saying it was a terrorist attack on the anniversary of your dad's group's disappearance or maybe an orchestrated attack on just you," Francis responds.

Harrison's mind becomes muddled at the mention of his father's disappearance, and he does not hear the last part of her sentence. The Destine Elder appears on the screen, commanding everyone's attention. His shrill, frail face is overtaken by wrinkles and is hidden by his dense, white neatly cropped beard. The top of his scalp is visible through his thinning white hair.

Seizing the podium, taking a deep breath, the Elder begins to talk.

"I want to first and foremost send my condolences to all the people that were injured during this incident two days ago. We are thankful that no one was fatally wounded. People in the small town of Eriz have a lot of questions as to what was behind the apparent attack in the antique shop. There are many rumors going around and I want to debunk some of those right now. We know for sure it was not a terrorist attack, and we know for sure it was not a planned attack on the young man, Harrison Grady. No one was trying to take his or anyone else's life. A student in the Academy who was helping the registration department accidentally transferred some energy from his Power Flow into the letter. As many of you know, Power Flow is what we use to create energy. He has been a student who has struggled in the Power Flow class, reported by his instructor Norman Drake. It is not uncommon for young students to release their energy into certain things without even knowing. Stating the obvious, the student's identity will not be revealed. He has sincerely apologized and feels bad for this. I truly apologize to Harrison Grady and I am sending my understudy, Sebastian Darby, and the Ragnar Council's leader, Adam Smalls, to the hospital to send my regards personally. May the Destine nation prosper!"

Francis cuts the TV off, looking dazed. Harrison, remembering what the letter had said when he opened it, began to wonder if they were lying and covering something up.

Did the Elder try to have me killed?

"Honey, was there anything suspicious, or that didn't seem right, on the letter when you looked at it?" Francis asks.

Harrison, thinking about what to say, spots the red-headed nurse enter the room.

"That is just great news to hear, knowing all this was just a terrible accident. I know all of you are relieved. I imagine that there is nothing more terrifying than knowing someone is out to kill you," she says while doing her routine checkup.

"Harrison, think, was there anything on the letter?" Francis asks again, ignoring the nurse.

"No, it was just an acceptance letter, that's it," Harrison replies back trying to act normal.

"Okay, thank goodness. I can believe the Elder then. Knowing all this, I am going to go get some rest for a while," Francis says.

She kisses his forehead.

"I hope you get some good rest, Ms. Grady," Victoria says, giving her another tight hug.

Harrison, still trying to process all of it, longs to get outside again.

"Ma'am, can I go outside for a couple of minutes. She will go with me and make sure I am okay."

Harrison points to Victoria.

"Sure, some fresh air might do you well," the nurse responds.

Unhooking the monitors, she and Victoria helps him up. Walking through the doorway, he felt a hand lay on his shoulder.

"If you need me, my name is Rena," the nurse says.

She comforts Harrison with her smile.

The sun tries to sneak below the horizon with soft strands of light shooting behind the buildings. Breathing heavily, Harrison could feel the difference between the sour air in the hospital and the fresh air outside.

Sitting next to Victoria in the middle of the rose garden, different colored roses surround them. The sweet, moist smell of the roses unclogs the stubborn odor of the hospital that is trapped in his nostrils.

"It feels so good out here. This is so much better than that room. And the funny thing is I just realized I was in it just a little bit ago," Harrison chuckles. He takes a rose from the bush next to him.

"Here, for you," he says, giving it to her.

"Always trying to charm someone, huh?"

She sniffs the small pink flower.

"I am sure everyone was probably scared and confused about what happened," Harrison says.

"Yeah, people have been talking around town. Like the Elder mentioned, a lot of rumors have been going around. Man, what are the chances a student struggling with his Power Flow control accidentally doing that?"

"Yeah, tell me about it! That kid sure does have some enormous power, maybe that's why he can't control it?" he says sarcastically.

"You don't believe him, do you? You must know something that we don't."

Harrison quickly defends himself. "No. I would tell you guys if I knew something. Why would I keep something from all of you? That would be stupid."

"Well that's good because if it was someone else that really did this, especially someone up at the Academy, that would be the last place you would need to be at," she says, spinning the rose in her fingers.

Abruptly, five men in gray robes with two red stripes running down the sides, walk up to them. Harrison grasps Victoria and brings her close to him. He sees two swords hanging from each of their backs. The one in the front waves his hand with two fingers pointing out.

"It's clear, only the boy and a young girl," the man gesturing says.

Moving behind them are two men also in gray, hooded robes but their stripes are white. Their hoods hide their faces in darkness.

"Thank you, Red Hawks, you may fall back," the one on the right says in a hoarse voice.

"Yes, sir! You heard him. Fall back Hawks!" the one in the front of the group says, signaling them all away from the garden.

Who are they? And why do they roll with a group of men that intimidating?

"You didn't tell me your nephew had a little girlfriend. Guess you can say he outdid himself though," the individual with the raspy voice says.

Nephew? Did he just say nephew?

They glide the hoods off their head, finally revealing their faces.

Harrison grins.

"I haven't seen him in a while, I guess his mom failed to mention that to me last time we talked," the one on the left responds back.

"Uncle Adam!" Harrison loudly hollers, leaping to embrace him.

His head bounces off his uncle Adam's solid chest. He barely gets his arms all the way around his back while hugging. His uncle's long, flimsy auburn hair is in a tight braid tickling Harrison's hand.

"Man, it's been too long, Uncle Adam," Harrison says, looking right into his shadowy brown eyes.

"Yeah, I think the last time I saw you was when you were about ten years old. Now look at you, fifteen years old, and you have a girlfriend. Wow!" his uncle Adam says.

"Oh no, she isn't my girlfriend, we are just good friends," Harrison responds awkwardly.

"Yeah, we aren't dating, but my name is Victoria, Victoria Grant, and it is nice to meet you guys. You must be from the Academy, aren't you?" she asks them.

"Yes, ma'am, you are right, as you heard, I am Harrison's uncle, his mom's favorite brother-"

"The only brother!" the other man interjects.

"Still makes me her favorite brother, thank you, but like I was saying. We are both from the Academy, I am on the Ragnar Council and Sebastian Darby right here, is our Elder's understudy for the last two years and may just be the next Destine Elder and leader of the Destine nation," his uncle Adam announces.

Sebastian smirks proudly. He holds his hands behind his back, constantly rubbing his thumbs around each other while swaying back and forth.

He comes up to about his uncle Adam's shoulders. His short black hair recedes in the front and his scalp forms a nice circle in the back that he is trying to cover up.

"Hey, Uncle Adam, I just got to know something since I really didn't get a confirmation since that energy bomb kind of tried to take me out the other day. I just want to know if I made the Academy. My letter didn't say if I did or didn't," Harrison asks.

Harrison notices Victoria through the side of his eye. He sees the misunderstanding on her face. She moves close to his ear so only he could hear.

"Why do you need to ask your uncle if you got in if you already know? I mean I heard you tell your mom that you saw it on the letter before it exploded," she whispers to him.

"What are you saying, young lady? See only couples tell secrets with each other, so you aren't selling it to us very well," Sebastian says, still bouncing and spinning his thumbs behind his back.

Harrison immediately responds, "Oh, it's nothing really-"

"Apparently we are just friends because we keep secrets from each other. We don't tell them," she says under her breath.

"Well, Harrison, what did your letter say then since it didn't say either one?" Sebastian asks fascinated.

"It was just a blank sheet of paper, that's it. That's why I was so confused," Harrison says.

"No wonder that boy that did this to you is struggling in Norman Drake's Power Flow class and doesn't know how to properly channel his energy throughout his body.

He is so intelligent that he puts a blank sheet of paper in the envelope," his uncle Adam says sarcastically.

"I mean, the students nowadays just don't have what the ones years ago had. I mean, our nation is in for some trouble with this generation. I guess they all can't be like your dad," his uncle Adam says, sounding disappointed.

"Yeah guess not, huh?" Victoria takes a couple of steps. "I got to go; my mom is probably worried about me. I guess I will see you around sometime, Harrison. I am glad you are alright and that energy bomb from the blank letter didn't hurt you worse than what it did."

"Well, we are thrilled to announce that you are accepted into the Destiny Academy and will begin classes in three months, at the beginning of fall," Sebastian announces cheerfully.

Harrison listens halfway, glaring at Victoria walking away upset.

"That's awesome! I can't believe I got in," Harrison says, trying to sound excited.

"In a couple of weeks, we will mail a list of items you will need to get for the upcoming school year," his uncle Adam says.

"Yeah, I have had enough fun from letters from the Academy already. Think you could just, like tell me now and let me write it down?" Harrison says, laughing but half serious.

"We promise nothing like that will happen again. And we came here to check up on you and send the Elder's condolences to you," Sebastian says confidently.

"Thanks, I appreciate that," Harrison replies.

Even though he may have been the one who tried to kill me!

Nudging his head through some of the roses, the Red Hawk leader whistles.

"It's time to go, my Honor," the Red Hawk leader says, as he sniffs the roses.

"I understand. I will see you when you get to the Academy. I am glad you are okay, and tell your mom I said hey, and I hope to come to eat some of her nasty cooking during the holidays this year," his uncle Adam says putting his hood back on.

"Yeah, I will," Harrison replies.

"It was finally nice to meet you. I look forward to seeing you again, young Grady," Sebastian says while also hiding his face with his hood.

Harrison sees Rena, his nurse, looking for him. Knocking into Sebastian's shoulder, she falls over. Sebastian catches her before she hits the ground.

"Sometimes we are in a hurry and aren't careful at what we are doing, huh?" Sebastian asks Rena.

"Look who is talking," Rena says walking towards Harrison.

"Are you okay?" Harrison asks Rena.

"I am the one who is supposed to ask you that. Come on, let's go back upstairs," Rena responds.

CHAPTER 5

Painful Decisions

The leaves begin to change colors for the fall. Harrison jogs around his neighborhood. Slowing down in front of Gavin's house, near his own house, he hears a door hurling open.

"Harrison, why don't you ever wake me up to run? I tell you every night to make sure you wake me up, so I can go running with you," Gavin says, pulling up his baggy pajama pants with various colorful cartoon characters.

"I promise I will remember to have you run with me one morning before I leave Thursday," Harrison responds, laughing under his breath.

"Well since you didn't let me go with you today, how about this evening you come over and train with me? Maybe you can help me with my martial art forms. The instructor I just know is about to fail me!"

"Sorry, buddy, but everyone is hanging out at the skating rink before the ones who made it into the Academy leave. It's our last time to get together before we start classes," Harrison responds walking back to his yard.

"Great! Well, have a great time skating around in a circle tonight knowing I am probably going to fail my mixed martial arts class. *THE FIRST ONE*! I mean it's embarrassing when you fail summer school," Gavin says.

"Thanks, man," Harrison chuckles and slowly waves at Gavin. "I appreciate it!"

Pulling up to the skating rink, the bright giant sign is visible all the way down the road, with *BACK TO SCHOOL BASH* written on it. People wait in a line stretched all the way around the building.

"Have a great time, honey, and make sure you are back here at 1:00 for me to pick you back up. Don't make me wait," Francis says.

"Thanks, I won't. I don't want to ride home with a black eye," Harrison says.

"Hush!" she says as he closes the door.

Heading to the back of the line, Harrison gazes JT, Jaylen, and Joseph.

"About time you got here," Jaylen says to Harrison.

"Late, as usual. We would think something is wrong if you were on time," Joseph says.

"Come on, I can't help that I got to wait on my mom. Just wait and see, when we're at the Academy, you will see how I am always going to be on time." Harrison responds.

"Hey! We aren't talking about the Academy or anything like that. We are going to go in there, talk to some girls, eat some nachos with extra cheese, and watch you bust your butt trying to skate. We worry about the Academy after tonight!" JT says.

They march into the skating rink.

The strobe lights paint the walls. The old dirty money smell rushes into Harrison's nose.

"Let's go get our skates before the line gets worse," Jaylen says, pointing at the line.

Harrison feels JT hit his chest with his backhand as he notices Victoria.

"Dude, there's Victoria. You won't believe it, but I heard she is dating Samuel Prince now," JT says.

"Really? I haven't talked to her since she came and saw me at the hospital three months ago," Harrison responds.

"Yeah, man, that stuck up fool got him another reason to be even more stuck up now," Joseph says, with disgust.

Harrison glares at Victoria as she leans against the little wall separating the lobby and the rink. Samuel skates over to her. Sliding in front of her, he kisses her.

She giggles. Harrison looks away at a girl in line trying on another pair of skates.

Harrison finally gets his skates.

"Okay, already? Let's get on the floor," JT says.

Losing his balance, JT starts swaying trying to gain his balance by gripping the wall. Missing the wall, falling into the rink head first, he rolls as two little boys' trip over him causing a mass pile-up on the floor.

"My bad, my bad! My wheels must be loose!" JT says, under the crowd of people that fell.

"C'mon guys, we got to help him," Jaylen says.

"Yeah, right. But I will meet you guys on the floor in a second," Harrison says.

He watches Samuel skate into the bathroom, leaving Victoria with just her two friends.

"Hey Victoria, haven't seen you in a while. How is everything?" Harrison asks.

"Fine. But I could actually mean something else by that, or I could be lying or hiding something. Oh, that's right I'm not you!" Victoria says.

"C'mon it's not like that Victoria. So, don't act that way-"

"What way? The way a friend would act when they were just told-"

"Told what?" Samuel says interrupting her as he skates next to her and Harrison.

"Nothing, I just told Harrison to leave," she says.

Coming close to him, Samuel is face to face with Harrison.

"You heard her. She told you to leave. So, go skate somewhere else, Grady." Samuel says not blinking as he gazes into Harrison's eyes.

"Yeah, I hear you. Maybe if you weren't so close, I could skate off," Harrison responds.

Samuel slowly moves back. Harrison starts to skate into the rink.

"Is that what your dad did?" Samuel grabs Victoria's hand. "Did he skate away that night because it was too much for him? That is what my dad says he did. Says he finally figured out he wasn't man enough for it. My Pops isn't wrong about much, but I think he is on that. I think your old man is dead."

"Samuel, shut up!" Victoria says as Harrison turns around.

He feels the anger escalating inside. His palms are sweaty and tingling with a warm sensation. Harrison races towards Samuel.

"What did you say? Don't you dare talk about my dad," Harrison says.

Samuel's two friends' step-in front of Samuel.

"Don't you ever say anything about him," he shouts continuously as the two friends are pushing him back and Samuel laughs behind them.

Suddenly the two giant plump boys being bodyguards push Harrison back.

"You heard him, skate on like your loser father!' one of the boys says.

Harrison leans forward and seizes each of them by the middle of their shirt.

41

A green glow covers Harrison's hands.

"*TAKE IT BACK, NOW*!" Harrison screams.

Pushing as hard as he can, the two boys go soaring backward crashing into the wall. Harrison, seeing both of his hands shining green, doesn't see Samuel charging at him.

Samuel tackles him. They fall over the wall into the skating rink. Landing on top of him, Samuel punches Harrison, hitting him in his left eye. Clutching his throat, Harrison sees his hands are back to normal now. Harrison pushes him off. Harrison sits up and sees JT.

"Harrison I am coming! You better get off my boy!" JT says falling down every couple of feet.

As soon as Samuel is back on top of Harrison, one of the workers snatches him dragging him back.

"This isn't over Grady! When we are at the Academy you won't be as lucky. Believe me!" Samuel shouts.

Being helped up by Joseph, Harrison sees Victoria, sobbing as she leaves. Jaylen, holding JT up, skates over to them.

"Dude, he was lucky, I was coming straight for him! Nobody messes with my friends," JT says.

"Yeah, it looked like you had a hard-enough time with the floor," Jaylen says.

A man working there skates over to them.

"Okay boys, turn in your skates. Your night is ending early," the man says.

The boys sit on the curb. Harrison's mom pulls up beside them, rolling the window down, looking surprised.

"I am fifteen minutes early, and you are already waiting? Wow, you are on it tonight," she says.

Getting in the car, Harrison sits down and knows his mom notices.

"Oh my gosh, you have a black eye. What happened?" she asks, concerned.

"Nothing really, just got in a little fight, that's it," he says staring forward.

"Oh, my goodness. Did you get in a fight too JT? You look worse than him," she says.

"Yeah, Momma. It was like seven of them, but I took them all out," JT says.

"Ms. Grady, he is lying. The floor did that too him," Jaylen says.

"Yeah, he took seven of them out all right, each time he fell," Joseph says.

Slowly rolling the window up, Francis smiles.

"Let me get him home. You boys have a good night," she says to them.

Pulling back into the road, Francis glares at Harrison.

"Well, I thought you said you didn't want to ride home with a black eye?"

Harrison stares at the bright sign in the mirror as they drive away.

Francis stops in front of *Hall-way Antiques*. Harrison observes the newly constructed building.

She hands him a list.

"Now make sure that you do not forget anything on that list. That's exactly what you need for this school year. Your uncle Adam got it to us late since he said, you mentioned something about you being nervous about getting another letter from the registration department. So, he wrote it for you," Francis says giving him the list.

"I was just playing around when I said that...kind of," Harrison responds getting out of the car.

"Now if you forget anything you won't have much time to come back and get it since you leave in two days. So, you and JT help each other remember to get everything."

"I won't forget anything mom, you don't have to be on my back so much, I can handle things like this."

"Okay. I will pick you up later when you guys get back from the shopping outlets. Be careful."

She drives off.

Harrison goes inside the antique shop for the first time since he was blown through the front of the store. The scent hasn't changed. The grubby timeworn smell attacks his nose as if it was showing it was still there.

"My boy, it is so good to see you!" Mr. Hall says.

JT walks out of his office.

"What's up Harrison?" JT says.

"Mr. Hall, it's good to see you too, and what's up JT, ready to go get this stuff for the school year?" Harrison asks.

"My goodness, son! Who gave you that black eye?" Mr. Hall points at Harrison's black eye.

"Oh, it's nothing really. A really insignificant story," he responds.

"All right Dad, enough asking about Harrison's black eye that he got from Samuel because I couldn't get there in time because of all the little kids falling in front of me. We got to get this stuff, so we are heading out," JT opens the door.

"Mr. Hall, I never got to apologize for damaging your shop so badly that day. I am sorry that your shop took so much damage," Harrison says.

"Son, don't worry about it, I am just glad you are all right and still with us. It's a miracle. No one survives a blast like you did. It's just remarkable you are alive."

"Thanks, Mr. Hall!" Harrison exits the shop.

Approaching the Shopping Outlet, Harrison opens his list to see the items.

This is what you will need to get for this year:

Destine Academy polo shirts and button ups. The only colors allowed is blue, white, green, red, orange, and Navy.

Khakis

Notebooks

Pencils

Pens

Destine Academy gym shorts and tee shirts.

Towels

Bed sheets

Pillows

Remember Harrison, the dress code states that during the school day you must wear a polo or dress shirt with Khakis. That is for male and female students. The only classes where you will wear something else is in Mr. Drake's Power Flow classes. The first year in his class you just learn the basics and are required to wear normal dress code clothing. Sebastian wanted me to tell you hello, and that he hopes you and your girlfriend are doing well. See you soon!

"This dress code stinks! I would rather be able to wear my own clothes and be comfortable," Harrison says as they walk past various stores.

"Yeah, they seem kind of strict up there about it. My dad says he heard that they make you tuck your shirts in too," JT says repulsed.

"Dang man, that's terrible," Harrison says upset.

"Hey, look over there. It's Victoria. She's coming out of the store," JT points at her.

"I need to go talk to her real quick. I will meet you in the Academy store when I get done," Harrison says.

Harrison walks towards her.

"All right, I see how it is! I am good enough to be around to save your butt when her boyfriend is clubbing you but not good enough now. Okay!" JT says, slowly going inside the store.

Harrison, grabbing Victoria's arm, turns her to face him. By her facial expression, he could tell she was stunned to see him.

"Victoria, I really want to talk to you for just a minute. Please listen to me. Please!" Harrison says, releasing her arm.

"I really shouldn't. Especially after how you and Samuel showed your butts at the skating rink, you really don't deserve to talk to me."

"Let me ask you. Are you still dating Samuel after what he did?"

She takes a deep breath and glares at Harrison, focusing on his black eye.

"Okay, let's go sit on the bench and talk for a minute," she says.

Moving towards the only empty black metal bench, they sit down.

"Listen, I am sorry I kept that thing about the letter back from you. I just didn't want you worried."

"You didn't just lie to me, but you lied to your mom. How do you think that would make her feel? She was just concerned about you. She doesn't want anything to happen to you either. That's why she asked you what was on the letter."

"I know, but if she knew what the letter really said she wouldn't let me go to the Academy. She would make me stay here and go to the local school with you and some of the others. I can't let that happen."

"What do you mean what was really on the letter? See! I knew you lied to your uncle and that Darby guy. You just can't stop lying, can you? And why do you have to go to the Academy that bad?"

"C'mon Victoria. It's not like that. I just can't say what was in the letter. I am afraid that if I tell you and somebody finds out that you know, then they will come after you."

"Who would come after me, Harrison?"

"Ummm, I really don't know for sure right now but-"

"But what? I mean, be honest with me Harrison!"

"Look, all I know right now is that whoever sent me that letter doesn't want me to go the Academy. I really think they are afraid that I will find out the truth about what happened to my dad. So that is why I have to go to the Academy. I am going to try to investigate and get some answers this school year. This is my only chance to find out what really happened to my dad. So that is why I lied. I didn't want my mom stopping me."

"Harrison, you could get killed. If what you are saying is true, then the person that tried to kill you is up at the Academy now. Don't you think that they will try to do it again somehow? You will be a walking target," she says, tears pooling in her eyes.

"I have thought about that. But I have to do this."

"Please, don't do this. For me, Harrison. Stay here. Just forget it all and move on," she says with tiny tears falling slowly down her face.

"I am sorry, Victoria. I can't. Just please try to understand."

"I have had feelings for you for the longest time," she wipes a tear going down her cheek. "Everyone noticed, except you. I always have adored you, and what always attracted me to you is your integrity. That is why it hit me so hard when you lied to all of us. I want to be with you and nobody else! But I can't back what you are doing. It's a suicide mission. So, if you decide to actually do this, then I am not going to talk to you. If you can't respect my feelings and my concern for you, then we just can't be friends."

She begins weeping harder. It starts to rain. He stands up, staring into her gorgeous eyes. The raindrops, combining with the tears running down his face, hid the fact that he is crying.

"Don't do that Victoria, that's not fair-"

"Well, what is it Harrison? Let me know right now!"

Harrison glares into her eyes, silent.

"Okay, I get it, I have your answer. Good luck Harrison."

She walks away, sobbing.

He still couldn't speak. Watching her walk away, he just stood there.

JT busts through the store's door.

"Dude, you are getting soaked, and you are just standing there like you just lost your best friend?" he shouts waving Harrison to get in the store.

I think I did just lose one of them!

CHAPTER
6

JT's Idea

Walking back to JT's dad's antique shop, their feet slush through the water laying on the ground from the recent downpour. Harrison thinks about Victoria.

Did I really just destroy a friendship over this?

What if I go and something does happen to me?

What if I go there and I am wrong about all of this?

Harrison can tell that JT suspects something is wrong with him. JT usually doesn't stop talking but he is silent.

"Hey man, you want to talk. You've looked sort of down ever since we went into the store and got our stuff for the Academy?" JT asks putting his hand on Harrison's shoulder.

"Well, I think Victoria is being really serious about not wanting to talk to me since I am going to the Academy. She says it will be too dangerous for me," Harrison answers, gazing at the water on the sidewalk.

"Why would she think it's too dangerous for you? That sounds crazy. What does she think, someone is out to get you up there?" he says, giggling.

"You remember when they said it was an accident that happened to me in your dad's shop?"

"Yeah, they said it was just a student that couldn't control his Power Flow. The Destine Elder himself said it."

"Well with what the letter said, that can't be true. I'm pretty sure they are lying."

Harrison kicks at the water while he walks.

"What did it say? I have heard from your mom that you told her it said you got in," JT replies.

"I don't want to tell anyone. I feel like if I tell and they find out that I told somebody, that person will be in danger. I told Victoria that and she got upset. I just don't want to feel responsible if something happens to any of you. I can't let that happen."

Harrison stops walking as JT places his hand on his chest.

"Listen, I understand you not wanting to tell her because of how you feel, but I think you shouldn't keep anything back from me. I deserve to know for a couple of reasons. First, I am your best friend. Second, I told you that I would help any way I can. I care about you and if I could help you find out what really happened to your dad then I would, no matter how dangerous it gets. And last, I deserve to know because it happened in my dad's shop and I see the stress it has caused my family trying to get that shop back up and running."

Noticing the twitch in JT's eyes, Harrison knows he is holding back the tears.

"I understand, I really do, but-"

"But nothing. If you understand what I said, then you will tell me what was really on that letter and let me help you," JT says, interrupting him angrily.

Taking a deep breath, Harrison feels the moisture still in the air from the rain.

"You are right. Okay, what it said only lasted a short time. The writing vanished. Then an energy ball came out and exploded. But it was handwritten, and it said that I wasn't ready for the truth and that I should thank them for keeping me from the truth because the truth would hurt worse than this."

Harrison, glaring at JT, could see the astonishment on his face.

"It just vanished, just like that? How does someone make something like that, a vanishing text and a hidden energy bomb?" JT asks.

"I don't know but I hope to get some type of answers up at the Academy. Whoever did that I feel knows something about what happened to my dad and his group," Harrison says.

"You know something else a lot of people don't understand? Is how you survived that blast head on like that? My dad said not many people are strong enough to take a direct hit like that. It doesn't make sense," JT says as they continue to walk again.

"I don't know. I have thought about that but also tried not to think about it. I guess I just wasn't destined to die then," Harrison says as they approach *Hall-way of Antiques*.

Walking up to the window, they look in, and the darkness is the only thing visible in the store.

What is he looking at?

JT puts his hand on the brand-new window.

"I think I know something that will help us get started when we get to the Academy," JT says.

"Yeah all this stuff we just had to buy, that's an easy one," Harrison replies chuckling.

"No, not that. I know something that will help us in trying to find out some information on your dad."

Harrison, stunned, turns facing him.

"What could that be?"

"Two months ago, I went with my dad to take something to the antique shop in Dosman, that small town outside of here about 15 minutes going south. And when we were there, I overheard my dad and the owner of the shop, Cecil Garner talking about something rare that he has in the shop."

"What was it?"

"I saw my dad go over to this drawing in a frame hanging up there. My dad was just so excited, which isn't rare when it comes to things like that. But what Mr. Garner said caught my attention. He said that thing in the frame was the original copy of the blueprint of the Academy. He said that it was rumored that the person who built the Academy built secret hallways, rooms, and bunkers that no one knew about," JT says as Harrison stops him.

"Why would he build hidden compartments in the Academy, what purpose would that serve?"

"Mr. Garner said that because of the Supreme Elder's prophecies of upcoming wars between the five great nations the Ragnar Council at that time wanted to have secret places in the Academy to hide the students just in case enemy forces attacked. So, he said the architect put the hidden rooms and such in the blueprints so that if they ever needed the rooms, they could find them in the blueprint."

Harrison runs his fingers through his damp hair.

"So, they must have used those rooms during the two different wars they were in?"

"Well, that's the thing. That's why they say it's rumored. They never got to use the original blueprint or the secret room's because the blueprint went missing and wasn't found till recently," JT responds.

Harrison tries to process what he just heard.

"Wait, so you are telling me that we don't even know if this is true or not? How is that supposed to help us then?" Harrison says, confused.

"It's worth a shot. I heard Mr. Garner say that it is rumored that if it is opened in the library at night then the secret room's entrances show up on the blueprint. I say tomorrow night we go to the antique shop in Dosman and take the blueprint and use it at the Academy. One night we can see where the secret rooms and things are, and we will be able to see if we could use those to help us sneak and spy on the Elder and other top officials there."

Harrison rubs his face roughly trying to think it through.

"Okay, but how are we supposed to take this blueprint from the antique shop," Harrison scratches his chin.

"Let me worry about that part. But what you need to do is go home and tell your mom that you are going to stay at my house tomorrow night. I will come up with something tonight on how we can pull this off," JT replies.

Harrison's stomach starts throbbing.

"Okay, if you think this is worth a shot, let's try it."

Harrison spots his mom pulling up to them.

"See you tomorrow then!" Harrison says getting into the car.

Pulling off, Harrison glares at JT putting his hand back on the window.

CHAPTER 7

The Blueprint in Dosman

Shining bright like little lights, the stars overtake the sky. Harrison's stomach still aches just as it was the night prior, maybe a little more.

I can't believe we are heading to steal an ancient map.

"What time is it?" Harrison asks JT, riding his bike next to him.

"Almost go time. We will be there in about five minutes, so this will be a good place to leave our bikes. We can walk the rest of the way," JT responds, slowing down.

Harrison steps off his bike and follows JT. They both try to hide their bikes secretly in the bushes. Harrison struggles to catch his breath.

"Okay, so what exactly is the plan again?" Harrison asks trying to focus on breathing.

"The last time I was there with my dad, I had to use the bathroom something serious. While I was in the bathroom, I noticed that there was a little window above the stall next to me that was opened halfway. When I was done with my business, I told Mr. Garner about it," JT replies rubbing the back of his neck.

"Seriously, that's how you got this idea? You remember sitting on his toilet and seeing the window? That is your brilliant idea? Great!" Harrison says.

"Hey, I believe the reason I was on that toilet is because of that terrible cereal I ate, and I am ninety-eight and half percent sure I ate that cereal from your house. So, think of it as us just being destined for this!" JT reasons back.

His body tingling, Harrison feels his nerves tensing with every step that got closer to the shop. They crouch at the end of the street where the shop is. Harrison spots the shop at the end of the road.

The store, smaller than *Hallway of Antiques*, shines brighter than all the taller buildings around as if it is signaling them there.

Sprinting behind the stores, Harrison thinks, *please don't get caught, please don't get caught...*

Getting close, Harrison notices the small sign become bigger now, *Garner Grand Antiques*. JT slides behind the building as Harrison follows.

Looking up, Harrison notices the tiny window halfway opened.

"Okay, help lift me up and I will go in there and unlock the side door and let you in," JT says as Harrison starts feeling like he is about to throw up.

"All right, let's hurry up and do this, and get back. I mean the last thing I thought I would be doing the night before I leave for the Academy would be stealing blueprints of the Academy," Harrison replies as he balances JT on his sweaty palms.

Swaying slightly, Harrison tries to plant his feet sturdier in the dirt. Harrison raises his lean arms up gradually as JT's legs dangle in the window. Harrison listens intently, anticipating JT's voice from inside.

Suddenly, a loud clang lingers through the window.

"Oh, you got to be kidding me, this is so gross," JT cries.

Harrison hits the wall signaling him to be quiet.

"No, you wouldn't be quiet either. I think Mr. Garner must have forgotten to flush the toilet, and I fell right in it, so don't shhhh me!"

"Which number was it, one or two?" Harrison asks giggling quietly under his breath.

"Shut up I can hear you laughing out there, it's not funny...and it was both."

Harrison hears JT open the door and leave the bathroom. Crouching, Harrison slowly walks over to a side door observing two tiny trash cans guarding it. The smell of expired tuna overwhelms his nose as he waits for JT to open it.

Finally, the door flings open. Water drips from JT's bangs. He combs his hair back, trying to keep the water from getting in his eyes.

"Wow, you really did eat that toilet, didn't you?" Harrison asks laughing as JT just stands there blinking.

JT doesn't move.

Harrison can tell he is thinking of an appropriate comeback.

"If I could harness energy from my Power Flow and create energy attacks right now, I would blast you with the biggest one I could create. And then kick your dog...twice," JT says, finally moving out of the way so Harrison can come in.

Moving in behind him, Harrison closes the door and thinks, *I don't even have a dog*, as he holds back a laugh.

Wandering into the store, Harrison observes the small tables full of old and dusty antiques.

Smaller than *Hall-way of Antiques*, the same grimy timeworn smell overwhelms Harrison's nose. JT walks over to the framed blueprint signaling Harrison.

"That thing is huge," Harrison says.

Touching the glass of the frame, Harrison glances at JT who is dripping toilet water from his hair onto the floor.

"Dude, you are making the floor wet," Harrison tells JT taking his hand off the glass.

"Well, what you want me to do about it? It doesn't matter though, because by the time Mr. Garner gets here in the morning it will be dry," JT responds.

Covering the whole wall, the frame is cheap looking. Harrison's reflection stares back with the blueprint overtaking his face in it. With part of the blueprint ripping in various spots, it looks as if a roadmap is showing up on his face.

Squinting to see the faded lines that made up the buildings on the page, Harrison moves in to see it better.

Suddenly, bright yellow lights rush through the store windows.

"Oh crap. You got to be kidding me," JT says

He begins looking for somewhere to hide.

"What the heck are we supposed to do now?" Harrison asks feeling his stomach throb again.

The lights vanish. Harrison hears a car door slam shut. Stuck in a daze gazing at the man walking to the door, he hears JT murmur at him.

Harrison spins and sees JT climbing up a ladder that led to a miniature balcony with just one tiny table. He runs to it. Standing up at the top, JT motions for Harrison to hurry. He can hear the man taking the keys out of his pocket and putting them into the door.

Harrison slips halfway with his leg hanging off. His body tingling, Harrison knows he is about to get caught. Suddenly, he hears the keys drop on the ground.

"Great now I got to bend over and get these stupid things, it's too late for all this mess," the voice complains.

Scurrying faster up the ladder now, he grabs JT's hand and hops up. They both hit the floor quickly. The man finally opens the door. They look over slightly to see who it is.

Cutting on the lights, the light gleams brightly off the top of the man's head. He pushes up his oversized glasses and wobbles like a penguin slowly to his desk.

"It's Mr. Garner," JT whispers softly. "Why would he be here right now?"

Unexpectedly, everything goes black. Closing the door behind him is a tall man with a long black robe with blood red streaks going down the sides. He locks the door. Harrison scoots closer to the edge trying to get a better look. With his huge hood over his head, the mysterious robed figure stands there as Mr. Garner waddles quickly to him.

"Who the heck is that?" JT whispers.

"Shhhhhh. Let's try to listen to what they say," Harrison responds.

"See I told you I would be here. Not many people would get me out of bed at midnight," Mr. Garner says.

The mysterious robed man stands there.

"Don't small talk me. You know why we are meeting. I have given you more than plenty of time to find what I am seeking," the mysterious robed man replies with his strong baritone voice carrying throughout the room.

Why does his voice sound like that?

It doesn't even sound normal.

"Now, I have been working hard to try to find-"

"Again, I said don't small talk me. You just answer yes or no. Which one is it?" the mysterious robed man interrupts sounding irritated.

"No, but please, please let me explain-"

"You said I could rely on you. That you are the most loyal follower amongst them all," the mysterious robed man answers.

He walks towards Mr. Garner.

"You can, but I just need a little bit more time to get some. I have learned that there is a cave in the forest by the Academy in Tespan. I just have to go and get some," Mr. Garner replies, shaking.

"I need to have a black gem in my hand for the next part of the plan. If someone tries to extract the energy from a black gem, unprepared and the wrong way, they will die. So, I need these couple of months to discover how to do that," the mysterious robed man replies.

Harrison feels JT bump his hip.

"What the heck is a black gem?" JT whispers.

Harrison shrugs.

"I understand and I know you are busy with your position at the Academy and all, so you need the time to find out. Even with your ability to control your Power Flow and the power you have I can imagine how difficult it must be then," Mr. Garner responds.

Harrison and JT stare at one another as their eyes enlarge.

"Well since you are so aware of my time frame then I encourage you to get it done. If not, I will get another follower to do my business. The numbers are growing," the mysterious robed man says.

The mysterious robed man strolls slowly over to the blueprint hanging on the wall.

Mr. Garner follows him, standing behind him as he observes it. Harrison lifts his head a little more.

"The good ole Academy. Putting out strong Destine elite warriors since it was created. I was always fascinated with the legend of this blueprint. I always wondered if it really worked if someone took it to the library at night. A fascinating legend in itself. When I was a student there, I wanted to find it and see for myself."

He reaches out to touch it.

"Yeah, I am just thankful you allowed me to have it when you found it. You are too kind," Mr. Garner responds.

The mysterious robed man inspects it.

"You shouldn't let people touch it and get their nasty fingerprints on it. It is too valuable to just let anybody touch," the mysterious robed man says, with anger in his voice.

Harrison views Mr. Garner stepping forward to examine it. He sees him stop, looking down with a confused look.

"Where did this water come from?" Mr. Garner looks up towards the ceiling. "Must have a leak in the roof."

The mysterious robed man heads to the front door.

Mr. Garner wipes the smudge off the blueprint.

"You know how passionate I am about history. It's one of my favorite things in the world. So, if you ever let anything happen to that blueprint, something bad will happen to you," the mysterious robed man announces, opening the door.

"Absolutely nothing will ever happen to this blueprint. You can trust me on that."

"I will be back at the end of the month, and I will also trust, you will have my black gem the next time we meet."

He slams the door.

Harrison and JT stay hidden as Mr. Garner exits. Harrison hears the car immediately drive away.

His body shaking, Harrison slides down the ladder. JT grabs the blueprint off the wall and heads to the bathroom. Jumping out the window, he lands next to JT. JT smashes the glass and takes the blueprint.

"Come on let's get going," JT says, shaking.

Harrison agrees and begins to jog behind JT, glancing up at the stars, trying to clear his mind.

CHAPTER
8

The Ferry to the Destine Academy

Harrison's back itches as he lays on the carpet without his shirt on. He glares at the wobbly ceiling fan slowly rotating in the bedroom over at JT's house. The annoying cracking noise gives Harrison a headache, or maybe it is JT snoring on the bed beside him. Mr. Hall raids through the door with a rousing look on his face and more energy than a five-year-old.

"Get up boys. What are you guys doing? It's 10:00 am and the ferry leaves for the Academy at 11:00. Let's hurry," Mr. Hall says.

"Okay, dad. We get it. It won't take us long to be ready," JT yawns.

"You guys are sleeping the morning away like you were up running the streets all night. Now come downstairs and meet me and your mom and be ready to leave," Mr. Hall closes the door.

Harrison, still laying in the same spot, sees JT stumbling around the mess in his room. JT kicks Harrison in the leg.

"Dude, get up we got to get going before my dad comes in again."

JT lifts his bags, putting them next to the door.

"What do you think will happen to Mr. Garner? Do you think that guy in the robe will actually come and do something since we took the blueprint? I mean you heard what he said," Harrison watches the fan spin.

"We can't worry about that. Apparently, he got himself around the wrong people. It would be his fault if something happened to him," JT answers, putting his shirt on.

Sitting up, Harrison walks to his bag and looks through it.

"Yeah but still, nobody would have ever tried to steal that blueprint. The only reason we did was because of what I am trying to do. And the bad thing is we don't even know if it's true or not. Even crazy sounding robe guy didn't know if it was. What if he does do something to him? Then it would be all my fault. I don't want to get people in trouble," Harrison says, lifting an old gray shirt out of his bag.

"Cool shirt, where did you get that from?"

"It's my dad's," Harrison smooths the front of the shirt. "My mom said he was wearing this shirt on the night he left. She found it on the porch. He must have changed into his battle gear before he left. She said it was the last thing she saw him in. So, I figured I would wear this today."

"I feel you," JT picks up his bags. "Come on let's get going."

Harrison sprints down the stairs behind him, and spots Mr. Hall on the phone, pacing in circles.

"No way…yeah…no…thanks for telling me, I could've never imagined that. If you need anything just let me know…yeah, alright thanks…talk to you later, Cecil," Mr. Hall hangs up the phone wearing a look of surprise.

"What happened honey?" she asks, sounding concerned.

Harrison and JT grip their bags tightly and walk towards JT's parents.

"You will never believe this. Someone broke into Cecil's shop last night and stole one of his rarest pieces, his original blueprint of the Academy," he responds.

Harrison's heart drops and his hands get sweaty.

"You can't be serious. That's terrible. How'd he sound over the phone?" she says, gasping.

"He seemed stressed about it. It almost sounded like he was in tears. He must be pretty depressed because when I said talk to you later, he got off the phone with, 'Yeah let's hope so,'" Mr. Hall answers.

Mrs. Hall opens the front door.

"Well, I hate hearing that, but let's hurry and get in the car and get to the dock. Harrison, your mom is supposed to meet us there."

"Yes, ma'am," Harrison replies strolling out the door first.

"Still can't get over that. Who would do something like that? I just don't get it," Mr. Hall says, locking the house.

"Probably some stupid kids up to no good," JT responds.

They throw their bags in the trunk and sit down in the back seat.

"You got that right. They sure aren't like you two boys. I can sleep well at night knowing that you would never do something like that."

Mr. Hall glances at them as he pulls out of the driveway.

"Yeah, you got that right," JT responds.

It began to rain and small raindrops land on Harrison's nose as he steps out of the car. His mom smiles as she stands waiting for him. Harrison's good friend Gavin is there, waving continuously amongst the crowds of people.

"Hey, mom," Harrison strolls towards them. "What's going on Gavin? I didn't expect to see you here."

Harrison messes with Gavin's hair.

"You just never know when I might pop up. And one day you may just need me to," Gavin replies, smiling.

JT moves in getting closer to Gavin.

"If we need you to ever help us, then just know that we are truly desperate and possibly dreaming," JT says.

Harrison giggles, but tries to hide it.

"You guys leave that boy alone," Francis interjects... "You never know, you just might need his help one day."

Suddenly, Francis gasps putting her hand over her mouth.

"Oh, my, gosh. Adam," she hollers, running to Harrison's uncle Adam.

Harrison follows his mom.

Francis hugs Adam tightly. Harrison notices the exhilaration in her voice.

"What are you doing here? Shouldn't you be at the Academy right now getting ready to welcome the students?" she asks.

"You think I would miss the opportunity to see my nephew off? Douglas would have wanted to be here so bad. So, in his honor, I came to see Harrison off. And I get to ride to the Academy with him for his first time. I couldn't pass that up. Plus, I was in the area, so try not to get all sentimental, kid."

Uncle Adam grasps Harrison's shoulder firmly, pulling him closer.

The strong grip numbs his whole left side.

"I like your shirt, man. I think it's pretty cool you are wearing your dad's old alumni shirt. I am sure he would have loved that. It's a little big though," he says, laughing.

"Yeah, you didn't tell me you packed his shirt," Francis says "You could've let me know. I didn't want to make a big deal about it, but it almost made me break down in tears."

Tears begin forming in her eyes.

"Yeah, well I just kind of thought about it recently. Sorry I forgot to mention it to you," he responds, staring at the ground.

Harrison feels his uncle's giant palm resting on his head.

"Your dad was the best ever. We all knew he was going to be the next Destine Elder. And I believe to this day that if that would have ever happened, he would've gone down as the best ever," Adam smiles down at Harrison.

Abruptly, a loud noise squeals from the colossal ferry. Startling Harrison, he glances over at the boat. Waves beat against the dark burgundy stripes of the boat as it cuts through the turbulent water.

"Well, that's the first horn. We better get moving," Adam says. "Your journey is about to begin nephew and it's going to be a wild ride. I will meet you there in a minute."

"Give me hug. It was so good seeing you," Francis says, pulling his uncle Adam close to her.

"It was great seeing you too. See you later, sis," his uncle Adam says, walking toward the ferry.

Harrison looks over and sees JT hugging his parents just like the rest of the crowd.

Gavin jogs over to them.

"Well, Harrison, good luck. I am going to miss you," Gavin says, staring at the ground.

"Thanks, man, I am going to miss you too. But I will keep in touch. You just make sure you keep working on those forms."

Harrison hugs him. Walking off, Gavin joins JT.

Harrison looks at his mom, tears pour down her face like a dam breaking.

"I am proud of you and I know your dad would be too. Go and work hard and try to be the best that you can be. And if you need anything, your uncle is up there," Francis says.

She pulls him close for a giant hug.

"Thanks, mom. I will," he replies.

The second horn blasts from the ferry. "Well, got to go."

Heading to the ferry, her hand touches his back.

"I almost forgot. I thought maybe you would want to take this with you. It might be helpful while you are up there. I found this in your pocket the night at the party when you were blasted through the window.," she says pulling out the old golden, aged compass that Mr. Hall gave him.

Harrison couldn't believe he forgot all about that compass.

"Wow thanks, I guess I forgot about it. But why didn't you give it to me sooner?" he says putting the compass in his pocket.

"I didn't know where I put it. But this morning for some odd reason, it was like it wanted me to find it. It was as if it had a mind of its own, calling me to it... weird huh?" she replies as they stand right in front of the dock for the ferry.

"Huh, yeah kind of. Oh well, I love you mom and see you later," he says hugging her.

"Bye honey, I love you too," she says.

Walking up to the ferry, he views the same agent that delivered the letters to the party, talking to his uncle. As soon as he gets on the ferry, JT, Jaylen, and Joseph rush toward him. The excitement is evident in their small talk as they walk towards his uncle.

Harrison looks over the edge as the boat begins to move.

The wind tousles his hair as the boat picks up speed.

"I must ask you, your honor. Why are you here in Eriz when the Ragnar council members are supposed to be at the Academy getting ready for the students to get back?" the agent asks his uncle Adam.

They all listen trying not to look obvious.

"I had to be somewhere last night for an important meeting. So, I figured I could just ride back with my nephew since this is his first time at the Academy," his uncle Adam replies with his arms leaning on the shiny silver rails.

"Oh okay. Where were you if you don't mind me asking?" the agent asks.

"I was in Dosman," his uncle Adam replies.

Harrison meets JT's eyes in shock.

"But I am not the only one gone from the Academy right now, so I can't get in too much trouble," his uncle Adam says laughing.

"Oh really. Who else from the Academy isn't there?"

"Two teachers, Norman Drake, and Buford Lloyd. Both of them had to go to Dosman too for some reason," Adam replies.

Harrison and JT turn their backs to them.

"Dude, the mysterious robed guy last night could have been your uncle," JT whispers as the wind picks up, blowing their hair in every direction.

"Yeah. But the problem is if what he is saying is true, it could be one of the other two teachers too," Harrison replies in disbelief.

"What are you guys talking about over there?" Jaylen asks.

"Let's go find a cabin in the ferry inside and we will fill you in on everything," Harrison says, motioning them to follow him.

The clouds begin to pour rain down, soaking Harrison's whole face, as they make their way down the stairs to the lower deck.

Harrison and his friends sit in a small room in the lower deck.

"You got to be kidding me. All that is true? That is wild," Jaylen says.

"Why couldn't you fill us in sooner? I mean we have all been friends for years. You should have known that we would have kept this secret and would have helped in any way," Joseph says, looking at Harrison and JT.

"Well I am glad that maybe we didn't go to that antique shop. That would have been kind of scary with weird robe guy. Plus, if I fell in a toilet, I think I would have cried," Jaylen says.

"Oh, JT did cry, you just couldn't tell because of the toilet water running down his face," Harrison replies, with a laugh.

"Funny, laugh it up. I can say I am the best friend you all got." JT folds his arms. "The crap I go through for you guys."

"Yeah, crap all right," Joseph responds.

Bending forward, Harrison signals them to come closer.

"I appreciate you all doing this for me. But I don't want you guys to feel like you have to," he whispers.

"Dude, we all know you would do this for us without hesitating," Joseph responds.

"Yeah, I mean if we can help you find out whatever happened to your dad then it's all worth it." Jaylen scoots closer to Harrison. "And it sounds like they are trying to hide something with the letter you got, so I want to find out what it is."

"We just got to be smart. We need to take our time, there is no need to rush. We are going to have a lot on our plate as it is with classes. Adding this is going to make everything harder, so we just got to handle all this carefully," JT says.

Jaylen leans back in his seat and places his hands behind his head.

"So as of now, we think maybe that guy who was in the antique shop could have sent the letter to you, Harrison because of that comment from Mr. Garner about him working at the Academy?" Jaylen says.

"Right now, that is what I am thinking. My uncle mentioned that there were three people from the Academy in Dosman that same night. Him, Norman Drake, and Buford Lloyd, so it could possibly be one of them," Harrison says.

Joseph stares at the ceiling, looking as if he is thinking hard. "Great, well two of these guys we have for classes. When I looked at my schedule the other day, I saw both of their names. So, two teachers and a Ragnar council member are on the list for possibly being weird robe guy. Absolutely awesome."

"At least we can maybe get to know the teachers and see which one it is," Harrison says, leaning back in his seat.

"Dude, what if it's your uncle? I mean you can't rule him out," JT says, leaning towards Harrison.

"It can't be him, though. I know him and he wouldn't do anything like that," Harrison replies.

Suddenly, Samuel and his two chubby bodyguards push the door open.

"What are you losers talking about?" Samuel says with a smirk. "Must be trying to hide something if you have to close the door."

Harrison walks toward them.

"Maybe we just close the door to keep the real losers out," Harrison says getting closer to them.

JT, Joseph, and Jaylen stand behind him.

"So, one of my friends talked to Victoria's close friend, and she told him how Victoria told her that she was not talking to you anymore. I feel bad for you, Grady." Samuel continues to mock him. "I mean, all you got are these three losers. It has to be terrible to be you. No girl wants you. I mean you chased one away. You chased your dad away. You must be like the biggest loser of all time."

Samuel breaks out into a laugh.

Instantly, Harrison's nostrils flare and he lunges toward Samuel. JT, Joseph and Jaylen, hold him back from attacking Samuel.

"If you mention my dad one more time, I swear it will be the last," Harrison replies pulling against his friends as they hold him tightly.

"Oh yeah, sorry. Don't want anybody from the Ragnar council or the Elder to hear. I forgot we are supposed to be silent about that whole thing," Samuel whispers, mocking him.

"Oh, by the way, that is so cute. You put your daddy's shirt on for today. It's too bad he couldn't see you it in and realize how much of a loser you look in it. Or actually, I guess what is really worse is you never got to see how much of a loser he probably looked in it."

Samuel stares straight into Harrison's eyes, as if daring him to fight back.

Harrison's whole body tenses up. He breaks free and throws a punch at Samuel's face. Samuel dodges it, grabs Harrison, and pulls him to the ground. Rolling down the hallway, they both exchange blows.

Harrison picks Samuel up, slamming him into the wall. The noise of the fight resonates through the whole cabin.

People start coming out to watch. The chubby boys close the door holding his friends in the room.

Samuel pushes Harrison into the opposite wall. Grabbing his throat tightly, he punches Harrison in the jaw. Harrison glances over and sees the two chubby boys holding the door closed so no one can leave.

Samuel punches him in the face again. Harrison drops to the ground. Then he curls into a ball while Samuel continues to kick him. His eyesight becomes blurry, making it difficult to block Samuel's kicks.

Suddenly, someone else slams Samuel against the wall. Harrison manages to slowly sit up. It's his uncle Adam.

"If I ever see you touch my nephew again, you will be kicked out the Academy so fast, you won't know what happened."

His uncle Adam pins Samuel up against the wall.

Samuel kicks his feet like a toddler having a tantrum. Onlookers start leaving. The chubby boys still hold the door closed. Harrison's friends holler and bang against the door, trying to reach him.

"Yes, sir," Samuel says, dropping back onto the floor.

The chubby boys shake as his Uncle Adam approaches.

"Open the door, boys, and get going," his Uncle Adam says.

"Yes sir," they reply in unison, moving quickly down the hallway with Samuel.

Opening the door, JT lunges with a heavy punch.

"Take this punk," JT says. He punches his Uncle Adam in the face.

JT falls to the ground in pain. His Uncle Adam stands unfazed.

"Holy crap, what is your chin made of, rock?" JT says.

"Well, maybe you will learn not to pick fights then, huh?" Adam says, helping him up.

"Pick fights? Shoot, I won't be able to use the fingers on this hand to pick my nose," JT says, trying to open his hand.

Harrison lays quietly on the ground. Jaylen and Joseph help Harrison stand up.

Uncle Adam points his finger in Harrison's face. "And if I ever see you fight that boy again, I will take you home myself. You have to be smarter than that, Harrison. You probably don't want to hear this, but you need to. You need to be more like your dad. You think he would have ever fought someone on the way to the Academy?" Uncle Adam says, looking intently at him.

"I don't know, I never got to know him, remember?" Harrison says quietly, staring at the floor.

Taking a deep breath, his Uncle Adam turns and begins to walk away.

"Go change and meet on the deck. We are about to be at the Academy," he says going up the stairs.

Why do I need to change?

Looking down, he sees his shirt. It has a giant rip from the collar to the middle splitting the word *Academy*. He closes his eyes and sighs.

You gotta be kidding me.

CHAPTER 9

Arriving at The Destine Academy

The ferry slows down and begins to bob in the perfect, blue water. Harrison walks up the stairs to meet everyone. The wind rushes through his hair, giving it a messy appearance. The deck is jam-packed with people looking straight towards his uncle Adam who is reclining at the front of the ferry.

Harrison glances around the crowd, trying to find his friends. The refreshing air calms him. Finally seeing, JT, Joseph and Jaylen, Harrison makes his way through the people as he tries to get to his friends.

"About time you got up here," Joseph says, looking at Harrison.

Harrison slides in-between them as they make room for him.

"I can't believe my shirt got ripped. Makes me so mad," Harrison announces sounding upset. Something cold rubs against his arm sending a bone-chilling sensation throughout the spot it hit. He glances down to see JT standing next to him with a large plastic ice bag on top of his hand.

"What?" JT says, looking at Harrison.

"Nothing, I was just wondering what in the world was touching me that was so cold," Harrison replies.

"While you were changing your shirt, I went to the nurse to get some ice because of the metal jaw that your uncle has," JT says.

They laugh at him then look up toward his uncle, awaiting his reply.

"Hey, it's not funny," JT moves the bag of ice off his hand. "It was the same pretty red-headed nurse you had looking over you when you were in the hospital, so I couldn't go in there saying I punched another man's face and almost broke my hand. So, I lied and said Jaylen almost fell off the ferry because he has a really bad sneezing condition and I had to catch him and pull him up. Thought it would sound better."

"Really the same nurse, huh? What're the chances of that?" Harrison says.

Adam stands up with a microphone.

"Alright everyone, I need your attention. My name is Adam Smalls and I am a member of the Ragnar Council.

We will be approaching the Academy in just a few minutes. To the returning students, I hope you are itching to get back to work and start another year at the Academy. Now for the new students, this first year is going to expose you to some new things that you have never experienced. You will be around many people that can harness and control their Power Flow which is within us all. You will learn more about that this year for yourselves. We come to a very special part of our nation. Because of all the energy the animals have been exposed to for hundreds of years, they have been affected by it. Which means... they can talk."

"Did he just say talk?" Jaylen whispers to Harrison.

Harrison nods, still listening intently.

"As you will see when we approach the Academy, you will be meeting our own little greeting crew, the Singing-Dancing ducks and geese. For years they fought over who controlled the water in front of the Academy because they both wanted to sing and dance to the students coming in on the ferry. It was quite a sight because not much singing got done. I am telling you; those ducks had a mean right hook."

Joseph nudges JT, "unlike someone I know."

"For the first couple of months, they couldn't get the students to focus because they all talked about the brawl they saw in front of the Academy. But that was all settled when our last Destine Elder helped them come to a peace treaty and join forces. Now we are treated to their wonderful singing and dancing. Now please, listen carefully. When you exit this ferry there will be a person from registration waiting to give you all the next instructions. Thank you and have a great year."

All the students push Harrison and his friends against the side rails trying to get a better look at the upcoming performance. Harrison is flattened against the side of the rail. The ducks and geese take his mind off the pain. They sing and dance in unison. Spinning and twirling with their wings spread.

Welcome, welcome, to another school year
Join us, join us, stand up and cheer

Singing, they all blast out of the water landing and standing on the water holding their last note while shaking their wings. Suddenly a tiny multicolored duck wearing an oversized hat on top of his head, lands in front of them. He holds a small stick, pretending it is a microphone.

Check, Check, welcome back it's time to put in that work,
you know
Young duckling on the mic, this is what I do, hear the flow
Grind hard so we all can make it to the top
Because all the people know, Destines don't flop

Dropping the stick in the water, the small duck folds his wings across his body. His hat droops over his eyes.

"We already told you we don't want that hippity hop stuff in our routine. It's not real music. We practiced this routine all summer and when it's show time you screw it up by pulling this prank," one of the angry ducks squeals at him as the ferry stations.

The other students release the boys from their painful position against the rail, as they scramble to get their belongings.

Heading downstairs to get their bags, JT looks at Harrison. "I don't know why they were mad. I thought the little guy was a pretty good rapper."

Strolling off the boat like a hungry herd, Harrison and his friends walk closely to one another. His nerves are beginning to rise with each step he takes closer to the Academy. Sweat drips from all over his body.

Approaching the lady from registration, her neatly charcoal straight hair captures everyone's attention. It is so long it touches her feet. Four enormous bronze statues stand behind her capturing the sunlight from the clear sky.

"Welcome to the Destine Academy where the elite warriors from the Destine nation are trained. We are trained to protect and defend the Destine people of our great nation. My name is Emily Bolton and I am in charge of registration, and it is my honor to welcome you all here today. I will be distributing colored wristbands to all of you. Each class will get a color to help us organize and put you in the right housing facility. We will break you all into lines. So, listen up. Let me refresh your memory. Each class has a unique title. First-year students are called Kadens, second-year students are called Cerdics. Third-year students are called Kylers, and fourth-year students are called Gideons. I want all the Kadens to line up in front of the first statue, which is the very first Elder. Cerdics you line up in front of the Second Elder statue. Kyler's line up in front of the Third Elder statue and Kyler's please line up in front of the fourth Elder statue. Go ahead and do that now, and I will have people coming to give you your colored wristbands," she announces.

Harrison gets in line behind his friends. With only two other people ahead of them, Harrison glances at the statue, waiting for the students to all get in the right line. He tunes out JT Jaylen and Joseph and concentrates on the statue of the First Elder.

Towering over them, Harrison has to lift his neck to observe all of it. Every detail is neatly defined. Something suddenly catches his attention. The statue is holding what looks to be a compass in its hand. His loses his breath.

That looks just like the compass I got from Mr. Hall. His heart beats faster. *So, what if the compass I have is really the Elder's compass?*

"*DUDE*!" JT screams, breaking Harrison out of his trance.

"Sorry, caught daydreaming, what's up?" Harrison says.

"I was screaming your name. You were daydreaming that hard?" JT says.

"Look at that statue of the First Destine Elder. Look at what he is holding in his right hand," Harrison whispers softly.

"Looks like a compass or something like that," Jaylen replies as they all observe it.

"I think I have that same compass in my pocket right now," Harrison declares.

"Okay, C'mon, now I know we didn't get to see what happened, but just how bad did Samuel hit you upside your head? You are talking crazy. How would you have the First Elder's compass?" Joseph says.

"I didn't tell you guys because I forgot about it. I first got it the night of the party. JT's dad gave it to me before we received our letters. He said he found it and told me that my dad came in asking if he had any leads on this compass because he needed it on his next mission. That next mission, Mr. Hall said was the Silent Mission."

"Hold up. How did you forget something like that? I mean that doesn't make sense," JT says.

"I just never thought about it when I woke up in the hospital. My mom said she found it in my pocket that day and just forgot to give it to me. She handed it to me before we got on the ferry," he responds.

A registration lady walks down the line. She hands Harrison his blue wristband then stops.

"Hey, you are Douglas Grady's son, aren't you?" she asks, staring at him curiously.

"Yes, ma'am, I am," Harrison replies, putting the wristband on.

"Wow you have grown up. I remember when he used to bring you to the office when you were just a baby. Wow, how time flies. Anyways, good luck this year. If you are Douglas' son, I am sure all this will come naturally to you," she replies.

She smiles gently and walks off.

"Okay. Kadens should all have a blue wristband. Cerdics should have a yellow one. Kylers should have green, and Gideons should have red. When you all get to your buildings there are dormitory areas for all the female students and an area for all the male students. This campus is broken up into sections. We have main buildings connecting to one another that you can visibly see now. Each one of those buildings is assigned to a certain class. This first building we see is the Gideon's classrooms and main offices for the Elder and The Ragnar Council. The building to the left of that one is for the Kylers. The one slightly behind that one is the Cerdics. Now behind those buildings is a long line of white huts. Those are where the Kaden's classes will be held," Mrs. Bolton announces.

Moans erupt from the first line.

Viewing the buildings behind the statues, Harrison can tell that it's a good walking distance to the buildings. Sitting high on top of a steep hill, they look massive. The grass is a lively dark green that looks perfect.

"The Destine Elder will speak to you all tonight after dinner. Right now, you may walk in a line to your dorms. Get situated and head to the cafeteria to eat," Mrs. Bolton says waving everyone to go.

The line begins to move. Harrison walks by the statue and stares at the compass in his hand. Observing the details quickly, he notices it has every detail that the compass in his pocket has.

I got to find out more information about this compass.

Harrison climbs the stairs to the Academy.

If my dad was looking for this to use for his mission, then I must find out what is so special about this. Maybe then it will reveal to me what the Destine Elder assigned his group to do that night.

Stepping inside, the cool air brushes against his face. It looks ancient inside but updated at the same time. Deep gray paint covers every wall, matching the dim lighting. The marble floor shines as if it was just polished. Behind the building, are small huts, lined up side by side.

"Well, a year of taking classes in those things should be fun, I guess," Jaylen says as they walk past the huts.

"I am starting to think a lot of things here are going to make this year interesting," Harrison replies.

CHAPTER
10

A Reserved Spot

The line for the buffet extends out of the cafeteria doors. Harrison, JT, Jaylen, and Joseph walk to the back of the line.

"Dang, did we take that long to get our room ready?" Jaylen says, straining his neck to see the front of the line.

"This is ridiculous," JT says.

Harrison observes the person in front of JT who keeps glancing back at them. The boy seems to be struggling to not make it obvious. His delicate brown eyes stare back at him every couple of seconds. He keeps turning around or moves his head toward them. He rubs his hands through his spiky light brown hair every couple of seconds.

Reaching out and grabbing their trays, Harrison nudges Jaylen as they race to grab the freshly cooked glazed chicken legs. The sweet aroma of the baby carrots and string beans fills their nostrils.

"You see that guy over there?" Harrison asks, pointing to the boy in front of JT.

"Yeah, what about him?" Jaylen replies, taking every food item from the line.

"You know who he is?" Harrison asks.

"Nope. I did see him in the dormitory, and I saw his blue wristband, so I know he is a Kaden like us. Why do you want to know?" Jaylen responds.

"When we were in line it seemed like he was trying to listen to us," Harrison answers.

"Dude, you are just being paranoid. I know that these last couple of months have been crazy for you, but I just want to tell you that not everyone is out to get you," Jaylen responds, holding two trays of food stacked high.

"Yeah, I guess you are right," Harrison holds his tray tightly. "Gosh man, do you really need that much food?"

They sit down at a table in the corner of the cafeteria.

Harrison spots a few people from different tables pointing over to their table.

Are they pointing at me because they saw me and Samuel fight on the ferry? he thinks, trying not to pay attention to them.

"Man, I cannot wait until the morning to see what types of cereal they have. I imagine this place would have plenty to choose from," JT says, looking around the cafeteria.

"You are already talking about breakfast and we haven't even got through dinner yet," Joseph responds, shaking his head.

Suddenly, a pretty girl with long, black, curly hair walks over to their table with two other girls. The girls stare as Harrison stuffs about fifty fries in his mouth.

"I don't mean to bother you but are you the son of the famous Douglas Grady? My dad went to school with your dad and he always speaks so highly of your dad," the girl with the curly hair says.

Struggling to swallow the half-chewed fries down quickly, Harrison takes a big gulp.

"Yeah, that's me," Harrison says not knowing if he should smile or not.

"Well I think it is really cool that I can tell my dad I go to school with the son of Douglas Grady," she says. "See you around."

"That was weird. But secretly, I wish I could use my dad to talk to girls," JT chews his food. "I mean, I don't know how well that would go if I tried. Not many girls are into antiques," JT says as they all laugh.

"Speaking of antiques, should we try to look at the blueprint tonight to see if it really works?" JT whispers.

"No, we need to wait a while before we try that. I am sure they are a little extra observant the first couple of days," Jaylen responds, packing a pile of fries in his mouth.

"I agree with Jaylen. We need to be strategic about all of this. We have so many questions that need answers. We got to see if this blueprint works and if it does, then we got to find the secret rooms. We have this compass that we don't really know anything about. And we are pretty certain that crazy robe guy is someone that is here. Plus, on top of all that, we start our first-year classes tomorrow," Harrison says.

"Yeah and there's another big question we need an answer to," JT says,

"What's that?" Harrison asks.

"What type of cereal do they serve for breakfast?" JT responds, smiling big.

At that moment a loud bell goes off signaling them to the auditorium.

"Guess it's time to go listen to the Elder speak," Joseph says standing up and stretching his arms.

They throw their trash away and walk towards the auditorium. Students clog the hallway as they wait to enter in the big room. Two security agents walk towards Harrison.

"Grady, right?" one of the agents asks Harrison.

"Yes, sir," he responds, sweating.

"Elder Dirk has requested that you sit in the front at the assigned spot that is reserved just for you," he replies.

"Okay, yes sir," Harrison says looking at his friends who seem nervous.

He watches, as they are escorted to their seats. Walking down the long aisle, Harrison feels the eyes staring at him.

Why would the Elder make me sit at the front in a reserved spot?

An empty seat at the end of the aisle sticks out with a huge sign that says:

Reserved for Grady, Harrison.

Harrison sits and notices the person sitting next to him. It is the guy who was staring at him in the lunch line. Looking straight ahead, waiting for the Elder to come and speak, gentle whispers erupt throughout the auditorium. Finally looking over, the boy puts his hand out to shake his hand.

"My name is Tommy Drake, you must be Harrison Grady," he says, waiting for Harrison to shake his hand.

"How did you know my name?" Harrison asks shaking his hand looking surprised.

"Well, I know this is going to sound crazy but I kind of was given a sign of who you were," Tommy responds, smirking.

"Really what type of sign were you given?" Harrison responds.

"Ummm, that big sign right there that says your name," Tommy replies pointing to the sign on the floor.

"Oh yeah, duh, I should have known that," Harrison says.

Sebastian Darby walks to the podium.

"Hello students, I welcome you here to another school year, my name is Sebastian Darby and I am the Destine Elder's apprentice," he says.

His hands are behind his back and he is twirling his thumbs.

"I want to introduce tonight, our great leader, the Destine Elder of our great Destine nation and new Headmaster, Jovan Dirk."

Everyone stands to clap. The Destine Elder walks slowly to the podium. He grabs the podium and smiles gently to the students. He motions them to sit. As Harrison sits The Elder stares at him.

The auditorium goes silent. Harrison, anticipating hearing what the Elder is going to say, hears a static buzzing in his ear because it is so quiet.

"It is a great day for our great nation. Today, a new class of Kadens begins their journey to become elite warriors of the Destine people, while a new class of Gideons enter their final year of the Academy and are one year away from joining our elite warriors. Some of you may join the regular ranks of the elite warrior army, while some of you maybe will get the opportunity to join an elite task force, like the famous Red Hawks who protect and oversee the Ragnar Council. Maybe some of you will one day be strong and wise enough to be on the Council yourself. Or maybe the next Destine Elder is sitting in this room right now."

Harrison sees people in the front row looking around at each other.

"I want to wish you all a prosperous year of studies and training. I am personally excited to see all of you grow. When I look out, I see individuals who wanted to be part of something bigger than themselves. I see young men and women who believe they are destined to protect the Destine people and help keep peace amongst the other two great nations. The world is safer when the Destines have strong elite warriors. You all are the future. This year is a special year also. I wanted to share with all of you that this year makes the 150th year since the first Destine Elder created this great nation. In the spring we will be celebrating with a huge celebration. So, Kylers, you will be in charge of helping put a group together and planning a celebration. I ask your class to do this since the Gideons are going to be busy with their graduating exams. So tomorrow before classes start, we will be doing our annual first-day tradition, The First Spar which was initiated by the First Elder himself. Tomorrow we will be witnessing history in this famous tradition as a Kaden will be sparring against a Gideon."

Harrison looks around seeing the shock on everyone's faces except for Tommy next to him. Tommy smiles.

"I know what many of you are thinking. You are thinking that I lost my mind. Some of our best students to go through this school, even Douglas Grady never sparred in the traditional First Spar as a Kaden. I assure you I would never put a Kaden in danger if I didn't believe they could not handle themselves. I know Kadens will just be learning this year the basics of harnessing energy from their Power Flow, and I understand that Gideons has up to this point had three years of training. But this is a special case. The young Kaden who will be sparring tomorrow is already close to the Gideon's Power Flow control."

Gasps fill the room. Harrison views the amazement on all the students' faces.

"The student representing the Gideon's is the student who is first in class. That student is Clark Bell."

Bursting out in a round of applause, The Elder signals him to stand. In the distance towards the middle of the room a boy stands up tightening his ponytail and waving to the student body.

"And the Kaden who will be making history tomorrow is...Tommy Drake, the son of the Academy's Power Flow Instructor, Norman Drake."

Tommy stands up beside him.

He is the Kaden who can control his Power Flow like that? That is crazy.

Minimal hand claps fill the room.

"Now, rest up and be ready for your first day tomorrow. May you all prosper this year in wisdom and strength," the Elder says, stepping away from the podium.

Instantly, the registration lady, Emily Bolton, steps to the podium as the place fills with many conversations, making a loud muffing noise.

"Okay, everyone is required to head to your rooms when you leave here. Have a great night," she says as everyone stands in unison.

Slowly standing up, Harrison gets up after Tommy.

"Well, good luck tomorrow, I guess," Harrison says, rubbing the back of his head.

"Thanks, I am excited. This is the first time I get to use my energy attacks in a fight with someone other than my dad. That gets kind of old just hanging out with your dad," Tommy says giggling softly.

"Yeah, I could imagine," Harrison replies glancing at the ground. "See you tomorrow."

"Okay, see you then," Tommy says as Harrison walks away.

Harrison walks to his room. When he arrives, the door is slightly open.

JT must have been in front of that crazy crowd to get here so fast.

He enters and notices the darkness overwhelming his room.

"JT, you in here?" Harrison says stepping on something that feels like paper. Picking it up he cuts the light on to see what is on it.

His eyes grow wide, losing his breath as he gazes at the paper. The paper looks like it is a copy of the original things on the page. He begins reading:

Dear Adam,

I am proud of you, not just as a brother-in-law but as a friend. Elder Dirk has informed me that I am going to be the captain of the new task force he is putting together, the Silver Falcons. As you finish your last year at the Academy, study, and train hard and I promise you, you have a reserved spot on the Silver Falcons.

Douglas Grady

He begins reading the next note.

Dear Adam,

I can't believe it's been two years since you graduated from the Academy. I am sorry that I haven't been able to get up with you. I have been slammed with missions, and this past month we have been training for a secret mission. I can't even tell Francis Anyways, your reserved spot is still there, and I wanted to tell you that it sounds like I may need some more help on this next mission. If you want, you can join the Silver Falcons for my next upcoming mission.

THE ARK OF POWER

Douglas Grady

Falling onto his bed, his back slams on the mattress that feels like rocks. Turning the paper around, big red letters cover the top.

THESE WERE TAKEN THE NIGHT HE LEFT FOR THE SILENT MISSION

Shooting his eyes to pictures at the bottom of the page. Harrison quits breathing as soon as he sees them. In the first picture, he sees his dad taking his Destine Academy Alumni shirt off on the front porch and putting on his battle gear. The next picture shows him meeting his uncle Adam at the end of the street with his battle gear on.

JT walks in. Harrison sits up.

"I got to show you this," Harrison says.

CHAPTER 11

Making History

Tucking in his navy-blue shirt, Harrison waits for JT to get out of the bathroom.

"Are you ready to head to breakfast yet?" Harrison says, through the door.

JT walks out grimacing.

"Yeah, yeah I am ready. I just can't stand this stupid shirt being tucked in. I can't believe we got four years of this crap," JT says, tugging at his shirt.

They head out the door. Jaylen and Joseph are waiting for them in the hallway.

"It's about time. We can't keep getting to the cafeteria late for every meal," Joseph says.

"Well, I almost overslept since we got to bed late. I mean we were up half the night looking at that note that was left in our room," JT replies as they walk to the cafeteria.

Approaching the cafeteria, they get right into line. Suddenly, JT, sprints off to the back of the room as if he was being chased by dogs.

"You got to be kidding me. Look at all this cereal," JT runs up and down the cereal line admiring all the different types of cereal. "There has to be at least seventy-five different types here."

Shaking his head, Harrison grabs a bowl of blueberry oatmeal and a ripe banana. He sits at a table next to a window that looks out over a huge field where people are preparing for the First Spar. His friends sit down. JT smiles and places four bowls of different kinds of cereal on the table.

"This place just got a little bit cooler to me," JT says.

"So, after sleeping on it, have you been able to wrap your head around that note?" Jaylen asks Harrison.

Harrison picks through his food.

"It just forms more questions. I feel like this whole thing is just going to present me with more questions than answers," Harrison replies.

"I just want to know who went in your room and laid it there, and how the heck did they get those notes and pictures if they are real," Jaylen says.

"That's what I think is key. How do you even know if they are trustworthy? Anybody can write a note and say it's someone else's handwriting. And the pictures could have been from any time. I am sure your dad took his shirt off more than once on the porch and met your uncle more than once," Joseph says.

"Yeah, the problem is I never saw my dad's handwriting before, so I have no way of really telling if it's fake or not," Harrison responds, spinning his spoon in his oatmeal.

"Maybe the Academy has something with your dad's handwriting on it. I mean it seems like he is an idol since he was the strongest and smartest Destine warrior to graduate from here," JT says, eating his third bowl of cereal.

"Yeah, that would help us find out. Next problem though, how do we find something he wrote?" Joseph asks.

"Good question," Harrison replies.

"Another thing. If the notes and pictures are real and your uncle did, in fact, go on the Silent Mission with them, then how did he never go missing and why would all the reports say that all the Silver Falcons went missing? Jaylen says.

"Yeah, I know. Why would my uncle not tell my mom about this? It just doesn't make sense right now. We got to figure this out, or it's going to drive me crazy," Harrison says.

The bell rings.

"Guess it's time to see that Tommy person get wrecked by that Clark guy," JT slurps the milk out of the last bowl. "Poor guy."

The stadium is full as they try to find a seat. Four seats open up in the middle section. Harrison squints, gazing down at the field and sees Tommy and Clark at opposite ends of the field with the Elder in the middle. They both are wearing the Academy's black gym shorts.

The orange shirt Tommy has on sticks out better compared to the plain white shirt Clark has on. Gripping the microphone, the Elder pats the top of it making the stadium instantly go silent.

"What an honor it is to continue this tradition. The rules are simple. The first one to get hit by an energy attack loses. Once the official declares it a hit then the match stops. The two participants understand the rules as the official has already talked to them. Good luck to both of you," the Elder says.

Moving off the field, he stops halfway, smacking himself in his head.

"I almost forgot, we need an energy field around the fighting area, or it could get really bad," the Elder says.

He lifts his right arm stretching towards the sky with his palm up. A small yellow energy ball hovers above his hand. He pushes it up quickly, shooting it into the air. It explodes into a large yellow energy net. It creates a barrier between the field and the seats.

The official calls for Tommy and Clark to take some steps closer. Motioning to see if they are both ready, they both nod.

"First Spar now!" the official says, jumping out of their way.

They both run towards one another. Clark throws a punch. Tommy pushes it up and flips backward invading it. Squatting low, Tommy is waiting for Clark to attack. Clark seems embarrassed as the student body is amazed at what they see from Tommy.

Clark runs at Tommy unleashing various punches and kicks. One finally connects, hitting Tommy in his face. He soars immediately into the energy wall. His body crashes into it.

Focusing quickly, Tommy's feet shine purple with energy covering them. He begins to run up the energy wall. Clark stands in the middle of the field watching. Running halfway up the wall, Tommy stops and stares at Clark who is now crouching slightly and beginning to power up for an energy move.

Clark is screaming as he is trying to bring his power out. The blue energy is circling him as it covers him. The crowd is in shock that Clark is about to unleash that powerful of a move on Tommy. Harrison hears people talking in front of him.

"I can't believe Clark is about to unleash his Brutal Ray Blast on this kid," one says.

"Yeah the kid is impressive to already be this far along, but this move is so crazy," the other replies.

Tommy begins to slightly crouch, screaming and powering up, standing on the wall. Purple energy starts to circle and cover his body. Suddenly, Clark forming a large blue energy ball in his hand launches it at Tommy.

"Brutal Ray Blast," he screams as the energy ball becomes a large blue energy beam coming towards Tommy. Tommy bends his legs and pushes off the wall flying to the beam holding a purple energy ball spinning quickly in both hands.

"Omega Supersonic Blast" he screams.

Splitting Clark's beam, Tommy pushes the energy ball into his chest. Tommy lets go of it pushing Clark into the ground bouncing off of it.

The crowd is silent.

"Tommy Drake is the winner," the official announces.

The place roars in applause.

"You all may head to class now," the official says.

Harrison glances at JT.

"Remind me not to mess with him," JT says as they stand up and head to class.

Staring towards the first hut, Harrison notices an older man bouncing up and down on his toes continually with his arms behind his back, cheerfully shouting at each student walking by.

"Good morning...Hello, Good morning!"

Every couple of moments, he scratches his shaggy gray beard and the top of his bald head that is sprouting various little gray hairs. on the back of his head.

Approaching his classroom, the excitement beams from his face with each bounce.

"Good morning young men!" the old man says to Harrison, JT, Jaylen, and Joseph. "History 1, room sixteen. If that is what you are looking for, you are in the right place. Just go in and take a seat."

Stepping in, the fruity smell of pineapples and bananas overwhelms Harrison's nose. Holding his nose, trying to stop the smell from entering in anymore, it makes his eyes squint gradually blurring the posters overtaking the walls around the classroom.

As soon as he sits, the guy from outside rushes into the classroom. Walking quickly with his robe on, he gets to the front of the room. Just gazing at the class for a couple moments, he suddenly hurls the robe off of him and on to his cluttered desk.

"I can't stand those robes while teaching, so I like to teach in what makes me comfortable," Mr. Lloyd says.

He brushes the wrinkles out of his flamboyant, short sleeve button up Hawaiian shirt and dingy khaki shorts. Giggles start to fill the room.

"And if you tell the administration or any other teacher, I teach in this, you will be history," Mr. Lloyd says.

The giggles stop instantly.

"Well, speaking of History, welcome to History 1. My name is Buford Lloyd and you may call me Mr. Lloyd. I will be your history teacher for the next four years," Mr. Lloyd says as he puts a miniature podium in front of him.

Tapping the board behind him, the board lights up with notes on it.

"Alrighty, go ahead and get some paper out, and please try to keep up," Mr. Lloyd says.

The board gleams bright with *How the Destine people nation started and why we are called Destines*. Harrison writes it down on his paper and is curious.

"Now, we need to understand the beginning to really understand the rest. If you don't understand the context of the beginning of the story, then the context will be messed up for the rest," Mr. Lloyd says bouncing on his toes as he talks.

"It all started like this. About one hundred and seventy years ago, all people lived on one mainland. Everybody was unified. Peace rested on the land. Two brothers grew up in the land and were the strongest. The power that they could generate from their Power Flow was unimaginable. The younger brother fell in love with a very beautiful young lady. To demonstrate his love, he went to the Purhara Mountains to search for a rare gem to place on her engagement ring. He spent three years there. It took him three and a half years to return. When he came back his power had increased immensely, and it grew dark somehow. He was bent on more power when he returned. The beautiful lady he loved grew scared of him. He was hurt and felt like she was betraying him. He planned to kill her until the older brother stepped in and saved her. Feeling betrayed by both of them he fled. Years went by and the older brother and the lovely lady fell in love and got married. Knowing that his brother may come back in revenge he trained 3 young men and 2 young ladies. He was given the title the Supreme Elder and they were known as his five disciples. They grew powerful learning from the Supreme Elder. Years later the younger brother returned vowing vengeance. His power was unlike anything ever seen. The Supreme Elder and his five disciples fought him. It took all of them to battle against him. They finally defeated him. Laying there about to die, he vowed vengeance still against his brother and his five disciples. The Supreme Elder was disturbed at what became of his brother. He knew that whatever his brother used to grow his power dark and evil, others could find too. He wanted to help prevent that, so he told his five disciples to form five clans that we now call nations. In those nations, they were to train and raise up warriors to keep peace and prevent anything like that from happening again. Each disciple was to become Elders of their nation. Each one went and did as their master told them. In the Supreme Elders last years, he began to have visions and he wrote the prophecies on scrolls. He sent the scroll to each of his disciples. He told of how one nation was destined to a great destiny and was going to prosper to enormous heights. That nation was the one you are a citizen of now, the Destine nation. The other nations were jealous and used the term Destines to make fun of us out of their jealousy. The word that they used as demeaning; the First Elder of this nation embraced it. He then made a decree that this clan would be called Destines."

The bell sounds, snapping the class out of the trance of the story he is telling.

"Alrighty, we will pick up with more notes next time we meet," Mr. Lloyd says as everyone heads out the door.

Harrison meets up with his friends.

"That was crazy!" Jaylen says.

"Yeah, I was listening like crazy, I never do that in class," Joseph says.

"Yeah I know, that is why you barely made it into here," Harrison says laughing and knocking shoulders with him.

"You know what I really took from that history class," JT says in deep thought.

"What's that?" Joseph asks as they walk towards their dorm rooms.

"Girls will take you down paths you shouldn't go on," JT says.

"Really? C'mon, that is the stupidest thing you could get out of that," Jaylen replies.

They laugh as they walk into the dormitory.

CHAPTER 12

Norman Drake's Power Flow Class

Harrison closes a window as the wind struggles back. His math homework sails across the room slapping and sticking to JT's face.

"I am so glad that after today, we get two days of break. We have only been in classes for a week, but it feels like an eternity," JT says, removing the math homework off his face.

"Yeah, no kidding. But I heard we go to the hardest class today, our Power Flow 1 class," Harrison packs his bags. "People say that Mr. Drake is the hardest teacher here."

"I heard that too, and all the horror stories, like how he has made people cry, quit, and need counseling. But, if he can teach his son to come up with a move like he did at the First Spar, then I will take the difficulty if he can teach me a move like that," JT says as they walk out of their room.

Shutting the door, Harrison turns around and is surprised. Standing right in front of their door is the janitor. On his right side is a pudgy gray cat with black stripes across his body. On his left side is a dingy white mouse with black spots. Sweeping the floor in front of the room, they all look up in unison.

The janitor smiles at them, stretching his wrinkles deeper into his pastel face. Brushing his dirty black hair away from his dark brown eyes, he puts his glasses on.

"Sorry, don't mean to be in the way. We usually don't clean these dorms this late, but I have been sick," the janitor says sweeping again.

"Yeah, every year we get sick the first week of school because of all these new kids coming here. It's starting to get old," the cat says.

"Quit complaining. If you aren't complaining about one thing, it's another," the mouse says.

"Hey, don't make me come over there. You don't talk to me like that," the cat replies pointing his broom at the mouse.

"Come over here, I dare you," the mouse responds, throwing his broom on the ground.

Staring at them, Harrison and JT watch intently as the cat takes a couple of steps toward the mouse.

"Y'all shut up and get back to work. Sorry about that, they get a little carried away sometimes," the janitor says, as the cat and mouse start sweeping again.

"My name is Felix Crane. The cat right here is named Sanford, and the mouse is named Edwin."

"Nice to meet you guys. My name is Harrison, and this right here is JT," Harrison replies.

"Oh, are you that Grady kid? Douglas Grady's own son?" Felix asks, squinting at him.

"Yes, sir, I am," Harrison replies.

"Huh, isn't that something. I remember your dad running these halls with Norman while they were students here. Man, how time flies. One time your dad and Norman were sparring in their Power Flow class and your dad shot an energy attack so big it took out a portion of the building. It took me two days to clean it up," Felix says, leaning both hands on top of his broom.

"Is the Norman you are talking about, Norman Drake, the Power Flow instructor now?" JT asks.

"Yeah, that's him. Douglas and he were inseparable here. He probably never thought he would be teaching Douglas' son one day though," Felix replies.

"Yeah, probably not," Harrison says. "Well, we better head to his class now. It was nice meeting you guys."

Walking away, the quarreling from Sanford and Edwin start back up. Leaving, Harrison hears Felix shout, "Will you two shut up for once?"

Approaching the hut, a large crowd is lining up on the small field in front of the hut. Joining the line beside Jaylen and Joseph, Harrison sees Norman Drake standing in front of the line of students.

The sky behind him makes the moment seem gloomy with the enormous black cloud covering the sun, not moving from its spot. Gusting heavy, the wind is making his gray robe flap continually in unison with his wavy brown hair.

The wind brings a tear to his left eye making a teardrop fall down into a large scar underneath it that looks like an x crossing out his whole cheek.

"My name is Norman Drake and I will be your Power Flow instructor for the next four years," he says. "This will be one of the hardest classes you take here. It will be frustrating and annoying at times. But it is vital every Destine warrior learns to create energy attacks from their Power Flow within them," he paces up and down the line.

"This is the basic class. You as Kadens are not allowed to learn how to create your own custom energy attack this year. That comes in class two. This year you will learn how to harness energy and control your Power Flow. That is all. In that process, you will learn how to form energy balls and beams, but just the simple basic ones. Do you all understand that?" Mr. Drake says.

"Yes, sir." the class replies.

"First, you need to know what Power Flow is. Power Flow is in everyone. We are all born with it. It is the life force of a person. We all have energy within us that we can harness and make into solid energy. That energy is created by your Power Flow. It's a lot like a muscle. We all have muscles. But you can only make your muscles stronger if you work out. If you don't work out your muscle, it will always stay small and you will be weak. That is how your Power Flow works," he says, stopping in front of Harrison and staring intently into his eyes.

"Now, this class of Kadens will not be able to grow their Power Flow as quickly as the other Kaden classes before you because of young Grady right here," Mr. Drake says smiling at him.

Harrison stares back at him in confusion as the class watches.

"You see, because of that student who almost killed young Grady by accidentally transmitting his energy into his acceptance letter, the Elder wants to assure that doesn't happen ever again. So as a precaution we created these gloves that are programmed to only filter a certain amount of energy at a time. If you surpass the set limit, the glove stops the energy from forming. These new toys are called Energy Filtering Gloves. Or as we will refer to them in class as, EFGs," Mr. Drake says walking away from Harrison.

Tommy, his son, strolls out with a huge vanilla brown box, setting it down next to his dad.

"Okay, let's assign you your EFG and get started," Mr. Drake says, while sunlight creeps onto the field as the wind finally pushes the cloud out of the sun's way.

Mr. Drake paces slowly in front of all the students as Tommy opens the box. Struggling to open it, Mr. Drake stares in frustration.

"As we all can see, my son Tommy here can beat somebody in a battle, but can't win against a box," Mr. Drake shakes his head.

"As we wait on Tommy to get the box open, which at the rate it's going, you all will be Cerdics by the time he gets it open, I'll share with all of you that you will see Tommy in all your other first-year Kaden classes except this one. He is enrolled in the fourth year Power Flow Class," he says as Tommy finally rips the box open. "As you all saw at the beginning of the week, his ability to harness energy from his Power Flow is beyond his years. It was signed off by Elder Dirk that I could start training him at eight years of age. So, putting him in this class would be similar to making him have to crawl instead of walk," he says, striding up and down the line.

"Make sure everyone gets one Tommy," Mr. Drake glances at the class. "And everyone, make sure you get one that fits well. And please keep up with yours. If you lose it, you will fail the class."

Harrison notices the concerned look on Jaylen's face.

Jaylen loses everything, he probably won't make it to the third class.

Dragging the box on the ground, the top progressively rips as Tommy pulls it. Stopping at each student, Tommy is a couple of people away from Harrison and his friends.

"Dude, this guy seems like a jerk. I mean, look how he treats his son," JT whispers so only they can hear him.

"Yeah, how could my dad be friends with someone like him? The way my mom explained how my dad was, there is no way he would hang out with someone like him," Harrison whispers.

Stopping in front of JT, Mr. Drake stares at them.

"What is your name young man?" he says waiting for an answer.

"Umm, JT Hall sir," JT replies nervously.

"Does JT stand for just talking? Because I was saying, why are you two talking?" Mr. Drake asks.

"We, uh, weren't..." JT says.

"Wow, Mr. Hall I am impressed by your guts to try to lie to me in my face," Mr. Drake replies.

"Sir, it was me that started talking to JT, I apologize," Harrison says.

Tommy gives Harrison his EFG.

"And may I ask what you wanted to talk to him about in the middle of my class?"

Sweat runs down his face from the heat and enters his mouth. The saltiness stops his words.

"I am waiting young Grady," Mr. Drake replies.

"I was just saying I was surprised my dad and you were friends, sir," Harrison responds. Out the corner of his eye, he notices JT and everyone's shock on their face.

"Is that right? And what makes you feel that way? I am curious," he says leaning to his side with his hands behind his back.

"I don't know. I just imagined my dad would have been around people more cheerful about life," Harrison responds.

Smirking slightly, Mr. Drake turns away as if trying to hold in laughter. Suddenly, turning quickly, Mr. Drake pushes a medium-size yellow energy ball into Harrison's stomach. Lifting up off his feet, Harrison feels the energy ball's warm sensation digging into his stomach.

Mr. Drake extends his arm sending Harrison flying through the air. Harrison hits the ground, bouncing a couple of feet. Harrison grabs his stomach, aching in pain from the attack. Mr. Drake walks slowly with his hands behind his back as the class gazes at Harrison on the ground.

"You see, young Grady, I did that because I know that's what your dad would want me to do if he heard what you just said to me," Mr. Drake replies, pacing in front of him.

Sitting up slowly, Harrison holds his stomach trying to stop the tingling sensation.

"I know how big your dad was on respecting and honoring those that are in authority. Your dad would have been disappointed in your actions and choice of words right then, young Grady," he says, turning his back to him.

Taking a couple of steps, he looks over his shoulder at Harrison.

"Apparently, I guess I know your dad better than you," he says walking back to the class.

"Go give young Grady his EFG and hurry up. We are wasting time," he says.

Tommy hands him a little black glove with the finger tips removed. Grabbing the glove, Harrison notices the thickness of a material he has never touched before. Expecting Tommy to help him up, he watches him walk off getting back to the line.

Dang, he could've at least helped me get up.

He rises to his feet and wobbles. Getting back in line, he notices how everyone is trying not to stare at him.

"Alright, put on your EFG. Get used to how it feels," Mr. Drake says. "This material was created by some of the top scientists we have, this past summer. It may feel weird at first, but you will get used to it."

Relief comes upon Harrison as he hears the bell sound loudly in the distance.

"Alright, see you guys next week. Meet me in the classroom as we will be taking notes for a couple of weeks. We won't be using these till the end of the month. I gave these to you now as a test to see who can keep up with them," Mr. Drake says as the class heads off.

Harrison walks gingerly with JT, Jaylen, and Joseph back up to the main building.

"Harrison, are you alright?" Jaylen asks.

"Yeah, but it hurt like crap," Harrison replies.

Harrison grimaces each step he takes.

"I can't believe you said that to him. Why didn't you just make something up?" JT says.

"I really don't know. To be honest, I wish I did now though," Harrison declares.

Walking into the main building, Harrison spots his uncle Adam with the Ragnar Council heading towards him.

"Harrison, why is your shirt tucked out? You know the dress code," his uncle Adam says. "And why do you have grass stains all over your back? You look terrible. I hope you can get those out of it since its white."

"Yeah, I was kind of pushed on the ground, nothing serious. But I am doing my laundry tonight so I will try and get it out," Harrison replies.

"Well that's good, looks like you need to. The washing machines and dryers are in the basement in this building.

They only stay open till 11:00. You don't want to be in there a minute late, or Felix the janitor will get you. Or his cat and mouse will, and I don't know who would be worse. Those helpers of his can't be much help to him since all they do is argue and fight," his uncle Adam says entering the Elder's office.

The Elder standing in the doorway welcomes the Ragnar Council. He makes eye contact with Harrison.

"You must be Harrison Grady. It's nice to finally meet you," he says smiling.

"Yes sir, it is a pleasure to meet you too, your Honor," Harrison replies.

"I can tell you are definitely a Grady by the way you respect and honor authority. I always respected that about your dad," he responds.

JT playfully coughs.

"Thank you, sir, that is a great compliment to be compared to my father. You know, I didn't really get to know him, so when I get compliments like that it feels good," he says, noticing the Elder's smile disappear.

"Well you all take care and study hard," he replies closing the door.

"Man, you are on it today. Taking shots at instructors and the Elder himself. I think if I keep hanging out with you, I am going to end up almost getting killed." JT says as they walk on.

Throwing his clothes into the washing machine, Harrison gazes at all the buttons to push.

Which button do I push? I have no idea what I am doing. My mom always did my laundry.

JT, Jaylen, and Joseph stroll in.

"Dude, did you even put detergent in it? Knowing you, you probably forgot," Joseph says, giggling.

"I didn't forget, I was doing that right now," Harrison replies, trying to find some detergent and play off the fact that he did forget.

"Here you go, use this," JT hands him a small pea-green cup of raspberry blue liquid. Harrison throws it into the washing machine.

"Thanks."

"So, we need to decide when we are going to try and find out if that blueprint works," JT says, sitting on a washing machine.

"How about tomorrow night we head to the library and do it?" Jaylen asks.

"Naw, I think we should wait till the end of the month," Harrison responds.

"What? Why wait a whole month to go by?" Joseph says.

"I just think it would be smart to let a couple of weeks go by and let us get our feet underneath us first," Harrison replies.

"Fair enough, we will do it then," JT says jumping off the washing machine. "Well, we better get going its 10:59."

"Crap, this place is about to close, and my clothes are just now done washing. I still got to dry them," Harrison says.

Leaving the room, JT, Jaylen, and Joseph encounter Felix, Sanford, and Edwin.

"Alright boys, time to get out. This place is closing," Felix the janitor says.

"Yeah, we know you had to read the sign outside the door that says, no one after 11," Sanford the cat says.

"I apologize, my clothes just got finished washing. All I have to do is dry them. Can I please do that?" Harrison pleads.

His friends giggle.

"Naw, Harrison, you still got some time before you need to dry your clothes," Jaylen says laughing.

"What are you talking about, you guys saw me put the detergent in and wash them," Harrison asks.

"No, I saw you wash your clothes with blue raspberry juice," JT walks off laughing. "Guess you shouldn't have had your mom do your laundry all the time," JT hollers in the hallway.

Feeling embarrassed, Harrison stares at Felix, Sanford, and Edwin with a blank stare.

"Wow, that's dirty. I think you need to learn how to pick your friends, kid," Edwin the mouse says.

"Yeah, me too," Harrison replies.

CHAPTER
13

Troubling News

Approaching the classroom, Harrison feels the temperature trying to switch from hot mugginess to a nice chill crisp. The cool air makes his arm hair begin to rise. As Harrison and his friends get closer to the hut, Mr. Lloyd's energetic voice reaches them.

"I can't believe he is still this excited a month into the school year. All the other instructors lost their excitement weeks ago," Jaylen says, as Mr. Lloyd bounces, welcoming every student that strolls by him.

"He is just as excited about greeting people as JT is about the cereal bar," Joseph says.

"Well, we know that isn't going to change," Harrison replies.

"You got that right," JT responds, with half his face inside his shirt, trying to avoid or evade the cool air.

Going into the classroom, Mr. Lloyd screams at them with excitement, "Good morning."

They laugh as they find their seats. Mr. Lloyd rushes to the front ready to start. As he is about to fling his robe off as normal, a student busts in the door, halting him.

"Mr. Lloyd, may I be excused for today's class?" the girl says. Standing there sobbing, she is gripping a newspaper, *The Tespan Observer*.

Her peach color eyes stand out as the makeup she is wearing runs down her face making it look like she has two black eyes. The bottom of her coffee colored hair is soaking from tears making it look like black coffee.

"What's wrong, Layla?" Mr. Lloyd says, walking to her.

Harrison tries to see what is written on the paper but can't make it out. Loosening her grip, she reveals to him what the paper says.

"I can't believe something like this would happen in my hometown, and to my neighbor of all people."

Mr. Lloyd takes the paper from her and reads the front page. Bringing her close to him, he hugs her tightly.

"Honey, I am so sorry. That is terrible." Mr. Lloyd responds.

"I used to swim in his pool every summer, and his wife would bring me lemonade popsicles as I swam. I just can't believe he is gone now. He was such a good man," she says.

Harrison and the rest of the class just sit there as he consoles her for a moment.

"You are excused, go ahead and go back to your room, and try to calm down," he says opening the door for her.

Walking by Harrison to get to the front of the classroom, Mr. Lloyd drops the paper on the floor by Harrison's foot. Reaching down to pick it up, Harrison stops mid-way, feeling his heart sink down to his chest as he reads the front of the paper.

The beloved, antique shop owner, Cecil Garner of Dosman, found brutally murdered and shop destroyed.

"Why did you stop? Are you going to make this old man pick it up?" Mr. Lloyd says, bending down and picking it up.

"Sorry, Mr. Lloyd, I was going to," Harrison says.

Harrison notices JT trying to get his attention secretly. He glares over at JT.

"What's wrong?" JT asks.

"Mr. Garner was found dead," Harrison whispers in disbelief. JT's eyes enlarge as they hear Mr. Lloyd beginning to teach.

Sitting in their dorm room, Harrison, JT, Jaylen, and Joseph all stay quiet. Gradually looking at each other, they each wait for the other one to speak up.

"Listen, guys, you can't keep thinking and feeling this way. His death isn't on us," Jaylen says.

"Yeah, it is unfortunate, but he was messing with a crazy guy from what it sounds like. It was probably bound to happen," Joseph says.

Resting on his stomach, Harrison picks at the beige carpet, trying to pull it out. JT sits up quickly, looking directly at Harrison.

"C'mon Harrison, we can't pout over this. Yes, it's tragic that Mr. Garner died, but who really knows if it was really because that blueprint is missing. It's not our fault," JT says.

"Then who's fault is it, JT? We are the ones that broke into his shop at midnight and stole the blueprint. His death is on our hands. And that should bother you. I mean, it bothers me that it doesn't bother you," Harrison says getting up and looking out the window.

"You want to know what bothers me?" JT asks, standing behind Harrison.

"Yeah, let me know since I sure can't tell what is bothering you. I guess I do need a little help, Harrison replies.

"What really bothers me is that if that crazy robe guy did kill him, then we both know that the killer is at this place working here right now," JT says.

"What if that guy that killed Mr. Garner is the one who sent you the letter and tried to kill you? If that's true, then

134

apparently according to the letter, that crazy robe guy knows the truth about what happened to your dad. We can't sit around anymore," JT says.

Getting up, Jaylen walks over to Harrison and grabs his shoulder.

"Hey, what JT is really trying to say, is that maybe it's time we start trying to find out some answers," Jaylen says.

"Dude, you been waiting your whole life for this opportunity. You always wanted to find out what happened to your dad. Don't get distracted now. This is not the time for cold feet," Joseph says.

"Tonight, is the night we go take the blueprint and see if it really works," JT says.

Rubbing his face, Harrison stares at his friends, noticing their concern.

"You guys are right. I just don't want anybody else to die. I don't want you guys losing your lives by helping me," Harrison replies.

"What are you talking about? We are the squad that people shouldn't mess with. We can do this. And we will find out what happened to your dad once and for all, together," JT says.

"Alright, let's get the blueprint and see if this thing works," Harrison says.

Opening his green backpack hiding in the corner, JT pulls out the giant blueprint, folding it up tightly.

"Remember we have to take it to the library to work," JT holds the blueprint with care. "Let's go find these secret rooms."

The dim lights make tiny circles of light that fill the hallway in the main building. The quietness seems odd and makes Harrison feel uneasy. Every step he takes seems to echo even more than the last one. Harrison is as nervous as the time they went to steal the blueprint.

The library is towards the exit leading to the Kyler's building. Walking to the door, Jaylen tries to open it. He shakes the doorknob. It doesn't open.

"It's locked," Jaylen whispers.

"You got to be kidding me. What school locks a library? I mean, who would want to break into a library anyway?" Joseph rubs his chin. "Oh yeah, don't answer that,"

"What do we do now?" Harrison asks.

JT leans against the wall, tapping the wall with his fingers as if it will help him think. Standing there for a couple moments, JT straightens up.

"We can go take the key from the janitor. He is sleeping now. We just go into his room and take it. After we get done, we will put it back," JT says

"Are you crazy? You know how difficult that will be?" Joseph says.

"Yeah, that's too dangerous. If we get caught, we would be in so much trouble," Jaylen replies.

"And what if the cat or mouse wake up? Those two are crazy," Joseph says.

Standing there, Harrison rubs his forehead.

"Okay, JT and I will go to the janitor's room and get the key. You two stay here and just keep watch. Look for us, so when we come back you can give us the signal if it is clear or not," Harrison replies.

Harrison and JT take the stairs to the basement. Every other light works down in the basement hallway. The buzzing sound from the barely lit lights makes it seem like they are dying. Harrison and JT walk slowly.

In-between every step, the darkness seems to snatch their feet away. Getting closer to the end of the hallway, Harrison spots the Janitor sign dangling halfway on the door, barely hanging on.

"Okay, be super quiet," Harrison whispers, slowly opening the door.

Harrison enters first. The smell of citrus invades his nose from all the cleaning products spread out through the tiny room. Felix, Sanford, and Edwin each are sleeping in three different beds, side by side but each one built for their own unique size.

Snoring in unison, all three of them blow their nightcaps up and down as the massive white cotton ball at the tip goes up and down with each snore. Looking around, Harrison searches for the keys. He finally spots them hanging on the wall by Sanford. Harrison signals JT to stay there.

He begins to tiptoe cautiously. Reaching the keys, he looks down at Sanford scratching his face with his hind leg.

"Shut up, just shut up, Edwin, and take out the trash," Sanford says, sleep talking.

Lifting the keys, he slowly takes them off the hook on the wall.

"What are you doing," Sanford says.

Harrison squints his eyes, knowing he just got caught. He looks down to face Sanford.

"I told you to take the trash out. I swear you are a good- for- nothing," Sanford says.

Oh man, that was a close one.

Exiting the room, Harrison takes a deep breath as he closes the door. Heading back up to the main building, Jaylen signals them over.

"Dude, I am so glad you guys made it back," Jaylen says.

"Yeah, me too," Harrison replies, looking for the right key.

Spotting a silvery key that has the word *library* written on it, he puts in the doorknob and turns the lock. The books all look depressed and lifeless. JT pulls the blueprint out and rolls it onto the long rectangle table in the middle of the room.

"Okay, so how does this work?" Joseph asks.

"Ummm, I really don't know. I never heard that part," JT says, rubbing his fingers through his hair.

"Interesting, so we just stole some keys from a poor old guy to get in here and we don't even know how to make it work? We must be the smartest squad then," Jaylen replies.

"So, what do we do now?" Joseph asks.

Harrison glares around the library trying to think what to do.

"I got it. You guys keep a lookout and I will go check and see if there is a book in here that mentions the legend of this blueprint. I mean being a Destine legend and being at the Destine Academy's library you would think maybe there is a book here about it," Harrison says.

"Well worth a shot I guess," JT says. "Hurry up."

Harrison paces the aisles looking at all the categories. Scanning the history section, he sees one that says *Destine Legends*. Pulling it out, another book falls down on the ground.

Bending over, he picks it up. The book is open to the middle. As he begins to close it, he notices the checkout log. The second name from the top says, *Douglas Grady*. The pages are faded and sticky, making them hard to read.

Chapter 2: The Compass of Destiny

Underneath that he sees handwritten initials spelling out *A.O.P*

Did my dad write that? And if he did what does it mean?

"Harrison, hurry up! Someone is coming," JT says.

Harrison rips the page out of the book and stuffs it in his pocket and puts both books back on the shelf. He returns to the table, seeing JT, Jaylen, and Joseph looking through the glass. The blueprint is in JT's hand.

"It's Sanford, his cat," JT says.

They listen closely with their ears up against the glass.

"I can't believe he gets up and goes to the bathroom, and sees his keys aren't on the wall. He forgets them somewhere, and he sends me on the search for them. Why couldn't he send Edwin?" Sanford says coming up to the library door.

Nervousness fills the room.

"Lock it, JT," Joseph says.

"I can't now, he is too close. If I do it now, he will hear it and know someone is in here," he replies.

Sanford approaches the door. Harrison holds his breath. Suddenly, he hears Sanford take his hand off of the doorknob.

"You know what, we didn't even clean the library today, so we were never in there. Boy, I really must be tired," Sanford says, heading down the hallway.

Harrison exhales a sigh of relief.

"We will wait a couple of minutes and head out. Just toss the keys in the middle of the hallway so he will eventually find them." Harrison says.

"Yeah, I got you," JT replies.

Minutes go by. Exiting the room, JT tosses the keys near the stairs that lead to the basement. They run quietly to their dorms.

CHAPTER
14

The Architect's Plan

The dew on the soft grass dampens Harrison's khakis. He puts his EFG on and off continually. JT looks at Harrison, Jaylen, and Joseph.

"It's been a week since we were at the library. Maybe we should try it again tonight."

"Man, I really don't feel like sneaking into Mr. Crane's room again to get that key. We have to figure out another way to get into the library," Harrison replies.

"You won't have to sneak into his room again. I got this covered," JT hops to his feet.

"How is that?" Jaylen stares at him.

"I took the library key off the keyring before I threw it the other night," JT replies.

"You did what?" Harrison responds. "Do you like stealing now?"

"It's not really stealing. I see it more as borrowing," JT scratches his head. "I'm gonna give it back."

Mr. Drake walks onto the field. The students form a straight line.

"Alright. Let me see everyone show me their EFG. Let's see who still has it."

Holding it up, Harrison dangles it from his hand. Mr. Drake paces slowly, inspecting each student. Stopping abruptly, he looks at a student without one.

"Mr. Kevin Wilson, may I ask where your EFG is?" Mr. Drake paces. "If you'd bothered to look at the board in my classroom you would've known you needed it today. I wrote a note about it two weeks ago!"

"I apologize Mr. Drake. I was up all night doing my language homework. I was so tired I accidentally forgot it in my room," Kevin shivers in fear.

"You know what I am tired of, Mr. Wilson?" Mr. Drake shakes his head. "I am tired of students who want to be future Destine warriors not being responsible. How can I rest at night knowing that the future generation that is supposed to protect our people are so irresponsible?"

Harrison notices the tears forming in Kevin's eyes.

"You fail," Mr. Drake paces slowly again. "You may leave the field, Mr. Wilson."

Bursting in tears with his head down, he slowly walks off the field.

"Okay, everyone else put on your EFG. It should go on your dominant hand, as most people harness energy better with their hand they usually write or eat with."

Pulling the thick glove on his right hand, Harrison squeezes his hand a couple of times to loosen the tight grip.

"Now, the ways these things work is simple. They are all programmed to only allow a certain amount of energy to form in your hand. If you accidentally try to bring forth too much energy from your Power Flow, the glove will automatically stop the energy. The EFGs only allow you to form small energy balls. That will be what you focus on this year," Mr. Drake stands still. "So, go ahead and partner up with someone and stand facing them."

Harrison moves next to JT, partnering with him. Everyone forms two lines facing their partners. Mr. Drake paces in-between the two lines.

"We will work on learning how to channel your energy from inside you. We want you to learn how to bring your energy into your EFG. When you properly do it, the glove should glow whatever color your energy is. This way we can distinguish what color your energy is," Mr. Drake puts his hands behind his back. "So, what you want to do is focus and clear your mind. Everyone starting out has to learn to focus and feel their Power Flow within them. After that, you want to direct the energy from your Power Flow to your hand," Mr. Drake smirks. "Everyone close your eyes and relax. I want you to clear your mind and just focus on your Power Flow."

Relaxing, Harrison closes his eyes and tries to figure out what his Power Flow feels like. Minutes go by, and the quietness on the field shows how much everyone is focusing. Finally, he feels a tingling sensation in-between his stomach and his chest. Breathing slowly, the warm tingly sensation starts to grow stronger.

I can feel it. It reminds me of what I felt at the skating rink that night.

He concentrates, feeling the energy creep through his arm.

"Okay, everyone should have an understanding of what your Power Flow feels like, and hopefully you have started trying to bring it into your hand," Mr. Drake says. "If you did it properly, when you open your eyes your hand will be glowing with the energy from your Power Flow."

Ready to see what color the energy is from his Power Flow; Harrison anxiously waits for the signal.

"Alright everyone open your eyes, now," Mr. Drake says.

Opening his eyes quickly, Harrison is amazed at what he sees in his hand.

Nothing.

Glancing across him, he sees JT's hand glowing blue. He looks around and sees Jaylen's hand glowing yellow and Joseph's hand glowing orange. All the student's hands are glowing with different colors, except his.

What? Why isn't my hand covered with my energy?

146

"Hmmm, I guess we see who is going to be the slower learner in this class," Mr. Drakes says mockingly.

"Everyone squeeze your hand tightly," he says.

Down the two lines, all of them squeeze their hands. Their hands go back to normal. Excitement emanates on their faces.

"Whoever you partnered with today will be your partner all year long as we continue to learn how to harness energy. You are dismissed."

Walking together back to the building, Harrison doesn't mention what just happened. Listening to them talk about it, Harrison sees Mr. Lloyd walking up to them as they are about to enter the building.

"Harrison, wait a second," Mr. Lloyd says.

Harrison closes the door and faces him.

"Yes, sir?" Harrison says.

"I know you are in Layla's class. She went back home to go to her neighbor's funeral so she will be gone until the middle of next week. I was wondering if you can make sure she gets the notes from you?"

"Yeah, that's no problem. I can do that," Harrison replies.

"Thanks. She has really taken his death hard. I met the guy a couple of times. He had the original blueprint of this place in his shop. It was amazing," Mr. Lloyd says.

"Really?"

"Yeah, a thing of historical beauty it was," Mr. Lloyd smiles. "Well, I will see you around."

Harrison sees him take a couple of steps.

"Mr. Lloyd, may I ask you a question?" Harrison says.

"Sure..."

"I read rumors that the blueprint is able to show some secret places here in the Academy. I heard that the original architect made it where you could only see them on the blueprint at night in the library. Do you think that is true?"

"I was always fascinated about that blueprint. Even when I was in school here, I wanted to find it and go and see if the rumor was true."

Harrison gets a weird feeling he heard that before.

Oh crap, that sounds like what that guy from the shop that night said.

"Harrison, are you paying attention?" Mr. Lloyd says.

"Yes, yes, sir," Harrison replies.

"Anyways, I don't know if it's true or not, but it is a fun legend."

"Just one last question," Harrison says. "Have you ever heard what the person with the map had to do once they were in the library with it?"

"I always heard there was a certain spot on the ceiling that the blueprint had to be on. Once it was laid flat on the exact spot, the blueprint was supposed to reveal the answers."

148

"Thanks, Mr. Lloyd. Things about history just interest me."

"No problem. When my friends try to apologize to me about talking about history too much, I always say the same thing to them, you know how much I love history," Mr. Lloyd waves as he walks off.

Harrison's eyes widen as he enters the building.

That guy that night said the same thing. Is Mr. Lloyd the mysterious robe guy?

Harrison comes up to his friends after math class. Conversations fill the hall, with students rushing to the cafeteria for dinner.

"I can't stand math. It doesn't make any sense," Joseph says.

"We know. You struggle with simple addition," Jaylen responds.

Joking with one another, Harrison looks around and stops them on their way to the cafeteria.

"Listen, earlier when Mr. Lloyd stopped me after our Power Flow class, I asked him if he knew anything about the blueprint," Harrison whispers.

"What? You told him we have the blueprint? Why?" JT says frantically.

"No, of course not. He was the one that brought it up, so I just asked," Harrison responds, looking at JT like he is crazy.

"Did he know anything about it?" Jaylen asks.

"Yeah, he said that it's rumored to get the blueprint to work, you have to put it in the exact spot on the ceiling. When you get the right spot, it reveals where the secret rooms are," Harrison replies.

"Okay great. So, what spot on the ceiling?" JT says.

"I don't know. And I don't think he knew either," Harrison says, grinning a little.

"Great. That's just fantastic," JT says.

"I say we go find out if it works tonight. Then come up with a plan on how to spy on the Elder and the Ragnar Council, and when the best time is to do it," Harrison says.

Walking up the stairs towards the cafeteria, they get into the back of the line and wait to get their food.

Staring at the clock, the green numbers stick out in the dark room.

"It's time. Jaylen and Joseph should be waiting in the hallway now," JT seizes the blueprint and places the key in his pocket.

Closing the door behind them quietly, Harrison motions to start walking. The scenery is the same as the last time. Harrison doesn't feel as nervous this time though, which kind of bothers him. Unlocking the door, they enter in swiftly, this time locking the door behind them. Rolling out the blueprint across the table, they all examine the length of it.

"One person can't hold this out by themselves. It's going to take two of us to stretch it wide," Jaylen says.

"To get it across every inch of the ceiling, two people are going to have to lift the other two," Joseph says.

"Wow. Coming from the person who isn't good at math, you sure you are counting right in this equation?" JT says, giggling.

Surveying the ceiling, Harrison bumps into a rack of books, making a couple of books fall. Bending down, he picks them up and puts them back. Picking up the last book on the floor, he notices it is the book he tore the page out of the other night.

I need to check the handwriting in the book. If they are the same, that means my dad really wrote the notes.

"That was a smooth move. Just take the whole bookshelf down why don't you?" JT says, sarcastically.

Harrison and JT each grasp opposite ends. The shrill slick paper keeps slipping through Harrison's fingers. He presses his fingers down harder to get a firmer grip.

"Alright, let's make this happen," JT bends his knees.

Joseph stands behind JT, while Jaylen stands behind Harrison.

"Okay on the count of three, we will lift them at the same time," Jaylen says as they bend their knees.

"You got that Joseph? I know that involves numbers and counting. Sure, you can handle it?" JT says, smiling at Harrison.

"One...two...three," they both say.

Instantly, Harrison flies up, feeling Jaylen wobble slightly.

"Whoa, get it together guys. Walk together, or this isn't going to work," JT says as Jaylen and Joseph direct them in different directions.

"Easy for you to say," Jaylen says as if he is struggling.

Harrison and JT push the blueprint against the ceiling.

Nothing happens.

"Slide it slowly," Harrison says.

"We are trying," Joseph replies, sliding it across the ceiling.

They keep going across the library, but nothing is happening. Harrison feels Jaylen struggling to hold him up. The sweat is dripping down Jaylen's face. They can't do it much longer.

"Let's just try this last spot right here, and then you guys can put us down," Harrison says.

"That sounds like an awesome plan," Joseph replies.

Placing the blueprint against the ceiling, JT loses his grip and drops it. Harrison holds his section in place as JT struggles.

"C'mon, really?" Joseph says, frustrated.

"My bad," JT says, grabbing the blueprint and placing it on the ceiling.

Harrison suddenly feels the blueprint stick to the ceiling. Immediately a figure made of paper emerges from the blueprint and drops out of it. The figure slams into them and they crash onto the floor. They all jump up, staring in shock with what is standing before them. A paper figure made out of the same paper as the blueprint is waving.

Harrison glances at the blueprint still sticking to the ceiling. The paper figure that fell out of the blueprint is still in front of them, waving.

"Hello, I am at your service. Are we under attack? Do we need a cover?" the paper figure says, looking concerned.

"Yes," JT says.

"No," Harrison says.

"Maybe," Joseph says.

"I want to touch it," Jaylen says, not blinking and pointing at the paper figure.

The paper figure looks around, surveying the library in confusion.

"So, we are under attack, or aren't we? Which one is it?" the paper figure asks.

"Ummm, listen we just wanted to see if it was true about the secret rooms. We didn't think that, umm, you would pop out," Harrison replies.

"Well, what did you think would happen?" The paper figure responds, with a look of bewilderment on his face.

"You know, like some cool holographic type thing," JT rubs the back of his head. "But, yeah, totally wrong on that one. Like way wrong."

"Hmmm, that is interesting. The architect, when asked to come up with the secret rooms, decided to put his subconscious into the blueprint so that I could be created. My job is to lead everyone to the secret room. He figured this would be the best way, just in case someone couldn't follow a map," the paper figure smiles. "I was created to make sure that all could arrive in the secret rooms."

"Great, well let's wait a couple of minutes and then we can head out and you can show us where the secret rooms are," Harrison says.

"Oh, I am sorry, but we cannot waste much time," the paper figure says, putting his hands on both hips.

"What, why can't we waste any time?" JT says, staring at the paper figure.

"Well, you see I am only programmed to be out of the blueprint for five minutes every two years," the paper figures walks toward the door. "And we have wasted two and a half minutes already."

Harrison stares at his friends in disbelief.

"Crap, we got to get going then," JT says, running to the window, looking out.

"Hurry up, just take us to the closest one," Harrison says, nervous that they will run out of time.

"Okay, there is the one by the Elder's office. Follow me."

The paper figure quickly opens the door and walks out. Traveling down the hallway, Harrison and his friends survey the halls, hoping no one sees this.

"Wow, they must have repainted these walls. It was not this gloomy looking when the architect chose the color of paint to go on these walls," the paper figure says.

"Now is not the time to talk about the color of the walls," JT whispers. "If we get spotted, I don't know how we can explain a piece of giant paper walking and talking."

Stepping beside the Elder's office, the paper figure turns and looks at them.

"This is all you have to do to get into this secret room," the paper figure taps the fourth brick on the wall five times with just his index finger.

A door appears that is bright and made of energy.

"Just do that and you can open this secret room anytime you want," the paper figure begins to crumble to the ground. "It was great meeting you."

He completely crumbles and vanishes. Harrison and the others open the door to the secret room, walking in.

CHAPTER 15

The Elder's Conversation

Moving into the room, the dense air takes some time to get adjusted to, making Harrison's lungs feel weighty. The yellowish energy glow around the long spacious room blinds him. Squinting his eyes, he surveys the room. He walks slowly, touching the rough walls. They feel like a miniature rollercoaster with bumps going up and down every few inches. The wall looks old, but as he feels it, it makes him think he is in a new room just recently added.

"This room is wild," Jaylen glances around the room.

"Yeah, I can't believe it actually is real," Joseph says.

"There is energy around the walls protecting it. It must be like the energy wall the Elder created during the First Spar," Harrison says.

"They must have put this energy around the walls just in case there was a war going on, and the Academy was attacked. It would protect the students," JT says.

"So, this is the room next to the Elder's office. At least we can use this room to try and listen in when he is talking to the Ragnar Council. They could slip up sometime and talk about the Silent Mission," Harrison says.

Harrison approaches the door, putting his hand on the doorknob shining with yellowish energy.

"Well since we have seen it, I guess we can head out, and head back to the room," Harrison says, waving the others to follow.

As he is turning the doorknob, he hears a door shutting through the walls. He gazes at his friends and realizes everyone is nervous. Two voices penetrate through the walls unclearly.

"It's the Elder and someone else is with him," JT walks to the wall and puts his ear up against it to listen.

Harrison hurries over to the wall pressing his ear against it. The coldness from the wall invades his ear taking the focus off of the conversation at first. Muffling sounds are the only thing he can hear.

"We can't hear what they are saying. The walls are too thick," Harrison says, lifting his ear on and off of different spots. He tries to find a place he could hear.

They all try to listen and switch to different spots, hoping to hear a bit of the Elder's conversation.

"Dang it," Harrison pounds his fist on the wall in frustration.

Suddenly, the energy on the wall vibrates and shakes the wall turning the solid bricks all into yellow energy. Harrison steps back nervous, as he sees the Elder sitting in his large brown chair. Sitting on the other side of the desk is Sebastian Darby.

"Oh crap, get down," JT says, as they all flop on the floor on their stomachs. Laying there for a couple seconds, Harrison gently stands.

"I don't think they can see us. The energy field must have been made so that the people here could see what was going on out there," Harrison says.

Harrison walks up gently to the wall. He waves slowly at them in the other room. He hears the conversation more clearly as he stands there.

"They can't see us. And the energy field makes it easier to hear them now," Harrison says.

The others stand up and walk next to him. They listen carefully.

"Well I am very thankful you were able to go to Mr. Garner's funeral for me," the Elder says.

"It was a pleasure for me to represent you there," Sebastian replies.

"Dosman is a nice little town. I always enjoyed going into his little antique shop when I was around the area," the Elder says.

"Well, I have never been there until this past week. It was almost completely destroyed by an energy attack, so I didn't get to see much," Sebastian responds.

"Were you able to examine the body before the funeral?" the Elder asks.

"Yes, Your Honor, the authorities allowed me to look at the body the day before," Sebastian replies.

"That's great, I am glad you were able to make it in time. So, were you able to find anything?" the Elder says.

"I found something interesting burned on his chest. The letters G.O.M. were across his whole upper chest," Sebastian hands over some pictures.

"So, whoever did this wanted to leave a message for us?" the Elder looks at them. "I wonder what G.O.M. stands for?"

"I don't know."

"I found something else alarming that I wanted to show you," Sebastian hands a picture over to him. "I took this picture when I found it. I was the only one who spotted it. It was written on the floor underneath all the debris."

The Elder examines the picture putting it in a drawer in his desk.

"It's a list of names of people that have been murdered in the past six months. Their names have a red line through them," the Elder replies.

"Yeah, I noticed that too. The last one who has a line through his name was Mr. Garner. But did you see one of the names at the bottom that didn't have a line through it?" Sebastian says.

"Yeah, Harrison Grady's name was one of them. I saw that" the Elder responds.

Harrison's heart drops. The numbness makes him not even feel the piercing stares from his friends.

"Your Honor, I think we need to keep a close eye on Young Grady. What if this person tries to come after him?" Sebastian says.

Leaning back into his chair, the Elder takes a deep breath.

"That might be a smart idea. The last thing we need in the news and in the papers is Douglas Grady's son being murdered. Then many people would demand more information about the Silent Mission, and we would have no choice but to tell them what we know. We can't let that happen," The Elder replies.

"Your Honor, if you don't mind me suggesting, I think it may be a wise idea to have the Red Hawks start following him and keeping a close eye on him," Sebastian says. "I mean, I and The Ragnar Council can take care of ourselves. And we don't have a hitman on us trying to kill us as young Grady does."

He is in deep thought.

"You are right, that is a wise suggestion. They are on a mission right now, but they should be back in two months. Until then we will just keep a close eye on him," the Elder responds.

Sebastian gets up heading to leave the Elder's office.

"I better get going, Your Honor, I will see you tomorrow," Sebastian says.

"Yes, of course. Thank you again for going to Mr. Garner's funeral for me," the Elder says.

Opening the door slightly, the Elder stops him.

"Sebastian."

"Yes, Your Honor?"

"That was wise thinking on your part. Your care for the boy and your wisdom on how to keep him safe just shows that you will be a fine Destine Elder one day," the Elder says, leaning forward in his seat.

"Thank you very much, sir," Sebastian smiles slightly as he walks out the door.

The Elder exits his office moments later.

Harrison stands there in disbelief. That person that killed Mr. Garner is really trying to kill me.

"Man, stuff just got real," Jaylen says, breaking the silence in the room.

"Come on, let's just head back to our rooms," Harrison says.

They open the door and walk out. He glares at the wall and sees a normal wall. Sprinting down the hallway quietly, they all head to their rooms.

After breakfast, Harrison lets out a monstrous yawn.

"You have been yawning all morning," Joseph says, as they walk to their Power Flow class.

"I couldn't sleep last night after what I heard. It upset me a little," Harrison replies.

"Yeah, I don't blame you," JT places his hand on Harrison's shoulder. "It upset me too."

Harrison gazes at him with a blank stare.

"What?" JT asks.

"Coming from the person that was snoring ten minutes after his head hit the pillow, I bet you were real upset," Harrison replies.

Jaylen and Joseph laugh as they all line up on the field. They wait for Mr. Drake to arrive.

"What are you all doing?" Mr. Drake walks on the field. "I told you that we are partnering up for now on. I should see two lines, not one."

The class rushes to form two lines.

"See, this is another reason why I can't sleep well at night-"

"Join the club," Harrison whispers under his breath while Mr. Drake is speaking.

"What was that young Grady?" Mr. Drake stands in front of him. "I know, I heard you say something."

Tommy and a group of friends walk by the field. They turn their heads away as if trying to avoid seeing Mr. Drake's class. "Tommy, come over here," Mr. Drake says, grinning.

Tommy walks over with his head down, standing next to his dad.

"Yes, sir?" Tommy says, fidgeting nervously as his dad signals him to wait a moment.

"Answer my question," Mr. Drake glares at Harrison.

"I just said join the club. But I wasn't meaning it in a bad way. I was just saying it because I didn't get any sleep last night either."

"You didn't get any sleep?" Mr. Drake laughs as he puts his hand on Harrison's shoulder. "What makes us lose sleep is completely two different things. You can't sleep at night because you probably are stressed over homework, tests, and your next class. I can't sleep because this generation doesn't know how to listen to directions."

Mr. Drake puts his hands behind his back. Harrison tightens his abs and squints his eyes slightly as he prepares for an energy blast. Mr. Drake chuckles as he looks at Harrison trying to prepare for a blast.

"Stop it, boy, you don't deserve another energy blast from me. You're not that worthy."

Harrison relaxes. He stares at Mr. Drake as he puts his hand on Tommy's shoulder.

"But I tell you what, we will do a little assignment just for you, young Grady, with the help of my son Tommy," Mr. Drake taps Tommy on the back.

Tommy glances down at his watch.

"Dad, I really need to get to math class. I'm already late-"

"Be quiet. I am an instructor. All I have to do is tell them you were helping me in my class for a little bit." Moving in front of Harrison, Mr. Drake looks down to him. "You were the only one who couldn't properly harness his energy into his hand the other day. That's disappointing, young Grady. I expect more coming from a Grady," Mr. Drake walks away from Harrison. "So, to help you out, I tell you what I am going to do." He moves in front of Tommy and puts his hands on both of his shoulders. "Everyone stand behind Tommy, now."

All the students move swiftly behind him.

"Son, I want you to create your Omega Supersonic Blast energy move right now," Mr. Drake clenches Tommy's shoulders tighter.

Harrison's eyes widen as he begins to sweat.

"What?" Tommy says.

Taking his hands off his shoulders, Mr. Drake turns and looks at Harrison.

"It's alright. Hopefully, you won't have to use it on him," Mr. Drake grins. "Young Grady, all you have to do is just harness energy into your hand and you are safe. But, if you don't...Tommy will hit you with his Omega Supersonic Blast."

"What?" Harrison and Tommy say in unison.

"You see, a prime example of this generation not listening. Did I stutter or something?" Mr. Drake itches the back of his head.

"I thought Kadens weren't allowed to participate in moves of that caliber until the second year?" Harrison shakes.

Standing face to face with Harrison, Mr. Drake stares into his eyes without blinking.

"This is my class. I make the rules," Mr. Drake points. "Tommy do it now,"

"Dad, please..."

"I said do it now," Mr. Drake screams, glaring at him.

Tommy bends his knees a little and turns slightly. Harrison hears a loud buzzing sound from the purple energy circulating around Tommy's feet. The wind shoots in different directions making Harrison's hair fly around. Tommy begins to scream, holding his hands out as he summons more energy for his move. The students behind him start to scoot back with fear in their eyes.

Purple energy spins around his whole body as he holds a shiny purple energy ball in his hands the size of a small bowling ball.

"Okay, young Grady, please put on your EFG and harness your energy into your hand. You have thirty seconds," Mr. Drake says. "Go."

Harrison pulls his EFG out. He fumbles and drops it. Picking it up quickly, he slides it on. Extending his right arm out, with his palm facing upward, he focuses and tries to send his energy to his hand.

C'mon, C'mon, C'mon.

"Times up. Nothing." Mr. Drake shakes his head. "Tommy hit him with it, now."

Tommy looks at his dad as if waiting for him to say he is joking.

A couple of seconds go by.

"What are you waiting for? Do it now," Mr. Drake screams.

Tommy grimaces.

"Omega Supersonic Blast," Tommy screams, as he moves quickly to Harrison.

Tommy pushes the purple energy ball into Harrison's stomach launching him into the air. Harrison's mouth bursts open with spit flying out. He loses his breath instantly. Sailing through the air, he finally slaps the ground and rolls a couple of feet.

His whole body feels as if it is on fire. He lifts up slowly and sees Mr. Drake and Tommy walking towards him. But everything gets blurrier with each blink. He sees them getting closer. His eyes shut and his head hits the ground.

CHAPTER 16

Harrison's Questions

O pening his eyes sluggishly, the wind from the slightly open window next to his bed tickles his eyes. Laying in a small twin sized bed, he surveys the tiny room. The room is blank and boring. Trying to sit up, Harrison feels his whole-body ache.

"Oh no, you don't need to get up yet. Lay back down," the nurse says, rushing to his bed.

Harrison is confused at who he sees. Rena Rush smiles at him.

"So how long have I been out of it this time?"

"Only one day," she says, walking around the room.

"Hey, at least it wasn't two days."

"Yeah, maybe next time you will be able to leave the same day," she says, giggling under her breath.

"Let's hope there isn't a next time."

"I agree with you on that one," she checks his monitor. "I will be back around later to check on you."

Harrison stops her as she is midway through the doorway.

"Why are you working here now?"

"The opening came up. I always wanted to come back and work at the Academy," she says, beaming from ear to ear.

"You were a student here at one point?"

"Yeah. I graduated from here," she says. "Oh well, rest up."

Closing his eyes, the cool wind from the window runs across his face. The chilly breeze relaxes him. He starts to fall asleep. Suddenly, his uncle Adam's voice sounds in the hallway. Uncle Adam and Sebastian Darby enter his room.

"Nephew, I am tired of coming to places like these to see you," Adam jokes.

Harrison cracks a little smile, feeling groggy from almost falling asleep. He doesn't feel the air anymore from the window since Sebastian Darby is standing in front of the window with his hands behind his back and bouncing on his toes. Harrison can see from the corner of his eye, Sebastian Darby's thumbs circling one another quickly.

"Yeah, seems like I haven't had the best of luck with energy blasts the last couple of months," Harrison sits up.

"How do you feel?" Sebastian says.

"I feel okay. Better than I did when I took that energy blast head on."

"Yeah, it's an impressive move. I imagine with being able to do energy attacks like that, he'll be teaching them one day, like his daddy," Adam replies.

"Let's hope not like his daddy," Harrison responds.

Adam and Sebastian chuckle, glancing at one another.

"Well get some rest. We will see you around," Adam says, beginning to walk towards the door.

"Uncle Adam, can I ask you something?"

"Sure, anything other than about your mother's cooking, because I don't like having to go on the record on that subject."

"No, it's not about that," Harrison giggles to set the tone. "Did you by chance meet my dad the night he left for the Silent Mission?"

Adam blinks for a couple of moments.

"I wish I did. Then maybe we would know now what happened," he smiles. "But you know we aren't supposed to talk about that whole situation."

"So, you didn't see him that night?"

"No, I didn't," Adam responds.

"Okay, I appreciate it, uncle Adam."

Adam and Sebastian walk out of his room. As they leave, Tommy walks in with a pack of red crème sodas.

"Hey, I just wanted to check on you," Tommy walks to his bed slowly.

"Thanks, I appreciate that."

171

"I heard you love red crème soda, so I thought the least I could do was bring you some," Tommy puts them in the chair next to his bed.

"Yeah, you heard right."

Tommy stands there rubbing his neck gradually. Harrison can tell he is uncomfortable at the moment.

"Listen, I just wanted to say I am sorry."

"Don't worry about it, man. I don't blame you or your dad. It's nothing to worry about. It just showed me not to mess with you," Harrison laughs.

"Yeah, I guess," Tommy grins.

"Well, I better get going. I hope you enjoy the red crème sodas-"

"Hey, before you leave, I want to ask you for a favor," Harrison sits up completely. "I mean it's the least you can do since you blasted me clear across the field, right?"

"Sure, anything."

"I want you to train me and teach me how to control my Power Flow," Harrison says.

"What, you want me to train you? Why?"

"I'm struggling at it right now. I can't even get the basics down," he says. "But it is important that I get it down, and quickly."

"I have never trained anybody. And where and when are we supposed to do this? It's not allowed. If we get caught, we both could be expelled."

"We can do a couple nights a week, late at night. We can go to the woods behind the school," Harrison points out the window. "Plus, you're so skilled. I know for sure you can teach me."

Tommy looks out the window. Harrison turns slightly so he can face him.

"Please. I can't go into great detail right now, but I believe someone really powerful is going to come and try to kill me. I have to be able to protect myself."

Tommy stares at Harrison as he continues to talk.

"With all that we learn in the first year Power Flow class, and having that EFG on, I will never be prepared for something like that. This is the only way. Please."

Tommy looks back out the window. Putting his head down, he grabs his nose in between his eyes, looking like he is thinking hard.

"Okay. I'll do it."

"Awesome," Harrison clenches his fist tightly.

"When would you like to start?"

"Tomorrow at midnight," Harrison replies.

"What? But you are still recovering."

"Hey. You didn't hit me that hard," Harrison smiles.

Tommy smiles and nods goodbye to Harrison. Harrison drops back into the bed. Closing his eyes, he falls asleep as the wind blows on his face.

A clanging noise captures Harrison's attention, waking him from his sleep. Glancing over at the window, he sees it is closed, preventing the cool morning air from entering in. His nurse walks beside him with her comforting smile and places his breakfast tray on his lap. The smell of overcooked pancakes and burnt sausage fills his nose.

"Here you go sweetie," she lifts the lid off the plate. "Eat up, and you are clear to head to your first class this morning."

"Yes ma'am."

"Let's hope we don't see you in here again for a while," she smiles and walks to the door.

"Yeah, I agree on that," Harrison responds, trying to choke down the dry pancakes.

"Well, till next time," she waves.

Man, she sure is nice.

Walking towards history class, the nimble gray clouds dominate the sky. Watching them as he walks, they help him relax. Noticing other students passing him, he can hear many of them whispering to one another.

"I was expecting more from him because of who his dad is-"

"I heard he couldn't even harness his energy into his palm. That's sad-"

"Yeah, my little brother is in his Power Flow class. He says he's so weak, it's not even funny-"

Harrison stares at the sidewalk, trying not to dwell on what he hears. He slams into Mr. Lloyd.

"Oh, I am so sorry Mr. Lloyd," Harrison stumbles. "I guess I wasn't paying attention."

Mr. Lloyd stops and faces Harrison.

"Good Morning. Glad you could make it to class," he bounces on his toes. "You were just so excited to attend my class you weren't paying attention. I understand."

Harrison nods his head and walks into the class as Mr. Lloyd follows.

JT, Jaylen, and Joseph smile, waving at him as he walks in.

"Well thank you, boys. I appreciate the excitement you have to see me," Mr. Lloyd says, chuckling as he heads to the front of the class.

JT scratches the back of his head.

"Yeah, anytime Mr. Lloyd."

"Alright, let's get your notes out. Today we start our new section," Mr. Lloyd flings his robe onto his desk. "Our new section is an important one. This section is about the Destine nation's most important artifacts. We are going to focus on some of the big ones. You will need to know all of them for your test in a couple of weeks."

Tapping his pen on his green notebook, Harrison tries to keep his eyes open. Even with Mr. Lloyd's earsplitting excitement in his voice, he can feel his eyes longing to shut.

"So, the first important artifact we will learn about, I believe is the most important of our rich history. It's the Ark of Power. The Ark of Power was known as the First Elder's greatest accomplishment."

Harrison sits up and raises his hand.

"Yes, Harrison" Mr. Lloyd leans against his wooden podium.

"I was just wondering how this Ark of Power could be considered a greater accomplishment over the creation of a nation?"

"That's a good question, Harrison. A lot of you may be thinking the same thing," Mr. Lloyd stands up. "The reason why I say it is considered the greatest accomplishment is for a couple of reasons. The first thing is because of who wanted it created. It is a long box, made of silver on the bottom, and gold across the top. It is one of the most beautiful things ever made. You see, the Ark was created while the Supreme Elder was nearing death. The Supreme Elder grew very sick and saw that he didn't have much time. Growing paranoid that someone would gain power similar to his brother's and try to destroy the five great nations, he came up with a plan. He went to his favorite disciple, our First Elder, and asked him to execute his plan. The Supreme Elder wanted the Ark made so he could transfer his energy onto the Ark."

Harrison raises his hand slowly.

"Yes, go ahead Harrison."

"How was he able to transfer his power into the Ark? I never heard of Power transfer."

"The Supreme Elder came up with a special way to transfer his energy. The only thing that he found that could sustain the strength of his power was gems. He transferred his energy into many gems while on his death bed. Since he transferred all the energy from his Power Flow into the gems, he died. So, the First Elder took the gems back home. When he got back, he cut the gems, pouring the Supreme Elder's energy on the Ark. The Ark became the greatest weapon that could be used against someone who gained the type of power his brother found," Mr. Lloyd takes a seat on a wobbly stool. "Any further questions?"

"What was inside of it?" Harrison says.

"Very good question. This is also why I think this is one of the most important artifacts in our history. The First Elder placed the Supreme Elder's bones inside of the box," Mr. Lloyd says.

Gasps fill the classroom as everyone looks around at each other.

"What is the purpose of his bones being in there?" Harrison says.

"We really don't know. All we really know about the Ark is a couple of things. We know that only Destine Elders are able to carry it. It is said that if anyone else touches it, they will die. Also, another thing we know is after the First Elder's death and his reign was over, the Ark went missing during the First Great War between the five great nations. No one has seen it. The Second Elder and the Ragnar Council are the ones responsible for losing it in a battle in the war."

"Wait, so no one knows where it is now? That is tragic," Harrison says.

"That is true, Harrison. But you know what is even more tragic than it being lost? It's that it was created to protect the five great nations against unimaginable evil and power, and yet it was used in a war against the Supreme Elder's disciple's nations. Quite sad I think," Mr. Lloyd says as the bell rings.

"See everyone next class," Mr. Lloyd puts his robe back on.

Harrison meets up with his friends as they walk out of the class.

"Man, it is so good to see you. I've been so lonely in that dorm room all by myself," JT grabs Harrison's shoulder and pulls him close to them as they walk.

"Well, I'm glad you missed me, I guess that means something," Harrison replies, giggling.

"Yeah, that room is kind of scary when you aren't there at night," JT replies.

"I hate to tell you, but you better get used to it a little. Some nights I'll be getting in late," Harrison says.

"What are you talking about? Where would you be in the middle of the night?" JT asks.

"I asked Tommy to train me secretly at night to help me get my Power Flow control down."

"What? Why would you do that?" Jaylen says.

"Yeah, that sounds crazy," Joseph says.

"Listen, if someone is out there trying to kill me, then I got to get stronger and be able to create energy attacks if I want to protect myself. I just need extra help with it, and Tommy is the only one that can do that right now."

Approaching the dorm room, the light gray clouds start dripping cold raindrops on them.

"I start training tonight."

CHAPTER
1 7

Training at Night

The rain beats against the roof like bricks falling from the sky. JT watches as Harrison packs a small backpack with extra clothes and puts his black hoodie on. JT cuts the light on. "You are really leaving to go and train with him?"

Harrison throws his backpack over his shoulders and heads to the door. "Yeah, I wasn't playing."

Harrison opens the door and peeks out.

"Don't get killed tonight then," JT lays back in the bed.

Suddenly, JT lifts his head up quickly, glaring at Harrison as he begins to step out.

"Dude, are those my grey sweat pants you have on?" JT says.

"Yeah, I needed a pair since I ruined mine when I washed my clothes with blue raspberry juice," Harrison shuts the door behind him.

Quickly exiting the backdoor of the dormitory, the fence separating the forest and the Academy towers over him. Harrison flings his hood up as he feels the rain attacking the top of his head. He starts climbing the fence, feeling it shake as he gets closer to the top.

Sliding his leg over the top, he slips on water. He crashes on the other side, landing on his back. The soft muddy ground helps soften his landing. Looking up, he sees Tommy looking over him. Extending his arm down, he helps Harrison up.

"You alright?" Tommy says.

"Yeah, never better," Harrison fixes his hood.

"Alright, let's go a little further in the forest. I found a spot we can use," Tommy says, signaling him to follow.

Traveling down a dirt trail, the woods tower over them. The rain falling off the trees makes a dripping sound that gets louder the further they go. Darkness hovers over the whole forest, making it hard to see.

"Here we are," Tommy says.

Harrison surveys his surroundings. The clear area without any large trees allows the rain to fall freely on them. Harrison takes his backpack off and throws it next to a broken log on the ground.

"Okay, so where should we start?" Harrison says.

"Well, just like in class you have to learn to harness the energy from your Power Flow into your hand. That is the basic part of the whole process," Tommy replies. "Once you learn that, then you can harness your energy to really any part of your body."

"I remember when you fought in the First Spar, you did that to your feet."

"Yeah, I sent my energy to my feet so I could run up the energy wall. To be honest, if I didn't do that, I knew I was going to lose. I had to get the high ground. If I didn't then the outcome would have been different," Tommy rubs the back of his head.

"Well, I want to learn a move like the one you used on Clark and me. I want you to be able to teach me in a couple of months my own personal move like your Omega Supersonic Blast."

"Whoa, you are way ahead of yourself. It takes time to learn and perfect an energy move of that caliber."

"Like how long are we talking about?"

"Like two years."

"Two years. I don't have two years."

"Let's just get the basics down first. You know, harnessing energy and doing simple energy ball attacks. Then we will worry about your own personal move," Tommy says. "Alright, I want you to focus and try to harness it into your hand now."

Harrison moves closer to Tommy. Closing his eyes, he begins to focus. He feels the energy heading towards his hand. Opening his eyes, his head drops in disappointment.

"The energy was starting to get there, it just didn't last," Tommy says.

"Dang it," Harrison says frustrated.

"Just keep trying, we got all night."

Harrison nods and starts to try again.

Harrison opens his eyes. The light green energy fizzles out of his hand.

"Dang it. Why can't I do this?" Harrison walks over and kicks his backpack. "It's been hours and it's almost time for us to stop."

Harrison sees Tommy rubbing the back of his neck as if he is trying to figure out something. "Okay, well I really didn't want to do this, but it's worth a shot."

"Do what?"

Tommy moves closer to him. Suddenly, Tommy punches Harrison in the face. Harrison wobbles to the left.

Holding his chin, Harrison looks up in confusion. "What the heck?"

Tommy rushes energy on his hands, turning them purple.

Immediately, he pushes Harrison. Harrison glides and slams into a tree. Harrison slides down the tree. His back throbs in pain.

"It's sad. I mean I agree with everyone else. I expect more out of the famous Douglas Grady's son," Tommy paces slowly. "I guess it's a good thing he's gone or dead because you would be an embarrassment to him."

Harrison feels the rage rushing through his body.

"How dare you say something like that? What gives you the right to say something about my dad?" Harrison stands up.

"You really took it hard huh? Was it hard growing up without him but having to hear all the famous stories?" Tommy stands still. "It has to be rough knowing that your dad cared more about his missions and his team than he did about you."

Harrison feels his whole-body tingling. He stands there staring at Tommy in anger.

"I guess to you, Douglas Grady isn't just the famous captain of the legendary Silver Falcons. He is also famous for being a father who didn't want anything to do with his own son," Tommy smiles. "I guess that is one heck of a legacy. I understand though, that would be a hard one for you to follow."

"Shut up, before I make you shut up," Harrison screams loudly.

"C' mon let's head back, I got to check in with my dad who actually wanted to be in my life."

Screaming in rage, Harrison's hands turn green as green energy circles his whole body.

Tommy stares at him, taking a step back with a look of concern.

"Take this!" Harrison screams.

Suddenly, two small green energy balls form in his hands. He launches them at Tommy. Tommy stares at them soaring towards him. He doesn't move, allowing them to smash into his chest. Soaring backward, Tommy pushes them off and does a backflip on to the ground. Harrison falls to one knee, and the energy disappears instantly. Tommy runs over to him, helping him up.

"Sorry about all that, but I had to say all that stuff and hit you to see something," Tommy brushes off the dirt on his black hoodie.

"What? All that was just part of your little test?"

"Yeah. I heard people talking on the first day when we arrived at the Academy. Some people were discussing how you and Samuel got in a fight again. I was curious about where you were at when it came to controlling your Power Flow so I asked a person who saw it if you used an energy attack on him," Tommy helps him up. "They told me not that time but said the first-time you guys fought at some skating rink, he talked about your dad and you got angry and you had energy come out."

"Yeah, but what does that matter? It was just some rare incident."

"It matters because it had me think that your power may be triggered off of your emotions."

"Wouldn't most people be?"

"Actually, you are the only one I have ever seen."

Harrison's heart races.

"That's a good thing though. That just shows me that you got something special about your power. That now has me really intrigued." Tommy says.

"Yeah, me and you both."

Harrison wobbles towards the dorms with a slight limp. Water squishes with every step he takes, from his soaked socks. His clothes are stained with dry mud.

"What time is it?" Harrison says.

Tommy gazes at his watch, squinting to see it. "5:15, we better hurry and wash up. Breakfast starts at 7:00."

As they approach the dorms, Harrison recognizes the Elder and captain from the Red Hawks walking towards the main building.

I thought the Elder said the Red Hawks wouldn't be back for two months.

"What are you staring at? Come on," Tommy opens the door.

Harrison heads up to the main building.

"Dude. What are you doing? Are you crazy?" Tommy says. "The Elder and the Red Hawk captain just went in there. If they see you, we are screwed."

"Just go to your room. I got to check something out. I won't get caught, I promise," Harrison creeps to the main building.

Quick footsteps sound behind him. Tommy is crouching along with Harrison. Entering the main building, the lights are barely lit, forming minor yellow rings on the floor. Tiptoeing down the hallway, a bright illumination gleams through the Elder's door.

"Yes. That is exactly where I wanted them to be," Harrison says.

"What are you talking about?" Tommy whispers. "This doesn't make any sense. You sure you didn't hit your head too hard on that tree?"

"Shhh. I'm fine. Just be quiet."

Approaching the entrance to the secret room, Harrison opens it. Harrison notices Tommy's mouth open wide like he is yawning. The yellow energy glows and lights up the whole room.

"You have to be kidding me. This is crazy," Tommy surveys the room. "How did you find this room?"

"Long story. I will fill you in some other time," Harrison walks to the wall and punches the same spot as last time. "Just be quiet so we can hear their conversation."

Reclining in his chair, the Elder glares at the Red Hawk captain who is standing in front of his desk. "Amazing that you managed to get this information in such a short time. I truly thought it would take the whole two months we planned for."

"We were able to get some leads faster than what we thought. After the intel we collected, I thought it was urgent that we report it to you immediately," the captain says.

The Elder sits up slowly, laying his elbows on the enormous desk. "What did you find out?"

"We found a letter from Douglas Grady to an unknown individual stating that the secret mission was, in fact, him going on a search to find the Ark of Power."

The Elder gently caresses the tight wrinkles on his forehead. "We can't let that get out. We must keep that piece of information secret."

"Yes, your Honor."

Lounging back into his giant chair, he removes the large hat from his head. "If people find out that the Silent Mission was, in fact, him searching for the Ark then some will worry that an impending war looms with the other nations. Also, if the other nations hear that we are seeking it they too would worry that we are planning an attack. Everyone is a little anxious since the War of Sorrows."

"Yes, Your Honor. I understand. I will protect this information with my life."

The Elder places his hat back on his head, hiding the wild, white strands of hair. "Thank you, captain."

The captain opens the door slightly.

"Captain. One more thing I need to ask of you and the Red Hawks."

"Yes, Your Honor."

"I need you to keep an eye on Harrison Grady. Sebastian found his name on a list indicating that the individual we are seeking is coming after him."

"Yes, Your Honor," he nods. "So, you believe this person also put an energy bomb in his acceptance letter?"

Pulling his hat down slightly the Elder walks towards the door. "Yes, I believe that."

Opening the door, they exit together. Harrison feels his clothes sticking to him as he helps Tommy up.

"You weren't playing when you said you thought someone was out to get you," Tommy says.

"Yeah, I wish I was," pulling his sweatpants from being attached to his thighs.

"I am just glad I heard them talking. Now I know that the Elder sent my dad and the Silver Falcons to find the Ark of Power."

"Yeah, but what did the Elder want the Ark for? It's been missing for a long time. Why did he send your dad to find it thirteen years ago? It doesn't make any sense."

"I don't know but the important thing is I got one more piece to this crazy puzzle," Harrison says. "C' mon, we got to get going."

Opening the door, Harrison peeks out. The sun rays start beaming through the windows. Harrison gestures Tommy to move out. Running towards the dorms, the sun rises behind the forest, shining a giant beam of sunshine. Before entering the dormitory, Harrison places his hand on

Tommy's shoulder. "Listen, I am going to lay low for a couple of months since the Red Hawks are going to be watching me. We will only meet when we have a chance."

"Okay, I understand. No problem."

Harrison removes his hand from his shoulder.

"Thanks for everything. I guess I should go up to the room and fill the guys in."

They head to their rooms. Harrison opens the door, hearing what sounds like a large drill cutting into a rock. Quickly, JT shoots up out the bed, stopping his loud snoring. Standing beside his bed, Harrison cuts the light on. "Dude, we have to talk."

JT sits up. "Darn right we have to talk. Look how you ruined my favorite pair of sweat pants," JT wipes his eyes. "What did you do roll in mud?"

"I rolled into something more than mud. I rolled into a little bit more of the truth."

C H A P T E R
1 8

The Compass of Destiny

S trong bangs sound at the bottom of the door. Harrison jumps out of bed, walks over, and opens it.

The door releases a screeching noise as Harrison gazes out. He surveys the area, but no one is there.

"Hey. We're down here, kid," a familiar voice says.

Sanford and Edwin stand there with neatly creased envelopes.

"Oh, hey, sorry about that," Harrison scratches the back of his head.

"Yeah, yeah, sure you are," Edwin crosses his tiny thin arms across his chest.

"Listen, we got your mail for you. So here you go," Sanford hands the envelopes to him.

Harrison stoops down and grabs them. "Thanks. But I got to ask where the guy is that normally delivers the mail? I haven't seen him since before the holidays."

"Don't get me started. That guy said he was attacked by a group of Chihuahuas at the beginning of the New Year and he is still in the hospital," Sanford says. "I mean come on, like those things could actually cause any harm to anyone."

"Yeah, so until he recovers, Elder Dirk said we are the team for the job," Edwin says.

"I hate my team. I wish I could be traded," Sanford says.

"Listen, if I could have a different teammate I would," Edwin says. "I saw a goldfish in one of the rooms and I was tempted to ask if he wanted a partner."

Resting against the door frame, Harrison stands there a couple seconds watching them argue.

"Okay, well it was great seeing you guys again. Happy New Year," Harrison closes the door.

"Wait, hold up kid," Sanford says.

"Yeah, what's up?"

"In the last two months we are always having to clean up dirt tracks that come from the forest. Apparently, someone is going into the woods at night a couple of times throughout the week," Sanford says.

"Yeah, and like he said we realized that it only happens when the Red Hawks are gone. We guess, that they are up to no good in those woods and are afraid to get caught. You see or hear anyone leave at night?" Edwin says.

Pretending to be in deep thought, Harrison caresses his smooth face. "No, sorry I haven't. But I will keep an eye out for you guys."

"Thanks, I know I am tired of cleaning all that dirt off the floor in here," Sanford says.

Harrison closes the door and flops on his bed. He looks at the two letters. One is from his mom and the other is from Gavin. He opens the one from Gavin first and reads.

Harrison,

Happy New Year. I hope you have been enjoying the last couple of months at the Academy. School is so boring right now. But when these winter months are over, we have a field trip planned for The Purhara mountains in the Golic nation. I can't wait to see you this summer and for you to show me all your cool energy moves. I hope I get to see you use them on somebody, just not me. Anyways, train and study hard.

Gavin

Harrison smiles and puts it back into the envelope. He rips open the one from his mom and starts to read.

Dear Harrison,

Hey sweetie, Happy New Year. I hope you are still enjoying your time up at the Academy. I sure do miss you around here. The holidays were really lonely since you didn't come back home on break, but I understand you have to do something for your Power Flow class. I can't wait till you get to come home in the summer. I am counting down the days. Write back this time, please.

I love you.

P.S. Here is a letter from your dad that you asked for. I think it's neat that you are doing an assignment on your dad. Tell me how it goes.

Mom

He snatches the other letter and hurries to a red notebook. He takes the ripped book page out and the letter that was left for him. Surveying the three side by side, he looks to see if they are all identical. His breathing ceases for a couple of moments, as he feels his heart pound in his chest.

I can't believe it. All three are the same handwriting. That means my dad really did write those notes to my uncle Adam and did write this down in the book.

Rubbing his hands continually through his hair, he paces slowly, gazing at the letters.

If the letters are real, then there is a great possibility those pictures are too. Which means my uncle Adam did meet my dad that night and he lied to me.

JT, Jaylen, and Joseph walk into the room. Harrison glances at them, picking the letters up.

"Man, Sanford and Edwin are outside arguing. Those two argue worse than my parents do," JT says.

"Forget that, look what I got," Harrison waves the letters.

"Okay, you got some letters. We get it," JT throws himself on his bed.

"No, my mom sent me a letter that my dad wrote to her. I asked her to send me one so I could see if the other two papers I had were in his handwriting."

"Whoa, so you told your mom that you wanted to do that?" Jaylen says.

"No, I told her I was doing an assignment on my dad for a class and needed something he wrote."

"Oh, so you lied to her the same way you lied to her about winter break. You told her you needed to do something for your Power Flow class," Joseph says.

"Yeah, and we know you just stayed here and trained with Tommy the whole time since you didn't leave for break," JT says.

197

"Listen, I was kind of working on my Power Flow class during that time. But I got a lot accomplished. I can now harness energy with ease and use energy balls better now," Harrison says.

"Okay, we get it. Back to it, you were saying the writing does match. So, the letter slid underneath our door a couple of months ago is real?" Jaylen says.

"Yes, that is what I was saying. Therefore, if the letters are authentic, then there is a great chance we can say the pictures are too," Harrison replies.

"Wow, so your uncle Adam lied to you," JT says. "So out of the three, who do you think is the crazy robe guy? Are you leaning more towards your uncle now over Mr. Drake and Mr. Lloyd?"

"I don't know yet. I haven't ruled out anyone, because it seems like Mr. Drake is always trying to kill me in class. Mr. Lloyd almost said the same exact thing the robe guy said about history," Harrison drops on his bed. "I'm so confused."

"Well, I know one thing we do know. We better get to Mr. Lloyd's class. We got to meet in front of the Elder statues today," Joseph says.

Harrison tucks in his dark green shirt, grabs his backpack, and follows the others out the door.

Small snowflakes gradually fall from the clouds. Every couple of steps Harrison feels a cold itch on his face. Mr. Lloyd's voice travels to them.

"Good morning. It's snowing," Mr. Lloyd says as the students approach him.

"Like we can't see that it's snowing," Jaylen throws his hood over his head. "Who decided to have class outside in the middle of winter when it's snowing?"

JT laughs and points at Mr. Lloyd who is springing on his toes. The snow makes the statues have a darker tint at the top of them.

Mr. Lloyd walks in front of the First Elder statue, lifting his hand up to it. "This right here is the First Elder, as you all know. The great disciple of the Supreme Elder. I thought it would be fitting to come and have my lecture out here in front of his statue since today is his birthday. We come out here to honor the First Elder who did so much for this nation."

The students around Harrison shiver as the snow gets fuller. Harrison puts on his dark gray hoodie throwing the hood over his head. The wind slashes quickly at times, making the First Elder statue seem like he is freezing. He tunes out Mr. Lloyd's lecture as he gazes at the First Elder's statue.

His eyes are fixed on the compass in his hand. Harrison's eye's grow heavy and he doesn't blink. Finally, he shoots his hand into the air. The students let out a sigh in unison as they see his hand up.

"Yes, Harrison. Do you have a question before we head back to the classroom since everyone is complaining about a little bit of snow?" Mr. Lloyd says.

"Yeah, just a quick question while it's on my mind," Harrison says. "That object in the First Elder's hand. What is he holding?"

Mr. Lloyd leans against the statue. "Great question. This thing in his hand is actually the Compass of Destiny. It's an important artifact in our history."

"Why is it so important? What does it do?" Harrison says.

"Well, you see this compass was given to the First Elder by the Supreme Elder himself. The Supreme Elder created it so that it would be able to lead the First Elder to him no matter where he was, just in case he needed him," Mr. Lloyd says.

"Wait, so how would the compass lead him to the Supreme Elder?" Harrison says.

Moans and groans grow louder as he asks more questions.

"It is said, that the Supreme Elder created the compass in order to be able to track him down by his energy. You see, the compass can locate where his energy is," Mr. Lloyd replies.

Harrison's heart races. "Wait. Mr. Lloyd that would mean that the Compass of Destiny could now lead someone to the Ark of Power since it was covered by his power."

"You are right, Harrison. That is why the First Elder made it so no one would be able to use the compass again."

Harrison's heart sinks to his stomach. "What? Why?"

"Because he was afraid someone might take the compass and try to find the Ark to use it sometime in the future. He didn't want to be responsible for that. So, he deactivated the compass by making it only able to work if his energy was placed on it. He actually did the same thing the Supreme Elder did and transferred his energy into gems, except they turned green. He then placed them in a cave deep in that forest behind the Academy," Mr. Lloyd says.

"Are the green gems still there in the cave?" Harrison says.

"No one in history has been stupid enough to go in there searching for them. It would be suicide with the type of different things in there," Mr. Lloyd says.

The snow starts coming down hard covering up the compass in the hand of the statue. Students begin to walk off complaining about Harrison asking questions.

"Okay, you all are dismissed," Mr. Lloyd says.

Walking slowly with his friends, Harrison stays back behind everyone else.

"Guys, it makes sense now," Harrison says. "My dad must have known that if he had the compass, he could find the Ark of Power on his mission. That is why he came to your dad's shop, JT, and asked if he had ever seen it. We have the one thing that can lead us to the Ark."

They slow down and stare at him.

"Dude, what are you trying to say? That we should use the compass to go find the Ark? Why?" Jaylen says.

"Because, if we find the Ark of Power, we might just find out what happened to my dad," Harrison says as they open the door and the warm air blasts out.

CHAPTER
19

The Plan

G rease gushes out of the crispy fried chicken as Harrison takes a large bite. Placing his chicken bone down into the rest of the collection, he glances at his friends at the table.

"You know that you are an absolute slob when you eat chicken," JT says.

"Yeah. It's pretty gross dude," Jaylen shakes his head. "About as gross as when JT eats cereal."

JT knocks Jaylen in the arm. "Shut up. I am not a slob when I eat cereal. I don't have it all over my face like he does."

"Listen. You both shouldn't take a girl out to eat on your first date. If they see you two eat, you would never get a second date," Joseph says.

"Whatever. At least I could get a date if I wanted, unlike you," JT responds.

JT, Jaylen, and Joseph keep bickering with each other, resulting in the whole cafeteria staring over at them. A screechy sound creeps toward them. Felix stops his cart at their table, watching them. Sanford and Edwin are carrying tiny brooms, shaking their heads as they watch them quarrel. Tapping the table continually, Harrison motions for their attention. They quickly stop arguing.

"WHAT" all three of them scream, gawking at Harrison. He slowly nods his head over to Felix and his crew. Sanford and Edwin both shake their heads in disgust.

"You three are something else. I can't believe you guys would have the nerve to argue like that in a public place," Sanford says.

"Yeah. It makes you three look bad. Get it together, " Edwin says.

Felix pushes the cart forward, releasing a screech with each push. Sitting at the table, they all remain silent, blinking at one another.

"Can I please blast that mouse and cat with an energy attack?" JT says.

Harrison pushes his dark blue tray full of greasy chicken bones to the side. Leaning forward, he lowers his voice, as the eyes around the cafeteria start moving away from them.

"Okay. I think I know what I want to do. I think I have the plan," Harrison whispers.

"The plan for what?" Joseph says.

204

"What do you mean for what? What we talked about after history class," Harrison replies.

"Yeah, I remember. So, what's the plan you came up with?" Jaylen says.

Sanford and Edwin clean chocolate milk off the floor near their table.

"JT, are you paying attention?" Joseph says, nudging him in the arm.

"I can't believe those two actually had the nerve to tell us we shouldn't argue. They argue worse than anyone I have ever met," JT says.

Slapping his own forehead, Harrison leans closer to JT. "Are you serious? You are worried about what they said to you just now?" Harrison shakes his head. "Worry about what we just found out."

"I am, it just made me mad," JT rests his chin in his palms.

"Anyways. So, like I said earlier. If we can find the Ark of Power, it could lead us to my dad. Whether he's dead or alive," Harrison says.

"Yeah, but what if it doesn't? What if we get lucky and find the Ark and your dad is nowhere around?" Jaylen says.

"Look, it's worth a shot. I know it's taking a chance, but I think it's the best option to find out what happened to him," Harrison replies.

"I understand all that, but we are still in a dilemma because the compass doesn't even work. We would need the gems that contain the First Elder's power and those are in a cave in the middle of the forest," Joseph says.

"I know. That is why we will have to go and get them first. Then we can activate the compass and it can lead us to the Ark of Power," Harrison responds.

"Whoa. You want us to go on a suicide mission and try to retrieve the gems? Dude. You heard what Mr. Lloyd said. No one has ever attempted that. It's too dangerous," Joseph says.

"Yeah, that does sound crazy," JT lifts his head.

"Oh, okay coming from the person who had us break into an antique shop and steal a blueprint in the middle of the night," Harrison replies.

"It worked, didn't it?" JT says.

"Yeah, and this may work too. We just won't know unless we try," Harrison replies. "C' mon."

Patiently waiting, Harrison sits quietly, watching the cafeteria empty out.

"Okay. Listen, if you guys don't want to do this I understand. It may be asking a lot. I can just ask Tommy to go with me," Harrison says.

All three of them lean closer to Harrison.

"What?" Harrison says.

"Dude, why would you ask him?" JT says.

"What are you talking about? I would ask him because you guys act like you don't want to really help," Harrison replies.

Pushing his tray aside, JT leans in closer. "What do you mean, we don't want to help? We are the ones that have been helping you for months," JT says. "Tommy helps you train a little and now you guys are all cool?"

"I didn't mean it like that. I know you guys have helped. I mean help now with this part-"

"We get it, just ditch your friends who you have known since you were younger and become best friends with the strongest Kaden in school. Makes perfect sense," JT says.

"What is your problem? It's not like that. Tommy is cool and all, but we aren't best friends. You guys are always going to be my best friends," Harrison says. "I mean I wasn't saying that in a bad way. I was just stating that if you guys didn't want to, I could just see if Tommy would help."

They stand quickly as Felix screeches towards them. Harrison gazes around and notices the emptiness in the room.

"Alright, boys. Let's get going. Everyone else has left, time for you guys to head back up to your rooms," Felix states.

Harrison and his friends exit the empty cafeteria. Not a word is uttered as they walk to their rooms.

"You aren't taking Tommy. We are part of this plan. We are going to be the ones that help you find the gems, then find the Ark, and see if it leads to your dad," JT says. "I told you the moment I found out that you were trying to do this that I would help any way I can. I mean that."

Harrison smiles.

"I am always going to be here for you," JT says.

"I know," Harrison replies.

Sanford and Edwin stroll by them. They shake their heads slowly.

"You guys are the most unique group of kids I have ever met. First, you're fighting, now you're getting emotional," Sanford walks off.

They stand there for a couple of moments watching them leave. Suddenly, all of them fill the hallway with laughter as they head to their rooms.

Harrison and Tommy walk to their typical training spot in the woods. Snow crunches with every step they take. The trees are buried in the pearl white snow as small snowflakes drop to help conceal them. Chilly wind rubs Harrison's nose, forming a numb feeling, as he stands to wait for Tommy's instructions.

"Okay. Another midnight training session. You got me out in the snow so you better accomplish something," Tommy hides his face in his coat. "Let's just pace ourselves before we dive in. Just create an energy ball and throw it at that tree."

Taking his fuzzy glove off, Harrison tosses it in a deep pile of snow. Closing his eyes, he extends his arm out with his palm facing up. Opening his eyes slowly, his hand shines green. Squeezing his fingers slightly, he snaps them straight as a small green energy ball the size of a tennis ball hovers over his hand. He grabs it and slings it at the tree. The green energy ball whistles through the air, slamming into a dense sturdy tree full of pearly white snow. It shakes the tree causing the snow to fall, making the tree bare.

Harrison forms another one effortlessly. He smiles slightly. He slings it at another tree, watching the snow tumble off. Energy ball after energy ball, he knocks all the snow off each tree circling them.

"Okay, well apparently you are just super excited that you have got that down, or you just hate seeing snow or trees," Tommy says.

"Yeah, I am pretty excited. Training over winter break was huge for me. If I didn't stay here, I would be further behind."

Tommy paces over to him. "Okay, well it's time to try and learn your own custom move then."

"Yes. This is what I have been waiting for," Harrison bounces up and down. "What should I name it? I want an awesome name for it so when I am about to hit an opponent with it, it strikes fear in their heart."

Scratching the back of his head, Tommy stares at Harrison as he continually bounces with excitement. "Ummm, I don't know. You can name it whatever you want. But before we name it why don't we learn how to do it?"

Harrison halts the quick bounces and looks over at him.

"Yeah. I guess," Harrison responds. "So how do we start?"

"Well with an elite attack you have to summon more energy from your Power Flow. It usually takes a little bit of time since you are trying to harness more energy. After you bring forth the energy into your hand or hands, this is where it gets interesting."

"What do you mean interesting? What do you do next?"

"You have to channel the energy into either a solid ball of energy or a ray. Like my Omega Supersonic Blast is a solid ball of energy that cuts through energy rays. That is why my move worked so well against Clark. His was a ray so it actually helped me out because it enhanced my move."

"Wow. Okay well, I think I know what I want my move to do. I want to form a solid energy ball about the size of maybe a volleyball and make it spin to create more force. Then it explodes on impact."

Tommy's eyes widen as he paces in front of Harrison, smashing snow with each slow step. "That would be a crazy move. Alright, I will sit, and you just start working,"

Harrison spreads his legs apart, balancing as he crouches a little. Clinching his fists tightly, the rushing of energy flows through his body. Opening his right hand, he channels the gushing energy to it.

"C' mon. You have to bring forth more energy from your Power Flow. Don't be scared, push all of it on your hand," Tommy says.

The snow lifts off the ground. His whole body vibrates as green energy circles faintly around him.

"This feels weird. I feel like it won't come out," Harrison screams.

Tommy grabs the dead limb on the tree. "Just let it out. Screaming enhances it because it takes pressure off of your muscles. The same way as when you lift weights. Screaming helps the process."

Tommy grips the tree as the wind picks up from the circulation of Harrison's energy.

Harrison yells. The energy flows rapidly through his body to his palm. His arm shakes overpoweringly. Grasping his wrist, his left hand seems as if it has joined in on a dance with his right hand. Harrison notices the green energy thickening around him, becoming more visible. A burning sensation forms in his right palm.

An energy ball the size of a golf ball forms. Moving slowly, he tries to spin it. As he starts to turn it and increase its size, a burning sensation overtakes his hand. Gazing at it, steam sizzles from the flesh on his hand.

Snow melts as it falls over his hand from the steam rising up from it. Suddenly, he drops to his knees, looking at the tiny scald in the middle of his palm. He slams it into the cold snow trying to stop the burning. "Oh. My. Gosh. That hurt like crap."

Tommy walks over to check on him. At that same time, crackling steps in the snow come from the darkness in the woods. Staring into the darkness, Harrison can't seem to focus as his hand feels as if it is on fire.

Abruptly, a voice comes from the woods, approaching them. "Oh. My. Gosh is what I should be saying."

Looking in the direction of the voice, Harrison spots Samuel and his two chubby friends walk out of the woods.

"This is too good to be true," Samuel strolls around them slowly. "When that cat and mouse asked me if I saw anyone leaving at night to go into the woods, and I told them I would catch them, I would have never imagined it would be you."

Harrison stands, tightening his hand. Aches trickle throughout his whole palm.

"And you two idiots made it so easy for us to catch you. All I had to do was follow your tracks in the snow. You are the ones that led us right to you," Samuel says.

"You can't tell anyone about this," Harrison says.

"What? You see that is not part of the plan. My plan is to catch the people sneaking out and report them, so it makes me look good in front of the Elder," Samuel says.

Tommy moves towards them as Samuel and the two chubby boys form energy balls in their hands.

"Wait. Slow down. I know you took down a Gideon, but you don't stand a chance against all three of us. Plus, your little back up over there looks like he hurt his hand pretty bad. So, let's just spare the time and get back to my plan," Samuel replies.

The snow flies off his shoes with each step as Harrison runs towards them.

"I will show you," Harrison screams.

Quickly, all three of them shoot energy balls at him. One is bright orange and two are red. Lifting his left hand, Harrison deflects the orange one into a tree causing it to shake. The two red ones knock into his chest, taking him off his feet and crashing him on the freezing ground.

Tommy's feet light up purple as he dashes up a tree. Flipping backward off the top of it, he hovers over them and launches a giant purple energy ball striking all three of them. Each of them take off into separate directions.

They bounce and roll on the snow. Tommy lands, crouching near Samuel. Bending over him, Tommy puts his hand on Samuel's chest. "Listen. We are going to follow my plan. The plan is that you aren't going to tell a soul who you saw out here. If you do, I promise you, you will be the person who receives the biggest Omega Supersonic Blast I have ever done. And I will tell my dad, who isn't too fond of you either, that you are lying and trying to destroy my reputation which reflects on him," Tommy stands up looking down at him. "So, what do you say? You like the plan?"

Samuel moans as he holds his head. "Yeah. Just leave us alone."

"That's a great choice."

Helping Harrison up, Tommy grabs their bags and leaves. The crunching of their steps in the beat-up snow drowns out the moans of agony behind them.

CHAPTER
20

The Akia Brothers' Treaty

S itting on an unstable violet plastic chair in the waiting area of the hospital, Harrison clenches his hand slowly. The sour air irritates the diamond shape burn in the middle of his right palm. Any movement sends jolts of pain from it, making him keep it half-way open. Two older girls stand in front of him, holding a giant poster.

Placing it against the wall, they giggle as one side keeps falling off as they try to tape it onto the wall. Minutes fly by before they get it up there. The extensive rectangular poster reminds Harrison of the *Hallway of Antiques* sign. Each letter on the poster is a different color, capturing every eye that walks by it. Harrison reads it.

The Cerdic class presents The 150 hours of Remembrance.
The Celebration of the 150th Anniversary of the Destine
Nation.

No Classes for 150 hours.

The whole 150 hours will be designed as a time of celebration of the First Elder creating our nation.

Just three months away.

Wow. One hundred and fifty hours of non-stop partying. That sounds so much better than my classes. Harrison thinks.

Suddenly, Rene Rush enters the waiting area holding a long brown board, flipping through papers. "Harrison Grady."

Harrison follows her to the back. She walks quickly, making it hard to keep up with her.

"This says it's your hand hurting, not your legs. So quit walking so slow," she says.

They enter a bare white room, with no windows. The noisy lights buzzing distract him from concentrating on her questions and even her smile.

She pokes around the burn, constantly looking at it and gazing into his eyes. Harrison smiles at her.

"This is an energy burn. Did this happen in your Power Flow class?"

Harrison's heart beats rapidly, making his chest feel like a drum. "Yeah. I just didn't report it to Mr. Drake. I figured it wasn't anything."

Grabbing a small pasty bottle, she stretches his hand out. Air jumps into his burn releasing a cringe on Harrison's face. She pours a thick clear gel in the wound. Harrison's hand throbs uncontrollably as the gel covers every inch of the area.

"Ouch."

She wraps his hand softly with a peach color bandage. "It will burn for a minute. I put a gel in the burn that will help it heal faster," she smiles gently. "Whatever you do, don't try to harness energy in that hand right now. It needs time to heal."

Harrison nods.

He glances over as she puts the bandage wrap back into the tiny cabinets.

"Well, at least this time, it wasn't an overnight stay," she says. "Plus, it was your energy attack and not someone else's that put you here."

Laughing, Harrison steps out and slams into Mr. Lloyd's chest. Off balance, Mr. Lloyd stares at Harrison.

"I am so sorry, Mr. Lloyd."

"It's okay. I guess you were just super excited to see me again," Mr. Lloyd says.

"Mr. Lloyd, what are you doing here?" Harrison says.

"I come and check on all my students in the hospital wing. But I was coming to see someone else. I didn't even know you were here, just like last time."

"Oh, it's okay, Mr. Lloyd, it's no big deal. I understand," Harrison responds. "But can I ask you a quick question?"

Mr. Lloyd fixes his robe as his colorful Hawaiian shirt peaks out a little. "Sure."

"What exactly makes that forest so dangerous that no one has ever attempted to go and find the green gems?"

"The only person to ever get to the middle of the forest where the cave is located is the First Elder," Mr. Lloyd leans against the wall. "There are dangerous animals that live in there. And that isn't the worse of it."

"Well, what is it, then?"

"The Akia brothers live in there. They are two giants who are the last remaining members of the giant clan who used to control the forest. The First Elder made a treaty with them, called the Akia Treaty. That treaty allowed the First Elder to build the Academy on the outskirts of the forest."

Rena Rush dashes out of the room, slamming into Mr. Lloyd. Papers scatter all across the greenish marble floor.

"I am so sorry. Excuse me," Rena bends down and picks them up.

Harrison and Mr. Lloyd bend down and help gather the thin pieces of paper.

"It's okay, young lady. I need to stretch my back throughout the day. This just helps me out," Mr. Lloyd moans in-between each word.

"So, Mr. Lloyd. What makes the Akia brothers so dangerous? I mean, I understand they are giants but what's the big deal?" Harrison hands the papers to Rena.

Cracks sound from Mr. Lloyd's back as he straightens up.

"Thank you," she organizes the papers back on her long clipboard.

"Well, Harrison, they are extremely powerful. They are fifty times stronger than we are. They may not be able to generate energy attacks, but their strength makes up for it," Mr. Lloyd says. "Well, I gotta get going, Harrison. I look forward to answering more of your questions next time. You are such a curious kid. I love that."

Mr. Lloyd walks off as Rena follows him, still organizing her papers. Harrison grabs his backpack and walks down the hallway.

Well, that isn't too bad. Two giants aren't too threatening.

We can handle two simple giants between all of us. So, I guess we can leave tomorrow.

Harrison approaches the snowy field, gazing at his Power Flow class tossing energy balls against a huge wall. Small rapid explosions constantly slam the old worn wall, making it look like they are trying to paint it with all different colors. Mr. Drake stands behind the line of students.

Harrison comes up behind him, clearing his throat. "Excuse me, Mr. Drake."

Mr. Drake turns his head slowly over his shoulder, glancing at Harrison with just one eye.

"Oh, young Grady. I was wondering where you were. Why are you so late to my class?" Mr. Drake looks away.

"I was at the hospital wing. I burned my dominant hand last night, so I have a signed medical note saying I can't participate in your class until it heals completely," Harrison takes the crinkled note out of his pocket.

"Keep the note, I don't need it," Mr. Drake walks towards the students. "This is going to put you behind in class, and you're already struggling. But go get some rest. I'll see you when you heal up."

Harrison waits, signaling for JT, Jaylen, and Joseph. They launch multiple energy balls at the wall. JT glances over at Harrison.

Harrison starts mouthing to him. "Meet me in the room. And tell them to get ready. We leave early tomorrow morning."

Mr. Drake looks over his shoulder at Harrison. Tensing up, Harrison waves at him.

"Sorry, I was watching them practice. I am leaving now," Harrison walks away as his heart beats through his chest.

Harrison wakes up to JT shaking him. Jaylen and Joseph stare at him as he blinks rapidly.

"About time you woke up," Jaylen says. "'You slept the whole day away. It's 10:00 at night."

Harrison rises quickly, knocking the heavy rosy striped blanket off his bed. Racing all around the room, he snatches his backpack, cramming different things into it. He gazes at them, staring at him with confusion written over their faces.

"Dude. What are you doing?" Joseph says.

"Why didn't you guys wake me up? You let me sleep the whole day away," Harrison zips his backpack.

"We tried to wake you for lunch and dinner, but you didn't even budge. Then we saw your nurse walking down the hallway. We asked her if she thought you would be okay, and she told us you probably needed the rest. Just to leave you alone and wake you up sometime tonight," JT puts the blanket back on his bed.

"What was she doing on our hallway? I never saw her around the dorms before?" Harrison pulls his gray hoodie over his head.

"She just said that she had to give a checkup to the Red Hawks before they left tonight on their mission. So, she must have been coming back from that," JT says.

Harrison focuses. "What? They weren't supposed to leave till tomorrow. That means they could come back tomorrow. So, we need to leave now and head to the cave before they get back. Harrison responds, grabbing his bag and rushing to the door. "C' mon. Meet me at the fence. You have ten minutes."

He closes the door.

Tapping the fence, Harrison waits for them to arrive.

C'mon. We have to get going.

Minutes go by and finally they appear.

"Hurry. Follow me and be quiet," Harrison says, ascending the fence.

They all climb the fence and drop over, falling into deep, thick snow. Walking into the woods, Harrison notices the nervousness on their faces.

"Just follow me. We are going to by-pass the area where Tommy and I train at. I believe the unrestricted part of the woods is just past that," Harrison says.

Snow crunches beneath their feet every time they take a step. The moonlight reflects off of the pearly snow.

"You know. I don't really like the sound of the unrestricted part. It just doesn't have a great ring to it," JT says.

Entering into Harrison's training area, the trees are now lightly covered with fresh snow. Harrison observes the ground seeing tracks of feet walking. He examines them.

"What's wrong?" Joseph walks up behind Harrison.

"Last night, we got in a fight with Samuel and his two friends-"

"What? Why didn't you tell us that?" JT says, interrupting Harrison.

Harrison gazes up at them.

"Tell me when I would have had time too? I was knocked out all day and haven't a chance to really talk to you," Harrison looks back at the tracks. "They found us because of our tracks in the snow. The problem is that was last night, and it has snowed more since then."

"Okay. So, what's the big deal?" Jaylen says.

"Our footprints we would have made from last night would have been covered by now, just like the trees around here are. I knocked all the snow off of them and look at them. They have fresh snow on them. The tracks right here are fresh," Harrison says, staring at the tracks that lead into the other end of the woods.

"Great. So, you are saying someone else is heading in the same direction we are?" Joseph says.

"Not just someone. Judging by how many different footprints there are, it's a small group," Harrison responds.

Their eyes enlarge as they look toward the woods. The wind rushes through making snow from the trees fly in front of them.

"C' mon. We will be fine. Let's go," Harrison says.

Walking further down, the trees seem to get older and larger each step they take. They approach an aged sign. The snow covers the greenish stains on the wooden sign. Brushing the snow off of it, JT exposes the sign's writing.

DO NOT PASS! THE AKIA BROTHER'S TREATY IS NOT IN EFFECT PAST THIS POINT!

"What the heck is the Akia brother's treaty?" JT says.

Harrison rubs his neck slowly. "It's nothing really. It's just something about two giants that live in here. It's really no big deal."

"No big deal? You just said, two giants. I think that's a big deal," JT says.

Harrison walks past the sign. "They can't be that bad. We probably won't cross them."

CHAPTER 21

A Giant Problem

The sun glimmers through the trees as they walk deeper into the woods. The light bouncing off the snow captures the bare, brown branches. The warmth from the sun keeps Harrison's eyelids from completely closing. Yawns sound every couple of seconds from behind Harrison.

JT, Jaylen, and Joseph have dark bags underneath their eyes. The trees seem to have overtaken the world. Suddenly, Harrison spots a bare area up ahead. "I think we are approaching something."

He speeds up but, the others keep moving at their same pace. Harrison stops, eyeing the clear area full of snow. The hill gives a changed look to the forest. Waiting for the others, a piercing scream rings in Harrison's ears.

Suddenly, a petrified man races over the other side of the hill. Arriving at the top, he stumbles trying to gain his balance. The man grips a black mask in his hand. His charcoal clothes are ripped throughout his whole outfit. JT, Jaylen, and Joseph hurry to where Harrison is, glancing up at the hill.

Suddenly, loud grunts echoes in the air. Instantly, the man is snatched up by a large hand. The reflection from the gold rings on the gigantic hand blinds Harrison's eyes as the sun hits them. Harrison views two large figures that are identical. They laugh. Their voices shake the trees that Harrison holds tightly to.

The vibration from the tree sends a burning sensation through his bandaged hand. The laughter gets louder as they play catch with the man. Flying through the air, the man's long black hair scatters everywhere. One of the giants grabs him by his hair with his thumb and index finger. Dangling him, the man's agonizing scream rattles their ears.

He swings him a little, launching him towards the woods where Harrison and his friends are. They crouch down as the man soars through the air. Sailing above their heads, he slashes through many trees. Slowing down, he falls and rolls on the ground, lifeless. The trees slam into other trees causing them to collapse. Harrison's legs vibrate as they fall.

The laughing stops. Harrison watches the giants still standing on the hill. Covering their eyes from the sun beaming down from them, their green skin brightens as the rays hit them. Their stringy black hair in ponytails sway in the wind in unison with their long brown fur coats that extend to their knees.

"Oh brother. I guess they are done playing," one of the giants says. "That was quick."

"Be quiet," the other one says. "They broke the treaty, and we deserved to break them. Makes me mad that they dare come in here. Let's get that body and put it with the others."

Harrison stares at his friends, scurrying back behind some of the broken trees. Bobbing lightly off the ground, Harrison feels the giants get closer. Pieces of large trees glide through the air as they clear a path.

"If I see anyone else. I will punish them worse than all of these," one of them picks up the lifeless body.

They stop at the end of the wood line. Their gigantic green toes are inches away from Harrison's face. Fungus in his toenails fills Harrison's nose with the most awful odor he has ever smelled. Grabbing his nose, he attempts to keep the foul odor out. His nose begins to sting throughout his nostrils. The giant takes a couple of steps.

Unexpectedly, Harrison sneezes.

Crap.

The giants glance down, throwing the trees he is hiding under. Standing straight up, he stares at them.

"Look. Another one brother," one of the giants says.

Their nostrils flare rapidly as they glare down at him. Harrison moves back slowly, showing his hands.

"My name is Harr-"

"I don't care what your name is. You broke the treaty and we must break you," one of them jumps towards him.

"Run," Harrison screams.

The others rise up following Harrison. Sprinting up the hill, they slip every couple of steps on the snow.

"I am going to pee myself. Oh. My. Gosh," Jaylen says.

"Look, there is more brother."

Harrison spots the giants soar to the other side of the hill as they make it to the top. Haltering immediately, they stare at the giants. Slinging his backpack off his shoulders, Harrison rushes through it, pulling his EFG out.

"What are you doing? You can't use your hand for energy attacks," JT says as Harrison slips the EGF over his bandage.

"I think this may help. I don't have a choice right now," Harrison tightens it on his hand. "Harness your energy. We have to attack."

Laughs erupt out of the giants as they listen. Bending over, they slap their knees and grab each other's shoulders. Pointing their huge index finger at them, they laugh harder.

"They are actually going to try and defend themselves," they say, repeatedly.

Moving beside Harrison, JT tightens his fist, shaking it. "You think this is so funny? Let's see how funny you think this is."

A blue energy ball hovers over his hand. He grabs the ball and launches it at one of them, hitting him in his left eye.

Grabbing his eye, the giant angrily leers at them.

"Please tell me you just didn't really hit a giant in his eye. Now you created a giant problem. Good job," Joseph says as the giants stomp their feet continually.

The giants sprint toward them. The boys create energy balls as they see the giants approaching. Harrison's hand burns as he feels the wound in his palm opening back up. Launching their attacks at them, the boys run right toward the giants.

"Go under," Harrison screams.

They slide in-between the giants' legs. Rolling down the hill, snow crashes into Harrison's face creating a cold burn. Screams erupt from the giants as they stand up on the bottom of the hill.

Suddenly, Harrison sees someone running up behind them with a bright light in his hand. Harrison's eyes grow wide at who he spots.

"Supersonic Omega Blast."

Slamming the energy ball into the one on the left's back, the giant raises up off the ground flying into the air. Thick spit falls on Harrison and them as they view the giant slamming into the cluster of trees.

"Brother!"

The giant throws a massive punch towards Tommy. Flipping sideways, Tommy evades the punch. Crouching on his knees, he blasts into the air with a long purple energy beam. The giant looks up at him soaring up. Releasing the beam, Tommy shoots two energy balls into both of the giant's eyes. Grabbing his eyes, the giant stomps around, screaming.

Tommy lands, bending his knees. Screaming loudly, purple energy circles Tommy. An energy ball forms in his hand. The giant squints as Tommy gains more energy.

"I will kill you," the giant charges at him.

"Supersonic Omega Blast," Tommy screams.

Slamming the energy attack into his stomach, the giant soars into the air towards the broken trees. Crashing on the ground, shocks run through the land. Both giants lay on top of trees passed out, with Tommy standing on top of the hill, still holding his stance. Standing there in complete silence, they gape at one another in shock. Wiping the slimy slobber from his face, he views Tommy standing on the top of the hill.

"This is so disgusting," JT throws heavy spit on the ground.

"I guess we are lucky he came. If not, we would have been in some serious trouble," Jaylen replies.

Harrison takes a couple of strides towards Tommy.

"Did you tell him to follow us?" JT follows Harrison.

"No. I never told him. But at this point, I am just glad he showed up," Harrison replies. "But I am going to find out how he knew we were out here."

The hum of energy zapping around Tommy is still sounding. He turns to face Harrison. Tommy's face goes pale and he collapses. Harrison catches him, slowly lowering him down to the soft snow.

"Tommy. Are you okay?" Harrison holds him in his arms.

His eyes flutter to the back of his head, as his mouth opens slightly. Harrison slaps his cheek softly on both sides.

"I think he may have used too much energy from his Power Flow," Joseph says.

"Well, what do we do?" Harrison says.

"If it's not too bad, he will be alright. He may have just passed out," Joseph replies.

Minutes go by and Harrison is still holding Tommy. Finally, he opens his eyes and sits up slowly. Tommy looks confused as he glances around. "Man. Using that second Supersonic Omega Blast took a toll on me more than I thought it would,"

"Are you alright?" Harrison helps him to his feet.

Wobbling around, Tommy gains his balance, surveying the giants he took out. "Yeah. I will be fine."

"Thanks for your help. But I got to ask. How did you know we were here?" Harrison says.

"We were supposed to train at midnight last night and you never showed up. I saw the tracks going into the forest, so I thought maybe something happened to you. So, I followed the tracks," Tommy says.

"Well I guess it's a good thing you did, or we would be goners right now," Jaylen says.

The giants are passed out, laying on top of broken trees.

"Let's go further in. They said they took care of others. They must be close," JT says.

Going into the other side of the woods, blood is spattered in various places. All of a sudden, they come upon many bodies spread out. Harrison glances at all of them. They are dressed the same as the man that was running. Their black outfits stick out in the snow, and each one is either holding a mask or has one on.

Some of them are guys and some are girls. Harrison stands over a small girl. Blood runs down her young face like teardrops.

She couldn't be older than eleven or twelve years old. What would she be doing out here with all these people?

Harrison flips the young girl over. Her sleeve is ripped, showing her shoulder. He observes something burned on her arm. Ripping the rest of her sleeve, he sees the whole thing.

Part of the ONE

"Hey, guys. Come check this out," Harrison shouts.

Hurrying over, they stand over him, studying the burn on her arm.

"I saw that on another person's back over there," JT says.

Harrison scratches his head. "There have to be fourteen people out here. I wonder if they all have that burned in their skin somewhere."

"The real question is what does it mean and why do they have it?" Joseph says.

"I don't know but apparently they are a part of some group," Tommy says. "Anyways I was wondering why you guys and this group are out here."

"We are going to go to the cave here in this forest to get a gem that has the First Elder's power in it," Harrison responds.

"Why?" Tommy says.

"We will tell you later. Let's just try to find the cave," JT walks on.

Harrison motions to the rest of them to follow. The trees decrease in size the further they walk. The branches are full of colorful leaves. Bright butterflies fly around the leaves. Healthy green grass overwhelms the ground. The snow is missing on the grass and trees.

"What the heck? Why isn't there any snow?" Jaylen says. "And why are the trees fully bloomed when it's the middle of winter?"

"I don't know," Harrison replies, as the butterflies fly around his head.

The sound of water loudly bounces off the trees. Exiting the woods, Harrison notices water slamming into rocks. Across the river is a large cave glistening in the bright sun.

Harrison smiles. "C' mon guys. We finally made it."

CHAPTER 22

The Wolfpack

Harrison and the others approach the huge silvery stone cave. Apple red cardinals rest on different stones sticking out of the cave. Swarms of honey-colored butterflies circle the cardinals continually. Harrison and his friends gaze around with their mouths drooping and eyes watering from staring at the sight of it all.

Harrison's body begins to tingle because of the warmth of the air. Sweat gently slides from the top of his brow, entering his eye. The giant cave's entrance feels welcoming to Harrison, despite the darkness that lays in it. Slowly, he moves closer to it with the rest following right behind.

"Harrison. We might want to be careful; we don't know how safe this place really is," Jaylen says.

Glancing over his shoulder, Harrison grins with a quick laugh. "C' mon look at this place. What can be dangerous about this place? Are the cardinals and butterflies going to attack us?"

Standing next to the cave, Harrison places his hand gently on the rock surrounding it. A coolness from the stone chills his hand through his bandage. His hand slides beside a beautiful cherry colored cardinal, that is bigger than the rest. The cardinal's burnt yellow eyes gaze into his.

The cardinal gingerly rises, extending its long wings straight out. Flapping gracefully, green waves of energy shimmer out. Heat from the energy rubs against Harrison's skin.

"Tommy. Have you ever seen or heard an animal being able to produce energy like that?" Joseph says, staring at it.

"I never saw anything like that, and my dad always told me that animals could never harness energy," Tommy scratches the back of his neck softly.

Extending his hand towards it, the warmth from the energy increases as it gets closer to the cardinal.

"Dude. I would be careful. Tommy said he never has seen anything like this, and his dad apparently said it's not possible," JT says.

Tuning the others out, Harrison puts his hand underneath it. The toughness of its feet tickles Harrison's finger.

"You guys are paranoid. What could possibly happen?" Harrison gazes at the cardinal resting on his finger.

Suddenly, the twitching of the other cardinal's heads scares away the butterflies. One by one they quickly soar off towards the colorful bloomed trees. The cardinals flying away takes Harrison's eyes off of the one relaxing on his finger.

"Harrison," JT screams.

Glaring back at it, Harrison sees the two spinning energy balls formed at each wing. Throwing the cardinal off his finger, it pushes its wings together blasting Harrison with a green energy ray. Slamming into his chest, Harrison soars to the ground and slides to the river. His head dangles into the water, soaking the top part of his hair.

"Harrison," they all scream, running over to him.

Sitting up, Harrison gazes at his friends running towards him as the cardinal flies in the same spot.

"Are you alright?" Tommy lifts him up.

Harrison stops them. "Shhhhh."

"What?" JT says, looking at him confused.

"Do you hear that?" Harrison slowly stands to his feet.

"Hear what?" Jaylen says concerned.

Suddenly, deep raspy growls linger in the air. Turning around, Harrison surveys the area to see where they are coming from.

"Okay. Someone, please tell me that I just didn't hear what I thought I heard," JT says.

"What did you think you heard?" Joseph replies.

"Like, some nasty growling coming from everywhere," JT says.

"Yeah, sorry to let you know, but you definitely heard that," Joseph replies.

Forming a circle, they gaze into different directions looking for where the growls are coming from. The shaking Harrison feels from the other's backs makes him realize that he isn't the only one nervous. Loud crunches from the wood line near the cave grab their attention.

A giant grayish paw with spotty black lines appears from the woods. Eyes the same color as the clear blue water from the river peak through. Old worn teeth show as slow forceful growls push through them. Finally, a big, old wolf steps out.

"Okay. I am not liking this. Flashbacks of the Chihuahuas are coming back to me," JT moves closer to Harrison. "But now they have bigger teeth."

"We are fine. Tommy took out two giants that were trying to add us to their collection. We should be fine," Jaylen says.

"True. What's just one wolf?" Joseph says.

All of a sudden, something lands on one of the giant rocks in the river. Harrison and the others spot another wolf, growling through his teeth.

"You got to be kidding me," Harrison scoots closer to the others.

The wolf on the rock creeps closer to them. Small circular glasses, tightly snugging the wolf's face reflects the sun, blinding Harrison as he creeps closer.

"Okay, so there are two. No big deal. Tommy, go take them out. Not like there are three or something," JT nudges Tommy

Harrison moves toward the one closer to the wood line. Deep raspy growling echoes from the cave.

"Okay. So apparently there are three," JT shakes his head.

One blueish green eye lights up the darkness from inside. A wolf exits the cave glaring at them with just one eye. A giant *x* replaces his left eye, making his right eye seem as if it is bulging out.

Harrison and the others close in tighter as the wolves approach them from different angles.

"Don't move. Maybe if we just stand here for a couple of moments they will go away," Jaylen says.

The wolves circle them slowly, releasing angry growls in between their teeth as they stare intently at them.

"Yeah. I think you can forget that plan," JT says.

Steadily pacing around them, Harrison feels their hot breath brush against his skin as one passes by. Their growls intensify, showing small yellow stains hugging the bottom of their teeth. Abruptly, the wolf with just one eye stops, glaring at Harrison.

"Why are you here?" the one-eyed wolf says.

His deep voice sends cold chills down Harrison's back. The scar replacing his eye intimidates him and makes it hard to focus on the wolf's determined stare.

"Great. They are crazy talking wolves now," JT whispers.

The wolf with glasses walks in front of JT, squinting his eyes at him.

"Hey, kid. We aren't known as crazy talking wolves. You better call us by our real title," The wolf with glasses says.

"What's your real title?" JT's voice cracks.

"We are the Wolfpack," the normal wolf says.

Lowering his head, the one-eyed wolf paws at his good eye. Lifting his head up, he moves closer to Harrison. "Okay kid. I already asked you once and this will be the last time. Why are you here?"

Taking a big gulp, Harrison feels his mouth go dry and a knot swell in his throat.

"We didn't come to cause trouble or bother you. We just came to get something from this cave," Harrison says.

The one-eyed wolf bounces back a couple of steps, spinning slowly in a circle. Lifting his head up quickly, the top of his head glows with green energy. Leaping at him, the one-eyed wolf slams his head into Harrison's chest, sending Harrison sliding on the ground.

Gliding on his back, the one-eyed wolf rides on Harrison's chest and stomach as he slides against the side of the cave. Knocking the top of his head against the cave, the throbbing sensation makes his eyes water making the wolf appear fuzzy.

"What are you trying to get from the cave?" the one-eyed wolf declares.

His lips stick together making it hard to utter a word. The wolf lowers his head closer to Harrison. "Answer me. Now."

"We were just here to get a green gem from the cave," Harrison replies nervously.

The wolves circling the others, glare at Harrison and the one-eyed wolf. Shocking gasps erupt from the wolves and the one on top of Harrison digs his paws harder into Harrison's chest. "Why are you trying to take one of the Elder's gems?"

"They are up to no good, boss. I think you should let me eat one," the wolf with the glasses licks his lips.

"Yeah, boss, that would be awesome. We haven't seen anybody around here since that time thirteen years ago when those two guys showed up. And remember you wouldn't let us eat them," the other wolf says.

"Yeah. The eating part doesn't sound like a cool option at all," JT says. "Plus, I guarantee we wouldn't taste good."

"Shut up," the one-eyed wolf screams, snapping his head, staring at them.

"Yup. You got it." JT glances at the ground.

"Now. Tell me why you want one of the Elder's gems," he says, inches away from Harrison's face.

"I can explain. We just need a gem so that it can activate the Elder's compass we have so that it will lead us to the Ark of Power," Harrison replies.

Ears on all the wolves twitch rapidly while their mouths dangle open.

"You have the Elder's compass?"

"Yeah. It's in my backpack underneath me," Harrison replies.

"Show me," he says, jumping off of him.

Harrison's lungs inflate as air rushes through his chest.

"Don't you try anything stupid either, or I will let those two over there eat your friends while you watch. Then we will eat you last."

"Yeah. Let's not try anything stupid, Harrison," JT says nervously.

Slowly sitting up, Harrison slides his backpack off. Feeling the one-eyed wolf gazing him down, he fumbles around inside the backpack. The zipper gets stuck, snagging on one spot. Out of the corner of his eye, he spots the other wolves crouching, ready to pounce.

Finally opening it, Harrison throws black gym shorts and two other gray shirts on the ground. Sitting on top of the compass is his dad's ripped shirt.

"Hurry up and take everything out. I don't want any surprises," the one-eyed wolf says.

Harrison slings his dad's shirt out of the backpack.

It lands in front of the wolf, who approaches the shirt and sniffs softly. "I have smelled that scent before," he stares at Harrison. "There are two scents on this shirt. Yours and one of the guys that came here thirteen years ago."

Harrison's eyes grow large at what he just said.

"That is my dad's shirt. You sure you smelled that scent before?" Harrison says, not worrying about the compass anymore.

"That was your dad?"

"Yes. He has been missing for the last thirteen years. That is why we are here. Apparently, my dad was sent on a mission to find the Ark of Power. I have the compass right here and if I can activate it then it could lead me to it and possibly him," Harrison stands up as the long compass dangles.

The one-eyed wolf's eye stays on the compass gently swaying. The other two wolves' ears lower, pointing sideways. Drool drops out of their mouths as they gaze at the compass. Taking short, slow strides, the one-eyed wolf moves towards Harrison.

"I have not seen that for a long time," he says, staring at it without blinking.

Clinching the compass tighter, Harrison pulls it up, hiding it. Stopping in his tracks, the one-eyed wolf glares in disgust.

"This is mine now. After I use it to see if I can find my dad, I promise I will return it," Harrison says, nervously.

His eye pierces into Harrison's, as he creeps closer to him. Feeling his mouth go dry, Harrison struggles to swallow as he takes a couple of steps backward.

"How dare you say it is yours? That belongs to the First Elder and him alone," the one-eyed wolf says crouching.

Suddenly, he lunges at Harrison. Harrison flips sideways evading him. Sliding on the ground, dust from the dirt fills the air. The one-eyed wolf dives at him again with more vigor. Quickly, Harrison forms a green energy ball, making his face squint in pain as he feels the burning sensation in his wound.

Flying through the air, Harrison sees the wolf's eye focus on the green energy ball. Suddenly, the wolf spins and lands behind Harrison, staring in amazement at the energy ball in Harrison's bandaged hand.

The other wolves' faces show the same distinct look as the other one. Harrison spots them creeping slowly towards him.

"It can't be," the wolf with glasses says.

"It's like the big boss said. I was starting to think maybe it wasn't true," the normal wolf says.

The one-eyed wolf gazes at Harrison without blinking, moving closer to him. Closing his hand, Harrison feels the energy ball evaporate. The one-eyed wolf stops, looking at Harrison's empty hand.

THE ARK OF POWER

"It has begun," the one-eyed wolf says.

CHAPTER
23

Old Memories

Sinking their heads, the wolves bow in reverence around Harrison. Glaring over to his friends, Harrison notices the awkward looks on their faces. Shrugging his shoulders in confusion, Harrison refocuses on the wolves.

"I apologize. If I knew you were the one that the Elder spoke about, then I would not have attacked you," the one-eyed wolf says. "My name is Tundra. The one in glasses is named Rocco, and over there, that is Toby."

Harrison squats down to their level. Scratching the side of his face, he gazes at Tundra with confusion.

"What do you mean by, it has begun?" Harrison replies.

Lifting his head up slowly, Tundra beams at him. Harrison sees a difference in the way his eyes look now. They offer a sincere glow of sweetness rather than the rage of anger that was evident earlier.

"To understand, you must know the whole context. You see, we were assigned by the First Elder to protect the gems in the cave. He dispersed this area and the animals that resided in this area with one of his gems. That is why ole' Peter the cardinal was able to blast you with an energy attack and why I was also able to," Tundra says.

"Okay, that makes sense. And you said he gave you guys the title, the Wolfpack?' Harrison asks.

"Yes. Before he passed away, he said we would be his mighty Wolfpack that would make sure no one would get the gems. It was important that no one got one of them in their hands and was able to activate the compass and find the Ark. He sacrificed himself to make sure the Ark was protected. But during his last days he developed a special power similar to that of the Supreme Elder," Tundra says.

The other wolves walk quietly over to them. Harrison glares up at them noticing the tranquility across their faces.

"What special power are you talking about?"

Tundra finally lifts his head up completely staring directly into Harrison's eyes.

"The gift of prophecy," Tundra replies. "He told us directly before he died that there would be a day that a young boy would show up seeking a gem for the compass. He told us to allow him to take one. He said that this boy was destined to bring harmony between the nations once and for all."

Bowing his head in respect, Tundra closes his eyes tightly. "You are that boy."

Taking a huge swallow, Harrison's chest tightens. Out of the corner of his right eye, he spots the amazement on his friends' faces.

"How do you know that I am the one he was talking about?"

"Because he said we would be given a sign that would help us distinguish who the boy was. He said that the boy would have the same type of dark green color to his energy that he had. I have only seen two people with that dark green energy. The First Elder and now you," Tundra lifts his head up.

Standing up, Harrison paces around in a small circle, rubbing his face with his hands.

"Okay. Whatever you say. But I want to know something. If you said you smelled my dad's scent, then he was here. He had to be here to get a gem. What happened, if you weren't allowed to have anyone get a gem other than me?" Harrison says.

"Those two that came that day asked us for one at first. I felt uncomfortable about it and told them that we couldn't allow anyone to receive one. They said they were summoned to get one by Elder Dirk for a special top-secret mission. I told them that the Elder had to come himself. They said he couldn't come and that they were leaving with one. We underestimated your father. I have never experienced that type of power since the First Elder. We attacked and they knocked us out. As they were leaving with one, I made a last-ditch effort by using my Energy Fang Bite. I bit your dad on his left forearm. He quickly knocked me out and went on." Tundra sits. "Something strange did happen though. I woke up with one of his memories replaying in my mind. The energy must have transferred a memory from his mind to mine somehow."

Harrison's eyes glow with excitement.

"What was the memory?" Harrison stoops back down to Tundra's level.

"It is hard to remember. I know I still have it. All I remember is that it was a memory with him and his son, which I assume was you."

Tears start to pile in Harrison's eyes. Extending his left arm out, he places it on Tundra's head. "Please tell me what the memory was."

"I can show you if you want. The only thing is I would have to bite you too in your left forearm. I can transfer it and you will be able to see it," Tundra says.

"Do it. I want to see it."

JT walks over and grabs Harrison's shoulder. "Dude are you sure you really want to do this? What if it isn't even your dad that he bit? I mean it sounds kind of crazy to just let a wolf bite you."

Wiping tears that are running down his face, Harrison closes his eyes tightly.

"Shut up. It may sound crazy to you but if it is really a chance that it is a memory of me and my dad, I want to see it. You have memories of you and your dad, so you don't know what it is like," Harrison responds back angrily. "Go ahead and do it Tundra. I want to see it for myself."

Harrison feels JT's hand come off his shoulder. Opening his eyes, the tears make Tundra seem like he is hidden in a giant wave. Tundra opens his mouth and his teeth shine with green energy. Harrison turns his arm over.

Tundra bites down hard on Harrison's left forearm. The heat from the energy runs through his arm and up to his head. Suddenly, a green energy cloud appears making Tundra and everything else go away. Instantly the green energy cloud explodes and Harrison gasps at what he sees.

Ironing a nice white collared shirt with thin blue stripes running down it, Douglas steps on a tiny car toy that is laying on the floor.

"Ouch," Douglas screams.

Hearing tiny footsteps racing down the hallway, Douglas gazes towards the door with a huge smile.

"Daddy...Daddy," a tiny two-year-old Harrison says with a concerned look on his face.

Picking up the toy car, he hands it to Harrison.

"Daddy, boo-boo?" Harrison points with concern at Douglas' foot.

"Yeah. But not a bad one. You just can't leave your toys around, okay?" Douglas says.

"Oh. Okay, my daddy," Harrison responds, grabbing the car toy from him.

Plopping on the floor in the room, Harrison plays with his car toys as Douglas continues to iron his shirt.

"Are you going to miss daddy when he is gone on his next mission?" Douglas says.

Crashing the cars into each other, Harrison makes a loud crash sound. Flopping on his back, Harrison holds the cars up pretending to make them fly.

Steam shoots out of the iron as Douglas stands it up on the iron board. Squatting down, he tickles Harrison, making him roll side to side and laugh hysterically.

"I said, are you going to miss daddy? Are you?" Douglas continually tickles Harrison's belly.

Harrison appears to be laughing without any sound coming out. Taking his hands away, Harrison sprouts up and hugs him tightly around his neck.

"So, are you going to miss daddy?" Douglas rubs his back as Harrison tightens his grip.

"Yes, my daddy," Harrison says sweetly.

Suddenly, darkness overtakes the room as the lights go out. Harrison breaks away from his bear hug, gazing towards the lights.

"Uh oh," Harrison surveys the darkness.

"Power must have gone out. But I know what we can do so we can see," Douglas pokes Harrison in the belly.

Grabbing his belly where his dad poked him, he takes his hands away and claps energetically.

"Power Light, daddy. Power Light," Harrison screams.

"Okay, watch closely."

Clapping continually, the smile on his little face makes Douglas grin.

"Okay, my daddy."

Lifting his palm towards the ceiling, a yellow energy ball pops into his hand, emitting a bright light around the room. His face beams with joy as the yellow light overtakes his face.

His mouth drops down as he marvels at the room glowing with a shiny radiance. Harrison's clapping intensifies and his smile goes from ear to ear.

"Daddy. Daddy," Harrison chants.

Suddenly, the power comes back on. They both glare around the room, staring at the lights. Douglas closes his hand, making the yellow energy ball disappear.

"Well, I guess we don't need this right now."

Harrison clings to Douglas' right leg.

"Daddy sure is going to miss you while I am gone," Douglas rubs the top of Harrison's head.

All of a sudden, Harrison blinks a couple of times and perceives Tundra in front of him. Tears race quickly down his cheeks as he falls on his face. JT, Jaylen, and Joseph rush to him. Harrison's legs feel weak as they pull him up. Glaring at his left arm, he spots the bite marks along his left forearm.

"It probably took a lot out of him. Just make sure you hold on to him for a while," Tundra says.

"I need that gem. Can you please give me one?" Harrison sobs.

"Sure," Tundra says. "Rocco. Toby. Go in the cave and bring back one of the gems in there."

"You got it, boss," Rocco goes into the dark cave.

Harrison stares towards the cave, patiently waiting for them to come back out.

"Now. When you are ready to activate the compass, you just place the gem on the back of it and it will make it work again," Tundra says.

Harrison feels his face tighten from the tears drying on his cheeks. He sees Rocco and Toby exiting the cave. Toby has the tiny green gem in between his teeth. He walks over to Harrison, dropping it at his feet. Tommy bends down and picks it up.

"Thank you. For everything," Harrison says.

"Yeah. Especially for not eating us," JT says.

Tundra steps closer to Harrison and the others. Rocco and Toby stand behind him forming a triangle.

"It was our pleasure to finally meet the one that the First Elder spoke about," Tundra says. "I am excited to see what you are destined for and I hope you find your father."

"Thank you," Harrison smiles as they turn to walk away.

JT and Jaylen hold Harrison up, walking slowly away from Tundra, Rocco, and Toby.

"Hold up," Tundra takes small strides to them. "The First Elder gave us the title of the Wolfpack. I think it is fitting to give you all the same title. It's just an old memory to us. But it's now who all of you are. You all are now the Wolfpack. We give you our title."

Harrison and the others stare at one another, grinning.

"We appreciate it," Harrison replies. "I will bring the compass back when we are done with it. So, till next time."

"Till next time," Tundra says.

Harrison and the others cross back over the river. Harrison looks back toward the cave and sees them still staring after them.

"Well. I am so glad we didn't end up getting eaten by wolves. That would have been tragic," Jaylen says.

"Yeah. I am not going to lie to you guys. I almost peed a little when he mentioned they wanted to eat us," JT says. "I kind of hated Harrison a little at that moment."

Laughter erupts from all of them. A tear runs down Harrison's face from laughing so hard. Walking past the dead bodies, the laughter stops abruptly. Silence comes from all of them as each of them gaze at all of the lifeless corpses.

"Come on guys. Let's get back. It's been a rough day. We could use some rest," Tommy says.

"I agree. I am ready for this moment to just be an old memory that we look back upon," Joseph says.

Taking his eyes off of the dead bodies, Harrison steps away from JT and Jaylen and begins to walk with the others back into the woods.

CHAPTER
24

The Cheerful Compass

Arriving at Harrison and Tommy's training spot, Harrison hears the horns from the Academy sounding. All of them gaze toward the direction of the Academy. Harrison's heart sinks at the sound.

"Oh man. They are signaling the horns for the return of the Elder and Red Hawks," Harrison runs his hands through his hair. "They weren't supposed to be back this early. We have to get back before the Red Hawks."

JT yanks him by his shoulder. "Harrison. Don't you want to activate the compass and see what it does?"

The beating of his heart makes JT sound muffled. The throbbing in his chest makes him feel anxious.

"No. Not now, they will be looking for me. It's too risky," Harrison throws JT's hand off his shoulder. "Just hold on to the green gem Tommy. It will be safer with you."

Hurrying to the fence, Harrison and the others peek through it to see if it is clear to jump over. Jaylen hits Harrison in the arm, motioning him to look to his right. Gazing over, Harrison spots Samuel and his two chubby friends. Samuel continually scratches the white bandage wrapped around his head.

"Crap. If they see us jump the fence, then they will know we were gone and will probably tell on us," Joseph stares at the ground in disappointment.

Silence fills the air as they gaze at Samuel scratching his head and the other boys slapping each other. Grabbing the fence, Tommy begins to climb up.

"What are you doing? Are you stupid?" Jaylen grabs Tommy.

Pulling away from Jaylen's grip, Tommy glares down at him. "Just trust me. Samuel and his friends won't say anything to me. I will distract them and then you guys can jump over."

Jaylen lets go of him. Tommy walks towards them. Samuel and his friends straighten up as they spot Tommy. Instantly, they walk off at the sight of him. Samuel strolls away staring at the ground the whole time.

"Is everybody afraid of this guy?" JT says.

Giggling as they climb, Joseph looks over at JT. "He did just take out two giants by himself. I think that makes him a pretty scary dude in my book."

Harrison and the others crouch and walk quietly behind the dorms. Harrison glances around the corner, noticing the Elder walking with Sebastian Darby, his uncle Adam and the Red Hawks marching behind him.

Where are they coming from?

Harrison and his friends enter the building. Rushing into the dorms, they dash to their rooms.

"We have to get cleaned up before anyone sees us," JT pulls his shirt off. "I will jump in the shower first, then you can get in. You two need to go to your room and do the same thing."

"Okay. Just hurry up. I don't want anybody to come to the room and see me filthy and nasty like this," Harrison says as Jaylen and Joseph leave.

"I will. Don't worry. Plus no one ever comes to our room," JT slams the door behind him.

Harrison grabs the compass out of his backpack. Suddenly, a loud banging sounds from the door. Harrison stops breathing, holding the air in his lungs.

You got to be kidding me.

Throwing the compass back into the bag, he tosses it behind his messy bed. Taking a deep breath, he opens the door. Standing there, ready to knock again is Tommy. Harrison sighs in relief. Closing the door behind him, Harrison takes deep breaths.

"Thank goodness it's you," Harrison says. "Did you already change your clothes?"

Tommy is wearing clean black gym shorts and a plain white t-shirt.

"Yeah, I didn't have time to get in the shower, so I had to just throw on some clean clothes and wash up," Tommy says.

Reaching into his pocket, Tommy pulls out the tiny green gem, spinning it with his fingers. "Should we try to activate it now?"

Searching for his backpack behind his bed, Harrison flings it to him.

"Yeah. Let's try it," Harrison pulls the compass back out.

Unexpectedly, a loud knocking noise erupts in the room. Harrison and Tommy stare at one another. Harrison throws the compass back in as Tommy places the green gem with it. The knocking grows louder on the door as Harrison struggles with zipping his backpack up.

Finally zipping it closed, Harrison takes his stained shirt off, wiping his face with it. Walking to the door, Harrison opens it, feeling the cold air hit his bare skin. Mr. Drake stands there gazing at him, with a blank stare.

"I saw Tommy walk this way. Is he in here?" Mr. Drake says placing his hand on the door, opening it wider.

Tommy rushes towards the door, standing in front of his dad. "Hey, dad. Sorry I had to come and ask Harrison something."

"Well come on. I need your help with something. I have been searching all around campus for you."

"Yes, sir. I am coming," Tommy says. "Thanks for your help, Harrison."

Nodding, Harrison smiles at Tommy as he walks behind his dad. Closing the door, Harrison sees JT drying his damp hair with a thick brown towel.

"You can get in the shower now," JT says, steadily rubbing his head with his towel.

Harrison grabs the shirt he took off and flings it at JT. Sticking to JT's face, he tosses the shirt off with a confused look.

"What the heck?" JT says.

"You said no one ever comes to our room," Harrison says sounding stressed. "You would say that and then Mr. Drake shows up knocking on the door."

Flopping on his bed, Harrison stares at the ceiling, replaying the last couple of hours. Jaylen and Joseph bust through the door with the smell of fresh soap following them. JT throws his towel on his bed.

"Let's go ahead and activate this thing and see what happens," JT says.

Harrison sits and grabs his backpack. Pulling the compass and green gem out, he gazes at his friends. "Might as well."

Rotating the tiny green gem with his fingers, Harrison examines every fine cut as it shines with each turn. Lifting

261

the compass closer to his face, he gazes at the unknown language written on it. Harrison places the gem on the back of the compass. Suddenly, the gem sticks on the compass as if it is glued to it.

All of them gasp as they perceive what is happening. Vibration shakes through his hand as the gem glows brightly. Harrison squints struggling to see the intense greenish glow coming from the gem. The gem sinks into the compass slowly, as if it is sinking into quicksand.

Harrison feels his hand sway gently as the compass pulsates stronger in his firm grip. Finally, the compass sucks the gem into itself, and is surrounded by shiny green energy. Harrison's hand tingles as he clutches the compass tighter. All of a sudden all of the glowing greenish energy expands, covering every inch of their room, painting everything green.

Instantly, the compass sucks every bit of energy into itself turning everything normal. Harrison's hand stops shaking, and he slowly opens it. Unexpectedly, Harrison gazes at the compass staring back at him with two big green eyes.

"What's going on everyone?" the compass says, energetically with a giant smile coming from a new mouth formed at the bottom of it.

Harrison jumps, flinging the talking compass on the floor. JT, Jaylen, and Joseph jump back in fear at the sight of the compass.

"Oh. My. Gosh. Did that thing just form a mouth and some eyeballs and talk to us?" JT says looking startled.

"Ouch. How disrespectful" the compass says. "We just met, and this is how you treat new friends?"

Covering his mouth, Harrison glances over at his friends, who stand there with disbelief on their faces.

"Okay. I am not losing it. That thing did just talk," JT says.

Harrison does not take his eyes off of the compass. The jubilant beam shines from it, almost scaring him.

"Harrison. What the heck are we supposed to do now?" Jaylen says.

Snatching it up, a soothing warmth radiates from it, comforting Harrison.

"I don't know. But we will figure something out," Harrison replies as the compass smirks back at him.

"Well, it is mighty nice of you to pick me up. I mean I was starting to wonder if you had any manners," the compass says.

A tiny laugh bursts out of Harrison. The compass' mouth enlarges at the sight of Harrison laughing.

"Wow. You guys do laugh and smile. I was worrying that I was about to be stuck with some depressing people," the compass says.

Standing next to Harrison, JT forcefully points his long index finger at the grinning compass. The compass goes cross-eyed staring at his finger.

"Hey. We are far from being depressed people. Just because we are not as cheerful as you are, doesn't mean we aren't happy," JT declares.

Following his finger, as he bounces it with each word, the compass' eyes spin quickly.

Harrison shoves JT back behind him. "Don't scare the poor compass JT."

A frenzied sound burst from the compass' mouth. Tears squeeze through its tightened eyelids. Harrison and his friends gaze at each other in confusion.

"He said don't scare...don't scare me," the compass says laughing hysterically.

"Maybe I should have said crazy instead of cheerful," JT says with a confused look.

Opening his eyes, streams of tears slide down his face as it tries to gain its composure. Small chuckles escape.

"Oh man. That was funny. You said he might scare the poor compass. You all are funny. Believe me, with all my adventures with the Supreme Elder and the First Destine Elder, I have seen a lot of scarier things than him."

Harrison sits the compass on his nightstand against the bare white wall.

"My name is Harrison. This is JT, Jaylen, and Joseph. We are the ones that activated you with the First Elder's energy gem."

"Well, it is my pleasure to meet you all. But if you don't mind me asking, why would you activate me? You look like young teenagers. What would be your purpose with me?"

"Well, we need you to help us locate the Ark of Power. Do you know where it is?" Harrison steps closer to the compass on the nightstand.

"Of course, I do. But what would you want with the Ark of Power?" the compass replies.

"It's a long story, but my dad went missing thirteen years ago while on a mission to find it. So, if we find the Ark then I might be able to find out what happened to him."

Silence fills the room. Harrison and the others wait for an answer from the smiling compass. Moments go as the compass continually blinks. Finally, the compass let's out a huge sigh. "Okay. I will help you. I feel like you all have pretty good character and are telling me the truth."

Harrison beams. "Thank you. You don't know how much this means to me."

"I just hope you guys are ready for a doozy of a trip," the compass says.

"What do you mean a doozy of a trip? Where exactly is the Ark right now?" Jaylen says.

Moving in closer, Harrison and the others focus on the compass.

"It's inside the Purhara Mountains."

Dropping his shoulders, Harrison sinks to the floor in disbelief. JT, Jaylen, and Joseph follow Harrison's reaction.

"You got to be kidding me. That is like a two-day journey from here," Joseph says.

"Yeah, that's just great. How the heck are we supposed to leave now without everyone at the Academy knowing we are gone?" Jaylen sits on one of the beds.

Running his hands through his hair, Harrison sits on the floor, struggling to think. "I don't know yet. That definitely makes it a little bit more difficult. We have to think about it for a little bit."

"What do we do with this cheerful compass then? We can't leave it in one of our rooms. It is really loud and if we get caught with it, we could get in some serious trouble," JT leans against the nightstand. "Unless it can deactivate itself."

"Sorry. But if you deactivate me you will have to get another gem with the First Elder's energy," the compass replies.

Harrison lays his head in between his knees glancing down at the old burgundy carpet. "Great."

Lifting his head up, Harrison gazes at the others, sensing their discouragement.

"Okay. So, this is what we will do to hide the compass. We will place it in the secret room and whenever we come up with a game plan and we're ready to go through with it, we'll get it out," Harrison stands to his feet.

Snatching the compass up, the others jump up. Cracking the door open slightly, Harrison peeks out.

"Alright. Listen compass. I am going to put you in my bag. I need you to be extremely quiet. Okay?" Harrison says.

"How disrespectful," the compass responds.

Harrison places the compass in his backpack. Throwing on a clean shirt, Harrison walks out the door. Students fill the hallway, hurrying to breakfast. Approaching the secret room, the Red Hawk captain stands there talking to Sebastian Darby and the Elder. Quickly halting at the sight of them, Harrison puts his head down and peeks around the corner, watching them.

"Crap," Harrison hits the wall with his backhand.

"What is it?" the compass says with a muffled voice through the backpack.

"Shhhhh. I said you can't talk." Harrison replies.

"So disrespectful."

Shaking his head, Harrison gazes around the corner to see if they are still there. Harrison notices they are walking outside. Immediately, Harrison heads over to the secret room and opens it. Out of the corner of his eye, he notices the Red Hawk captain.

Slinging the backpack off his shoulders, he throws it into the room, slamming the door instantly. As the door closes, the Red Hawk comes around the corner, entering the main the building. Harrison walks by him.

"How are you doing, Mr. Grady?" the Red Hawk Captain says passing by him.

"I'm fine. Thanks for asking," Harrison replies, walking out of the building.

CHAPTER
25

150 Hours

Sweat glides down Harrison's face as he stretches with Tommy in their normal training spot. Lightning bugs shine every couple of seconds, following the heat of the lightning brightening up the sky. Wiping his face, Harrison takes a sip of water, tasting the salty sweat from his chapped lips mixing with the water.

"I thought Spring wasn't supposed to be this hot. This is crazy," Harrison throws his water bottle next to his backpack on the dry ground.

"It builds character," Tommy takes a sip of water. "Plus, you sound like JT with all that whining."

"You got that right. He has been constantly complaining that in these last three months we haven't come up with a plan for how to get to the Purhara Mountains without anybody noticing that we are missing. I feel bad that the compass is still in my backpack in the secret room though."

Walking to the middle of the cleared area, the wind smoothly blows the fresh green leaves on all the trees circling them.

"Alright. You ready?" Tommy stretches a little more.

Harrison touches his toes and bounces on them lightly. "I am telling you, I got you this time. You better not take it easy on me."

Harrison hunkers down to his stance gazing at Tommy preparing to attack. Harrison rushes at Tommy throwing a punch at his face. Tommy snatches his hand, flinging him to the small nearby tree. Soaring towards it, Harrison sends energy to his feet making them illuminate green. He places his feet on the tree, crouches, and launches at Tommy. At the same time, Tommy runs at Harrison. Harrison extends his arm with a flying fist.

Tommy rolls underneath Harrison. Flipping through the air, Harrison lands on his feet crouching slightly. Tommy winks at Harrison, making Harrison grin back. Harrison forms a green energy ball the size of a soccer ball in his right hand.

Hovering above his palm slightly, he takes a couple of steps and launches it at Tommy. As he catches it with both hands, Harrison launches into the air with a spinning roundhouse kick, kicking through the energy ball that Tommy is holding inches away from his face.

Harrison's kick lands on the side of Tommy's face making him soar to one of the trees. Landing softly,

Harrison spots Tommy laying on the ground, rising up slowly.

"Nice one. I tell you what. Since you landed one, I will let you try your move and if you create it, you can try and hit me with it," Tommy knocks the dirt off his clothes.

"Well, you just messed up because I am feeling good about it tonight," Harrison smiles.

Bending his knees, Harrison extends his right arm with his palm facing the sky. Grabbing his right wrist with his left arm, he senses the energy rushing from his Power Flow and racing to his right hand.

Tiny strings of green energy form from his clammy palm. Harrison feels the pressure of energy ready to explode from his hand, so he lets out a screeching roar. Suddenly, more green energy strings form and starts intermingling with the other ones.

I can do this. I got it this time,

Harrison focuses harder.

Out of the corner of his eye, Harrison notices the amazing look painted upon Tommy's face. Gazing back down, the green energy strings spin faster and expand to about the width of a volleyball. All of a sudden, a burning sensation erupts through his hand and makes the middle of his palm sting with pain.

Steam rises up through the green energy strings spinning quickly in his palm. Harrison drops down to his knees and stops the process of creating the movement.

Sweat pours off of his dirty brow as he takes deep breaths. Tommy walks over and puts his hand on his shoulder, squeezing it softly.

"You almost had it that time. That is the closest you got to it," Tommy says with excitement. "I think you will get it down in a couple more tries."

Harrison stands. The draining feeling flows throughout his whole body. Swaying side to side, Harrison gazes at the trees bouncing around.

"Dang it. I thought I was going to get it that time," Harrison says disappointedly.

Harrison glances down at his right palm that has burned a little. "Dang."

Tommy pats his back softly, grabbing his bag and giving it to Harrison.

"You probably want to go and get some ointment for it," Tommy surveys his hand.

"Yeah, you are right. At least it's not as bad as last time."

Walking to the fence dividing the Academy and the woods, Tommy seems bothered by something as he places his hands on the fence.

"What's wrong, man?" Harrison watches Tommy stare at the ground.

"You know, I have heard you and the others saying that maybe my dad is the one that you and JT thought you saw at that guy's antique shop that night. That would make him the one who killed the owner of the shop," Tommy stares at the ground without blinking.

Harrison lets go of the fence and gazes at Tommy.

"Tommy, don't even worry about it. I am sure it's not your dad. We were just talking."

"Yeah, but we heard the conversation in the secret room that night. That guy who killed the owner wants you dead. We both know my dad doesn't think very highly of you. I mean he made me hit you with my Supersonic Omega Blast."

Harrison giggles. "Yeah. That sure wasn't fun. But don't beat yourself up about it. It could be either of the three. They were all there that night. So really, it's between my uncle, Mr. Lloyd, and your dad. Personally, I hate to admit it, but I am leaning more towards my uncle."

Tommy stares back at the ground kicking dirt with his foot. "I just want you to know that if it is my dad, I promise you that no matter what, I will be there to help you. You are like a brother to me now."

"That means a lot. I consider you a brother also. If you ever need help, I will do my best to be there for you too," Harrison grabs Tommy's shoulder gently.

Harrison and Tommy climb up the fence and head toward their rooms.

The fresh paint smell from the walls in the hospital clogs up Harrison's nostrils as he walks down the hallway. He waits patiently for his name to be called by the nurse. Dwindling his thumbs, gawking at the drying mopped floor, he hears the nurses mumbling through the door. He looks up to see the poster still hanging on the wall from the time he saw the girls put it up last time he was waiting.

The Cerdic class presents The 150 hours of Remembrance. The Celebration of the 150th Anniversary of the Destine Nation.

No Classes for 150 hours.
The whole 150 hours will be designed as a time of celebration of the First Elder creating our nation...

Starts in 1 day!

All of a sudden, Sebastian Darby steps out of the door with his right arm in a tight white sling. Standing up, Harrison walks over to him, noticing Rena Rush standing behind him.

"Mr. Darby. What happened to you?" Harrison says concerned.

Rena slides beside his good arm, stepping in front of him.

"Picking fights with people he shouldn't be," she grabs Harrison's files.

Sebastian giggles, moving his arm in the sling slowly.

"Yeah. What she said, young Grady," Sebastian replies sarcastically as he walks off.

Harrison walks into the room. She glances at his chart. He sits down on the elevated chair, folding up the thin crisp paper covering it.

"So, you got a slight burn in that same palm again, huh?"

"Yeah. But at least it's not as bad as last time."

She tosses the small tube at him. Catching it, he looks at her as she opens the door.

"You might as well just take the whole tube with you. I am sure you are going to burn it again somehow."

"Thanks. I appreciate it. But hopefully, you are wrong."

Wind from Rena closing the door makes the paper on the wall flap at the bottom. Harrison glances at the poster, pushing it back on the wall.

"Hey. How long are one hundred and fifty hours?" Harrison says.

"I think it is like six days," she puts the clipboard back on the shelf. "But I won't be here. I am heading to see some family at that time. So, don't get hurt when you are partying. We both know what happened the last time you were at a party."

"Yes, ma'am. You got it," Harrison replies slightly grinning.

Smiling back at him, she walks into another room.

Harrison stands in deep thought, as he reads the poster again.

I got it. This is our chance to leave. Nobody will be keeping attendance during these six days. Nobody will know that we are gone.

Slapping the wall with excitement, Harrison rushes down the hallway leaving the hospital wing. He hits Rena Rush with a huge smile as she walks out of the room

I can't wait to tell the others.

Harrison hears an annoying screech from his door. Stuffing clothes into his backpack, he glances over his shoulder and sees JT, Jaylen, and Joseph.

"Guys. Listen. I got something I want to tell you," Harrison struggles to zip his backpack shut.

"Let me guess. You are moving out?" JT replies with a confused look on his face.

"What? No. Why would you say that?" Harrison responds.

"Oh, I don't know. I mean, you're putting a lot of clothes in your backpack there." JT says.

Finally, he zips the overstuffed backpack up. Joseph lifts the bag up.

"Dude. How much did you need to put in this bag?" Joseph lifts it up and down.

Harrison snatches his bag from him and throws it by the door.

"If you guys would just shut up and listen, I would be able to tell you what I need to," Harrison says. "I know when we can leave and find the Ark."

A form of excitement and confusion comes over all of their faces.

"When?" Jaylen says.

"Tomorrow morning."

"What? How the heck are we supposed to do that?" Joseph sits on the bed.

Harrison glows with excitement. "The school-wide celebration of the anniversary of the nation starts tomorrow. It lasts for about six days. That gives up plenty of time to go find the Ark and come back."

JT, Jaylen, and Joseph gaze at one another with a confused look.

"Ummm. You sure that is a good idea?" JT says.

"It's our only chance. If we miss this opportunity, we may not have another one. This may be our only shot." Harrison says. "We are doing this. Go pack up and do whatever you need to do. We leave early in the morning."

JT, Jaylen, and Joseph stare at him. Moving them out of the way to the door, he cracks it open.

"Where are you going?" Joseph says.

"I am going to go get the compass from the secret room while you guys get your stuff ready," Harrison says scooting out the door.

Closing the door behind him, the muffled conversation from the room can be heard from the hallway. "Well, he has officially lost it-"

"Dang. I was going to try to talk to some girls finally since we have a week off. He just had to ruin that-"

"What girls were you going to talk to? Your mom and sister?"

"Shut up!"

Harrison hears the slams and pushes coming from inside the room. A quick smile shines on his face as he walks off. The hallways empty out. Looking around the corner, Harrison views the Elder and his uncle walk into his office.

Harrison rushes to the secret door, opening it quickly.

"Is someone here?" the compass shouts through the backpack laying on the ground.

"Hold up a sec," Harrison says pounding the wall.

The Elder and his uncle are reclining and are in the middle of a conversation.

"Yes, sir. I understand that takes me and Buford Lloyd away from the Academy during this week. But I believe it is important for me to go attend this ceremony in the Sendek nation," Adam says, tapping his thumb on his knee.

The Elder sits up, rubbing his forehead. After a couple of moments of silence, he drops back gently in his chair.

"I understand. It is probably a very good political move that needs to be made. Buford will be gone this week to see his sick sister. Plus, Norman is leaving for an urgent family situation. So, we will be missing three people from the staff during this celebration."

"Well, I apologize sir. But I truly think it is the wisest move for us to send someone to represent you in the Sendek nation's celebration. I know that Sebastian has been visiting the Golic nation in the last couple of days and is scheduled to return soon."

The Elder places his hat on the desk, running his frail fingers through his thin hair. "I know, Adam. You are right. It will help sustain the peace between the other two remaining nations."

Adam places his hand out as he rises from his seat. The Elder shakes his hand, grinning slightly. "Be safe on your journey."

Adam nods and walks out the door. Tapping the yellow energy hovering the wall, the Elder and his room disappear from his sight. Harrison snatches his backpack up and heads to the door.

"Don't worry. I will be safe," Harrison says, as he opens the door.

CHAPTER
26

The Abandoned Skunk

Harrison trips on the sodden russet dirt road. Falling out of his hand, the compass yelps as he catches it before it slams on the ground.

"Watch it. You have done that three times today since we left. It's only been seven to eight hours," the compass says. Wiping the bit of dirt that splattered on it, he tightens the chain to keep it from hanging.

"Sorry. I accidentally tripped," Harrison says leading the group.

Continuing on a lonely, dark brown trail surrounded by towering pine trees. Harrison can sense the others getting tired. Harrison sees all of them staring at the ground with each stride.

A strong vibration from the compass rattles his palm.

"What's up?" Harrison asks the compass.

The compass' eyes shoot straight into Harrison's. "We are entering an area that is called the Heart Pines. We will be traveling through here for the next six hours and that will bring us into the Golic nation. We are now out of Destine jurisdiction."

JT, Jaylen, and Joseph groan when they hear the compass's words.

Stopping quickly, Harrison stares at them with concern. "What's wrong?"

JT, Jaylen, and Joseph look up at Harrison.

"Dude. We are tired. We have been walking all day, non-stop. Let's just take a break tonight and rest," JT says.

"He is right Harrison. A little bit of rest wouldn't hurt any of us," Jaylen tries to get his attention.

"It looks like there is a small cave behind those trees. We can camp there for the night," Joseph points towards the woods beside them.

Harrison kicks the rock across the dirt road, watching it skip across the soggy dirt. "I just think it would be a better plan to keep going," Harrison says with an attitude. "But let's go ahead and start a fire close to the cave and set up camp."

Snatching his backpack off the ground, Harrison starts walking toward the woods.

"You don't have to have such an attitude," JT says.

"I don't have an attitude. I am just focused."

Harrison's hand vibrates rapidly as he is walking. Glancing down at his palm, the compass smiles back. "This cave is a special one."

"Why is that?" Harrison says with an attitude as he gets closer to the small dark cave.

"Because this cave is one of the only places that still have black gems inside."

Harrison's chest tightens.

That guy that night at the antique shop asked about those.

Harrison glances back at JT who is staring back at him with a shock on his face.

"Why do you guys look like you have seen a ghost?" Joseph says walking past them both, touching the cave and peeking in.

"Please tell me you didn't see a ghost. I think I would literally cry. I don't even like the thought of that," Jaylen looks back and forth between Harrison and JT.

"You got something worse to worry about in these woods than ghosts," the compass says joyfully.

All eyes shoot toward the compass with much concern.

"What are you talking about?" JT says nervously.

Squinting, the compass' eyes are not visible as it smiles.

"You see these woods here got the name Heart Pines not because of the pine trees but because of a group of creatures that live here. They eat a person's energy flow. The way they do that is by consuming their heart. They are called The Pine Tribe,"

"You know what...this adventure is just getting better by the second," Jaylen says.

Suddenly, creepy noises explode throughout the woods surrounding them. Harrison and the others gaze around quickly observing the darkness overtaking the woods. Each of them scurries quickly into the small, dark cave. Feeling his heart throb and beating through his chest, Harrison sees that the others seem to be experiencing the same feeling.

"This is great. Maybe we will get to see some of them. I haven't seen one of them in years," the compass says with eagerness. "The last time I saw one, it ripped a warrior from the Golic nation's heart out and chewed it."

JT blinks with a straight face, staring directly at the compass. "Why does the stupid compass sound excited about that?"

Stepping outside the cave, Harrison picks up a couple of small thin branches laying on the ground. He throws them on the ground in the cave. Extending his arm out with his palm facing out, he shoots a tiny green energy ball on the branches, causing a small fire.

"Let's just try not to stress about what could happen," Harrison throws his bags on the ground.

Harrison lays his head on the backpack. The warmth of the fire makes his face tingle as it grows.

"Get some rest so we can reach the Purhara Mountains tomorrow," Harrison watches the others follow his lead by laying on their backpacks. "I will let you guys sleep first for a couple of hours since you all are so tired, and I will keep watch. I will get some rest after you guys sleep a little."

"Sounds like a plan to me," Jaylen says.

"Me too," Joseph replies.

Loud snoring booms from JT's direction as his back is turned toward Harrison.

Slightly giggling, Harrison stares at the top of the cave, rolling the compass over his chest. Strong snoring sounds come from Jaylen and Joseph.

Harrison feels his eyelids start to droop gradually. Both of his eyelids feel as if they have weights attached to them. Rubbing his eyes, he tries to keep himself awake. All of a sudden, he doesn't see the ceiling of the cave anymore.

Unexpectedly, Harrison feels a strong tugging on his right leg along with cold dirt rubbing on his lower back as he feels his shirt rising up. Opening his eyes slowly, he hears the compass' joyful voice talking to someone.

All of a sudden, an outline of something is in front of him pulling him out of the cave forcefully. Harrison feels himself lifting off the ground. The moonlight penetrates through the woods, shining on the sky-blue skin of the creature throwing him in the air.

Hurling towards the giant pine trees, Harrison observes the moonlight bounce off the bald heads of about twenty blue individuals. He slams into a tree and slides down face first into the thick grass. The air in his lungs vanishes on contact. Catching his breath, a calloused huge hand clutches his shirt tightly.

"Alright. Looks like we are going for another ride," the compass shouts as Harrison grips it tightly.

Being lifted up, he looks back slightly and views another sky-blue creature smiling at him with teeth as black as charcoal. It throws him back towards the cave. Flying face forward towards the cave, another one jumps off the cave and leg drops Harrison before he gets to a cave he's never seen before. High pitch screeches erupt from all of them as Harrison crashes into the ground. Harrison coughs as it gets off of him. Flipping over to his back, he gazes at JT, Jaylen, and Joseph soaring through the air. Screaming as they fly across towards the trees, three creatures fall out of the trees into leg drops on each of them.

Harrison stands quickly spinning around swiftly with his eyes opened wide. Ten more light blue creatures emerge from the woods as the moonlight dances on their bald heads.

Harrison extends his hand out and forms a green energy ball in his palm. He launches at the creature sitting on top of JT slamming it into its chest. Screeching erupts out of the creature as it falls off of JT and rolls a couple of feet.

JT pushes himself up and throws an energy ball at the one sitting on Jaylen. The energy attack hits the creature on the side of its head. It falls off of Jaylen and jumps up into a tree. The creature on Joseph follows and jumps into the trees with the rest of them. JT, Jaylen, and Joseph race over to Harrison in-between the woods and the cave.

"This is amazing. Who would have thought that we would see the Pine Tribe? This sure is a treat," the compass says with a huge smile.

Harrison and the others observe all the creatures surrounding them in the trees. Roaring shrieks blast out of them as they each stretch their neck back and gaze at the moon.

"If we don't do something, we are going to be the treat," JT replies as he positions his hand, ready to form an energy ball.

Two of them jump down from the trees towards all of them.

"Watch out," Joseph yells.

All of them form energy balls quickly, launching them at the two running. The creatures roll on the ground, trying to evade the four energy attacks. Sprinting at them, as the creature on the right rolls up and jumps towards them, Harrison flies through the air and kicks it in the chest. Landing and rolling on the ground, Harrison sits up quickly, pushing two energy balls into one.

A larger than normal sized green energy ball forms in between both of Harrison's hands. He throws it at the creature running at the others. The energy ball slams into the creature's back, launching it into the air and into the tree.

JT, Jaylen, and Joseph's eyes widen as they stare at Harrison.

"Holy crap. Maybe we should call you Tommy from now on," Jaylen says.

Suddenly, all the creatures jump out of the tree, screaming in high pitched voices.

"C' mon," Harrison motions to the others as he sprints back to the cave.

Stopping at the entrance of the cave, he observes about thirty creatures chasing the others.

Harrison throws multiple energy balls at the creatures. Finally, they get to the cave. Harrison launches one last energy ball towards them. He turns around and runs into darkness. Blackness covers the cave as he gets further in. They stop at a dead end.

"Crap. What do we do now? We are going to be cornered," Jaylen slaps the wall.

Shrills start to creep closer as the moments go by.

Scratching the back of his head, Harrison struggles to figure out a plan. All of a sudden, a small hand firmly tugs his pants leg. Gazing down, Harrison observes a creature coming out of the floor.

"Follow me. Quickly," the animal says.

The animal pushes a large door up, motioning them to come in. Harrison and the others jump into the hole as fast as they can. The animal slams the door shut which follows with hard stomps on top of them. They can hear the creatures on top screaming loudly, spitefully.

JT and Jaylen drop to their knees as Harrison and Joseph leans against the icy stone wall.

"Thank you so much," Harrison tries to catch his breath.

The animal lights a huge wooden torch. "No problem. I have been lonely lately since my master abandoned me, so it's awesome to see some more people."

"Aww man. Who would abandon a...?" JT says as the light shines against the dark fur, brightening the white fur streaks across its back and face.

"Skunk," JT says as he fully sees him.

Laughing loudly, the skunk rubs his face where a giant scar runs down his right eye.

"The name is Ripper. I will rather be called that than a skunk," Ripper replies.

"Don't skunks stink?" the compass says to Harrison.

"Whoa. What did you say?" Ripper says, moving towards Harrison. "All skunks don't stink."

The compass looks back and forth between Harrison and Ripper appearing confused.

"Well, maybe he is one of the skunks that stink since his master abandoned him," the compass whispers to Harrison.

"What? I still hear you, you stupid compass," Ripper yells.

Harrison stuffs the compass into his pocket. Mumblings arise from his pocket.

"Sorry about that. He doesn't mean it," Harrison says. "So again, thank you. We are just glad you were here."

Ripper walks around with his head down, kicking the dirt gently.

"Yeah, yeah. I mean I don't have nothing else to do since I am by myself. I have been here in this cave for a while now," Ripper says.

"Well, what happened to your master?" JT stands to his feet.

"He just told me we were meeting someone he knew in this cave. When we got here, a black hooded figure was waiting for us. He asked my master to find the black gem for him. I found it for my master in the wall and when I handed it to my master, he knocked me out. As I was passing out, I saw my master walk out with the hooded figure," Ripper says, emotion filling his voice.

Harrison and JT lock eyes. Harrison feels his heart speed up.

"You said the black figure did get the black gem?" Harrison says, concerned.

"Yeah. Must have left with it," Ripper replies.

"Great," Harrison says. "Oh well. Where does this little secret tunnel lead to?"

Ripper walks past them, lifting the torch up higher, laminating further down the tunnel. "To the Purhara Mountains."

CHAPTER 27

The Master's Plan

Ripper leads in the front of a crooked line. Turning his head to the right slightly every couple of minutes, he gazes back to check on Harrison and the others. Harrison stares back to see the others also. All three of them slide their feet making dusty lines in the dirt.

The throbbing in Harrison's feet distracts him from the striking silver-gray stone surrounding them. The sparkly stone makes him squint every couple of steps.

"You guys sure are a slow bunch," Ripper says chuckling. "I mean I heard Destines were slow in a lot of ways, but shucks. I didn't think it was like this."

Harrison leans against the smooth wall with his right shoulder. JT, Jaylen, and Joseph halt at Harrison's abrupt stop.

Ripper turns around glaring at them in confusion. "Why are you guys stopping? I hope you aren't showing me just how slow you can be."

Harrison runs his hand down his face in confusion. "How did you know we are Destines?"

JT, Jaylen, and Joseph gaze at him. Harrison waits patiently waiting for him to answer.

"Oh. That's easy. I saw you guys walking toward the cave. I knew by the direction you were coming from and by you guys following that stupid compass that you were from another nation," Ripper says

Harrison and the others exchange eye contact trying to figure out whether to believe him or not.

"Listen. If you think I am out to get you or trying to set you up, why would I rescue you from the Pine tribe? I would have let them take you guys out," Ripper declares. "Now if you guys are done taking a break, can we get going? I hate being in this tunnel this long. When the Golic Nation built it in the Second Great War, they didn't intend it to be around this long. Kind of scares me that it might fall in at any moment."

"Yeah. Right. Let's keep moving," Harrison walks slowly.

Restless groans sound from JT, Jaylen, and Joseph and they begin to slide their feet again as they follow Harrison's lead.

"So, this tunnel was built during the Second Great War, huh? You got to be pretty smart to know that," Harrison grimaces with each step.

"Yeah pretty impressive, eh?" Ripper observes both sides of the walls. "I am not real smart in a lot of areas. My master just really loves history, so I always hear random historical facts."

Suddenly, Harrison stops, halting the others with his arm extended out. Harrison creates a bright green energy ball in his hand as he watches Ripper walk. Quickly, he launches it at Ripper. Slamming into Ripper's back he drops the torch, flying forward with the energy ball stuck on his back. Being driven through the air about thirty feet, he crashes on the ground, rolling continuously.

"What the heck Harrison?" Joseph yells.

"What are you doing?" JT asks.

Harrison takes quick strides towards Ripper who is trying to push himself up.

"That's not a way to treat someone who saved your tail from getting eaten," Ripper yells in anger.

"We all have been boys for years, but did I maybe miss something about Harrison maybe not liking skunks?" Jaylen says.

Loud coughs burst out with brown dust. His black fur is blasted with brown dirt. Grimacing, he tries to look up at Harrison who stares down at him as he stands over him.

"You aren't here to help us. You are trying to set us up. You said earlier that your master left you here when he met a hooded figure who was asking for a black gem. Your master never left you. Your master is the hooded figure who wanted the black gem. He told you to stay here and wait for us because somehow he knows we were coming," Harrison squats down to get closer to him.

Ripper opens his eye with the scar going down it and giggles in pain. "How can you possibly prove that?"

Harrison turns him over on his back, glaring down at him.

"You see, you gave it away when you said your master really enjoyed history. It just so happens that I saw your master one night in an antique store in Dosman, and he said the same thing about loving history. Plus, that night he was looking for a black gem. If I wasn't there, then I wouldn't have been able to figure you out," Harrison replies.

Ripper closes his eyes in disgust. "You are going to get what is coming to you, Grady. My master is going to make sure of it."

JT, Jaylen, and Joseph stand behind Harrison. Ripper rolls onto his back, gradually crawling slowly away from them. Harrison stands straight up gazing at Ripper attempting to crawl away.

"Who is he?" Harrison asks as Ripper agonizes in pain with each stride.

"You think I would actually tell you my master's name? Believe me, you will learn soon enough, and you are going to regret it," Ripper responds.

Jaylen places his hand on Harrison's tense shoulder. "Just let him go. He isn't going to say anything. We just need to let him be and get out of here'."

Watching him struggle to crawl, Harrison walks slowly towards him. Constant groans of pain come from Ripper.

"You better hope he doesn't find out that you did this to me. If he finds out that you injured me and killed me, he really won't take that too kindly," Ripper stretches his arm out to the torch on the ground.

"You may be injured but you aren't dead," Harrison replies.

Grabbing the torch, Ripper sits up. His whole upper body shakes greatly as he holds the torch firmly. "Not yet."

Suddenly, he turns the torch upside down, letting the flame jump on to the hair on his head. The fire spreads quickly covering his whole body in a giant flame. Ripper cries in misery. Harrison and his friend's eyes widen at Ripper being on fire.

"Let's get away from him," JT screams tugging on the others.

Harrison sprints with them down the dark hallway. Looking back, he sees a faint light from Ripper on fire.

"I see light coming from the end of the tunnel. We are close," Jaylen says.

The morning light peeks through what looks like an exit as a gentle breeze lingers through it. Approaching the shiny glistening door, JT and Joseph open it. As the door slides open gently, Harrison hears water rushing. Closing his eyes, the smell of the fresh water soothes him for a moment.

"Holy crap," JT says.

Opening his eyes slowly, Harrison loses his breath at what he sees. He blinks rapidly for a second to see if he is really seeing what is in front of him. Tommy stands with the warm sun rising over him on the other side.

"Hurry. We got to get going. Now," Tommy says.

Thin gangly trees surround them from every side as they hurry through them. Every couple of quick strides, the sun slices in between the trees, slashing on Tommy's face. Gazing towards the top of the trees, Harrison spots gigantic mountains piercing through them.

That must be the Purhara Mountains.

Snatching the compass out of his pocket, he wipes the small dry lint balls off of the snoring compass.

"Whoa. What's going on? What did I miss?" the compass says, glancing around as they keep a steady pace. "Hey, where's the skunk? I liked that guy. Funny little critter, that guy is."

"Don't worry about him right now. Are we near the Purhara Mountains?" Harrison asks.

The compass beams with joy as it continues to view the area. "You betcha. We are on the outskirts of Purhara City, which is the city right underneath the mountains and the Lake of Hope."

Tommy gazes back swiftly at Harrison with a troubled expression.

"Get that thing to be quiet. They will hear us and know where we are," Tommy whispers.

Shoving it back in his pocket, Harrison dashes faster to get closer to Tommy.

"Who will hear us?" Harrison whispers back.

Pushing Harrison down, Tommy stops the others, throwing them to the ground behind two large green bushes and a couple of lanky trees. Tommy drops down next to them, laying on his stomach and peeking through the bushes.

"Them," Tommy whispers pointing on the other side of the bush.

Loud chatter erupts through the other side as about thirty people talk around a large map on a giant stump. They are all dressed in black outfits with gray and white straight-faced masks.

Those outfits and masks look familiar. Where did I see those before?

Struggling to ponder, Harrison drops his head on his arms, keeping his eyes shut to think better.

In the restricted forest. The dead bodies we came across were dressed like these people.

"We know that Ripper will bring them into this general area," one of the guys says. "Just remember people. Master wants the Grady kid alive. The others we either take them or kill them. Doesn't matter."

Jaylen grabs his lower left leg and rolls on Harrison. Harrison rolls over to his back, putting his hands underneath Jaylen. Jaylen rubs his leg continually.

Crap. He gets a cramp in his leg now.

Jaylen thrusts on top of Harrison's leg pushing against his pocket with the compass in it.

"Hey," the compass screams. "Is that the skunk rolling around on me? I can tell by its smell that it's a skunk. I knew they stink."

Harrison glares through the bushes and sees that the group hears it.

"Who is there?" Multiple people with masks on walk towards the bushes.

Tommy stands quickly, throwing a medium-sized energy ball towards them. Exploding behind most of them, many of them fly forward from the explosion.

"It must be them. They are here. Get them," one of the guys shouts.

300

Harrison stands up holding Jaylen up. Placing him against a tree, Harrison launches multiple energy ball attacks at the masked crowd. JT rolls with Joseph to the other trees a couple of feet away from them and launches energy balls towards the group.

The masked people throw multiple energy balls towards them. Harrison and the others take cover. Harrison glances at Tommy who is forming an energy ball.

"Cover me," Harrison tells Tommy.

"Wait. What are you doing?" Tommy responds in disbelief.

"I got a plan," Harrison replies.

Harrison flips backward, running towards two of the masked people. Tommy throws the energy ball in between the two Harrison is running at. They jump sideways, creating space between one another. Harrison takes two steps on the tree and bounces off it, kicking one of the men in the throat.

He lands and rolls towards the other one. Tommy, JT, and Joseph continually throw energy balls towards the other masked people getting closer to Harrison. Leaping in the air, Harrison heaves two kicks at the other one that was separated. He blocks both of Harrison's kicks, throwing a punch at Harrison.

Grabbing his hand, Harrison pulls him forward and smashes an energy ball into his face. JT and Joseph come flying in with strong kicks to two of the masked people.

Jaylen limps from behind the tree and launches an energy ball hitting a couple of the masked people.

Suddenly, a person grabs Harrison from behind, clasping him tightly. JT and Joseph try to get to Harrison, but they are throwing multiple back and forth punches with one of the masked people. Out of nowhere, a masked individual forms a medium sized energy ball and slams it into Harrison.

"No. Harrison," Tommy screams running towards him.

Harrison can't move. He feels the energy ball slam into his chest. All of a sudden, Harrison sees the energy ball being absorbed into his pocket. Turning his head in confusion, the masked person turns his head sideways looking for his attack.

"What happened?" the masked person who is holding him says.

Suddenly, the energy attack blasts both of the masked people, in front and behind Harrison. Dropping to the ground, Harrison watches them glide into trees.

"Whoa," Harrison says.

Tommy stops next to Harrison.

"What just happened?" Harrison says to Tommy staring at his pocket.

"It has to be the compass. It absorbs energy, remember?" Tommy says. "It intensified that guy's energy ball. Get it out your pocket and throw it in the air," Tommy declares.

"What?" Harrison says confused.

"Just do it," Tommy shouts.

Harrison's hand gets stuck as he tries to yank it out of his pocket. Pulling it out, he tosses it in the air as the last five masked people run towards them.

"Wait. Why am I flying in the air?" the compass says.

"Supersonic Omega Blast," Tommy screams jumping towards the compass.

"Oh. Great. This is going to sting," the compass says.

Pressing the energy attack against the compass, it gradually gets sucked into it. The compass flies right in front of the five masked people sprinting at them.

"Get down," Harrison screams at JT and Joseph.

Dropping quickly to the ground, they each cover their heads. Finally, a giant explosion shoots from the compass blasting the five masked people into each direction in the air. Tree limbs and branches drop from many of the trees landing all over the nice calming area. Grass and dirt linger in the air for moments after the blast. The compass coughs several times as the debris settles around it.

"Okay. That is a new one in my book. Being used as a weapon. You would think I was the Ark of Power," the compass says still coughing sporadically.

Harrison walks over, picking it up. Tommy, JT, Jaylen, and Joseph circle around him.

"That was an awesome plan, Tommy," Harrison says.

"Yeah but I think I have a better one than that," Tommy responds.

"What is that?" Jaylen says rubbing his leg where he had the cramp.

Tommy points through the thinning wood line to a beautiful village sitting between giant blueish gray mountains.

"Let's go there," Tommy steps over the bodies on the ground.

CHAPTER
28

The Suspicious Person

A sweet, crisp breeze cuts through Harrison's clammy hair. Running his hands through it, Harrison drops to the ground with the others as they rinse off the dirt sticking to them in a small creek that runs into the giant lake. Harrison rests against the tree with Tommy joining him. JT and Joseph splash water on their face as Jaylen sleeps on the tree next to them.

The heaviness of Harrison's eyes makes him struggle to stay up and watch the others. The dirt sticks to his skin as if it has become a part of him. Collapsing on his back, the sound of the water jumping and the wind whipping delicately relaxes him. He stares at dark auburn birds flying in the sunny sapphire sky.

Man. What a time already. I feel like I can't go on anymore, Harrison thinks struggling to blink.

Unexpectedly, Harrison's eyelids drop down and he falls into a deep slumber.

Strong stabs dig into Harrison's right side. Waking up swiftly, Harrison views the sun beaming off of a man's dense glasses, blinding him. Squinting and positioning himself up, Harrison puts his hand over his eyes to block the shine. Harrison perceives a tall man standing above him.

"Son. You and your friends just going to sleep on my property?" the man says leaning against a giant pitchfork, rubbing it gently against his clean-shaven face. His nimble lime eyes appear bigger through the thick lenses.

"I am sorry. We didn't know it was your land. Really, we didn't know it was anybody's," Harrison says observing him tighten his navy jean overall straps.

Flipping the pitchfork around, he stabs it into the soft ground making it stick straight up. Quickly pulling his leg in, Harrison gazes at it.

"Son, I am not going to stab you unless you give me a reason to do so. But as it appears, you look like you have been through some crap. Matter of a fact, you look like crap," the man spits out sunflower seeds.

Standing up slowly, throbbing pain beats in his lower back as he rises to get on eye level with the man.

"The name is Stew. Stew Fields. But all my friends and family just call me Stew."

Harrison takes a moment to comprehend what he should do. Stew smiles gently, looking into Harrison's wearisome eyes.

"Son, I am not going to hurt you. You can trust me. I know you guys aren't dangerous. I saw what you guys did to that masked group."

"How do you know that we aren't the bad guys? You don't know us," Harrison responds. "I am learning you need to be careful who you trust."

Stew lowers his hand, snatching his pitchfork back up. Harrison tenses, ready to defend himself.

"What's your name son?"

"Harrison."

Stew takes a couple of steps and glances back at Harrison.

"Get your friends up and meet me at my house right over there. You guys can clean up, get something to eat, and get some real rest," Stew walks toward a small log cabin in the background. "And you are going to have to just trust me, Harrison."

Harrison watches Stew stroll towards the timeworn cabin in the distance. Looking down, he sees his friends knocked out on the ground.

They have sacrificed so much for me. They shouldn't have to sleep like this, and I am sure they are hungry.

Harrison wakes Tommy up.

"What's going on?" Tommy says waking up slowly.

"Get up and help me get the others up. We are going to that cabin over there to get some food and to get some real rest," Harrison grabs his backpack from the ground.

"Sounds like a plan to me," Tommy rises up.

Approaching the small wood cabin, the logs are the same coffee color as the trees surrounding the back of it. Walking to the front of the cabin, a small city can be seen in the distance with the Purhara Mountains overshadowing it. Harrison and the others stand in awe of the beauty of the pearl white seagulls soaring towards the city.

"You sure this guy isn't crazy? I mean we did just meet a skunk who lit himself on fire who acted as if he was going to help us," JT says.

"We will keep our guard up. It's our best option right now," Harrison replies. "Plus, there are five of us now since Tommy showed up so I think we can take him."

"With that being said, I was wondering how you knew we were there," Jaylen says to Tommy.

Stew busts through the front screen door which squeaks loudly as it flings open. Grabbing his pitchfork in his right hand tightly, he taps it on the wooden porch twice. They gaze upon Stew smiling from ear to ear.

JT's eyes widen glaring upon Stew spinning his pitchfork in his hand.

"Great. He has a nice sharp pitchfork. Why wouldn't he have a sharp pitchfork," JT says.

Stew takes a couple steps halfway down the uneven stairs. "Harrison, I am glad you and your friends decided to come. Hurry up and wash up. I am cooking some fish I caught yesterday. I guarantee you have never tasted fish as good as the fish from the Lake of Hope."

"Yes, sir. Thank you," Harrison replies.

Stew holds the door open for them as they enter the house. The room feels bare to Harrison, as he glances around. An old worn blue cloth couch sits in the middle of the room with five old blankets spread around it.

Closing the door behind him, Stew comes beside him and the others as they observe the emptiness of the room.

"I already put blankets out for each of ya. I will go to the kitchen and start cooking the fish," Stew says, strolling to the kitchen.

"Is there a reason why you only have a couch in the house?" Joseph says.

"This old cabin use to be my father's. He was drafted into the Golic warrior army during the Second Great War. Before he was drafted, he built this house. The couch was the only thing he got in the house. He was killed by one of those Destine bums in battle. So, in his honor, I never bought anything else for the house," Stew says from the kitchen.

"Oh. I am sorry to hear that," Joseph says.

"It's okay. I just wish the Destine nation was one of the two nations that got destroyed during the Second Great War. They are the worst group of people and if I ever see one, I would let him meet my pitchfork," Stew replies.

Harrison and the other's eyes widen and stop breathing for a second.

"So, are you boys attending the Golic Academy?" Stew asks dropping pans on the floor.

"Yes. Yes, we are," Harrison replies quickly.

Waking up from a long nap, Harrison throws the thin blanket with blue and white polka dots. Stretching his arms straight in the air, he takes a deep breath. Rubbing his face, he feels groggy as he stands up. JT, Jaylen, and Joseph snore in unison on the floor still. Glancing at them, Harrison observes that Tommy is missing.

Walking towards the door, the sun hides behind the mountains as if it was trying to hide from everything. Harrison sees Tommy sitting on the steps outside looking toward the water. Stepping outside, Harrison closes the door quietly, taking a seat next to him.

"Have you seen Stew?" Harrison says.

"He left about thirty minutes ago. I don't know where he went through," Tommy replies picking his fingernails.

Harrison sits there for a couple of moments in silence. Tommy continues to pick his nails. Harrison finally breaks the silence. "So, how exactly did you know where we were? That is the second time you showed up out of nowhere. I mean don't get me wrong, I appreciate that you did, especially the first time against those giants. But you had no idea that we were heading here."

Spitting out a piece of his fingernail, Tommy stretches his legs out across the steps.

"I guess I should be honest with you now," Tommy replies not looking at Harrison.

"I mean that would be nice. I consider you a good friend, Tommy. I think I deserve to know."

Tommy lifts up gazing at Harrison directly in his eyes. "I was assigned to follow you and keep an eye on you since school started. The Elder knew that you would probably try to find some answers when you arrived at the Academy. So, he had a game plan for years. The reason I was trained the way I was by my dad was because the Elder commanded him to get me ready to watch over you. It was his mission to get me ready for my mission. Keeping you safe is my mission."

Harrison's heart sinks to his stomach. "Why would the Elder assign you this mission? Why not someone else? Why go to the extent to have another teenager take this mission?"

"He told me and my dad when I was eleven years old that you would trust another student more than an adult at the Academy," Tommy replies.

"So that is the reason he reserved me the seat next to you the first day at the Academy? He must have set that up so we could meet each other," Harrison says.

"Yeah. He wanted to make sure we met. He figured that would be the best way to make sure I was introduced to you," Tommy pulls his legs back in close to his body.

Abruptly, a loud noise rattles from the bushes near the house. Harrison and Tommy look toward their right.

"You hear that?" Tommy asks.

Harrison rises slowly, inspecting the area better. Nodding his head in agreement, Harrison and Tommy walk off the porch quietly. They creep slowly. The bush sways in the wind gently. Tommy sneaks around, looking behind it. Glancing back at Harrison, he motions nothing was there.

Suddenly, a yellow energy ball slams near Harrison's feet. Jumping away from it, Harrison rolls towards Tommy. Gazing up towards the roof, a masked individual in all black jumps off the roof flinging another yellow energy ball at them.

Heading directly at Harrison, Tommy quickly steps in the way slapping the energy ball on the lake. Harrison watches it skip across the lake a couple of times before it disappears.

The masked individual lands on the ground and rolls onto his feet and sprints towards the city.

"Make sure he doesn't get away," Tommy runs after him.

THE ARK OF POWER

Harrison sprints behind Tommy following the masked person. Harrison doesn't worry about the aching pain at the bottom of his feet. The masked person runs towards a giant pier that sits on top of the crystal-clear water.

Forming an energy ball, Tommy throws it at the masked person. Tommy misses him. Harrison falls back, not being able to keep up.

"We can't lose him," Harrison shouts running faster to catch up.

The masked person stops, turning around sharply. Putting his hands together, he forms a yellow energy ball. Harrison and Tommy stop quickly, glaring at him forming his attack.

"It's an energy beam. Get out of the way. Quick," Tommy screams.

Pushing his hands out, a giant yellow energy beam shoots across the long pier, racing towards Tommy and Harrison. Tommy jumps off the pier into the water. Harrison jumps off the pier on the other side.

Crashing into the water, Harrison observes the yellow beam covering the whole pier as he is under the water. Swimming to the surface, all of a sudden Harrison sees a pitchfork covered in purple energy flying through the energy beam. Screams erupt from the masked man following the energy beam disappearing.

Harrison pulls himself up. The water drips off of him, trickling back into the lake. He observes Stew walking slowly to the masked person who is crying in pain as the pitchfork is sticking through his right lower calf. Tommy pulls himself up and helps Harrison up. Standing next to each other, Stew looks back towards them.

"Come on. Let's take him back to the house and figure out what we are going to do with him," Stew says determinedly.

CHAPTER
29

Ghost

S tew slings the door open, holding the masked person by the back of his black shirt. Harrison and Tommy follow the trail of blood that is dripping from his leg that was stabbed with Stew's pitchfork. JT, Jaylen, and Joseph raise up rapidly from a deep slumber. Stew throws the man onto the floor, next to JT.

"Harrison. Go get a chair and get some black tape from the drawer next to the fridge," Stew says.

JT gets up and scurries toward the couch. Jaylen and Joseph stand up with a look of confusion on their face.

"Gotcha," Harrison moves toward the kitchen.

"Okay. What the heck did I miss? Why are we throwing a masked guy into the living room?" JT asks.

Harrison flings the drawer open. Running his hand through packets of ketchup and mustard, he finally grabs the dense black tape. Shutting the drawer, he grabs the tarnished wooden chair and runs back into the living room.

The masked person clutches his leg tightly where the three wounds are. Stew lifts him up while Harrison places the chair in the middle of the floor. Placing him on the chair, Stew takes the tape, wrapping his arms behind it.

"Alright. It's cool. Don't answer my question. We will just wake up and watch you guys keep some guy hostage," JT announces sarcastically.

"He attacked us," Tommy says. "We chased him down and Stew captured him and brought him back so we can figure out what to do with him."

"Let's see who he is underneath this mask," Stew snatches the mask off of his face.

Long dirty blonde hair that looks as if it hasn't been washed in months, drops down to the pale freckled boy's shoulders.

"I have seen this kid before. He lives around here. Haven't seen him much in the last three years since he attends the Golic Academy," Stew says shocked and disappointed. "You boys probably saw him at the academy since you all go there."

Harrison's heart drops as the guy in the chair grins and stares in his eyes.

Crap. We can't let Stew find out that we lied to him and that we are Destines or we are in trouble.

"Yeah...kind of looks familiar but hard to tell since there are so many students there," Harrison replies.

The injured boy giggles as he tries to get comfortable on the chair. "You got to be kidding me. You have no idea who they are, do you?"

Harrison swallows hard, worrying about what they are going to do.

Stew stands right in front of the injured boy. "Son. I know who they are, I want to know who you are and why you are dressed like this and trying to attack them."

Turning his head sideways to avoid eye contact with Stew, the injured boy glares at the wall.

"It's none of your business now why I am trying to attack them and why I am dressed like this. That time will come soon enough and when it does, you are going to be begging that I don't remember your face," he replies looking straight ahead. "The real question you should be asking is why are they lying to you about who they really are."

Stew bends down and leans in close to his face, taking his glasses off. "What's your name son?"

Smiling back at him, the injured boy gapes in his eyes without blinking. "If I tell you, it's going to hurt either me or you."

"I doubt that. Try me," Stew smiles back.

"Okay. My name is Ghost."

All of a sudden, he slams his head into Stew's face. Blood gushes out of Stew's nose as he falls on his back.

Stew rolls on the ground in pain, holding his face as the blood pours on to the floor. Ghost squints his face as blood drips down his forehead. "Guess it was you."

Harrison and Tommy help Stew up. Holding his nose, blood rushes down his face running onto his blue overalls.

"Jaylen, take Stew in the bathroom and help him get cleaned up," Harrison says.

Jaylen grabs Stew's arm gently and helps guide him towards the bathroom.

Harrison and the others stare at each other for a moment.

"What the heck are we going to do? If this guy tells Stew we are Destines, we are dead. Especially since he just had his nose busted. He isn't going to be happy," JT whispers.

Gathering together, Ghost looks towards them trying to eavesdrop.

"We can't let that happen," Harrison whispers. "We got to do something to make sure he doesn't talk."

Scoffing under his breath, Ghost kicks his good foot on the floor.

"You think I am not going to tell him? You are going to have to kill me to make sure I don't say anything. Believe me," Ghost interrupts loudly.

"We can't kill him. We aren't killers," Joseph whispers.

"Joseph is right. We can't kill him. That's not us," Harrison whispers.

"Then what do we do to make sure he doesn't talk?" JT whispers.

Moments go by in silence as they gaze at the bloody floor.

"It is my mission to protect you no matter what, Harrison. The Elder and my dad told me that there would be times where I would have to do things that I didn't want to do. This is one of them, I guess," Tommy whispers, walking towards Ghost.

Grabbing Tommy's shoulder, Harrison stops him as he stands in front of Ghost.

"That doesn't mean you have to kill to protect me. I won't let you," Harrison says.

Tommy grabs and throws Harrison's hand off of his shoulder. "I'm not going to kill him. I am just going to make sure he isn't able to tell him."

Harrison takes a step back next to JT and Joseph. Tommy takes the tape off of him as Ghost glares confused at Harrison.

"What are you planning to do?" Ghost asks.

"All I can say is it is going to hurt either you or me," Tommy lifts Ghost as he tries to balance on one foot. "And it's not going to be me."

Suddenly, Tommy raises him up and tackles him through the window. Glass shatters and flies everywhere.

Landing on top of him, Tommy punches him continuously in the face as he sits on top of him. Right hook after right hook makes Ghost's face swell the size of an apple. He coughs up blood trying to breathe.

Standing up, Tommy lifts him up and leans him against a dense tree. Ghost slides slowly down the tree. Tommy slams an energy ball the size of melon into his stomach. Bouncing off the tree, Ghost falls face first into the ground, moaning in whimpers. Harrison, JT, and Joseph make it outside the same time as Jaylen and Stew who is holding a white bloody rag on his face.

"What the heck happened?" Stew says.

Tommy kicks him in the back of the head and turns to face them.

"He attacked us. While we were tending to you, he ripped the tape and attacked us. He set us up. So, I had to defend myself," Tommy wipes the blood on his knuckles on his pants.

"Gosh. Look at my window," Stew walks over to it.

Tommy stares down at Ghost whose fingers are twitching. "I told you it was going to be you."

JT and Jaylen carry Ghost back into the living room. Joseph dashes over with a beige towel placing it on the floor. Lowering him easily on his stomach, the blood continues to rush from his face. His puffed-up nose pushes his head up higher on the towel. Harrison closes the door softly behind Tommy.

Entering the living room, they all gaze around in silence. Suddenly, Stew opens the door holding the towel pressed against his face.

"We can't let him just sit in my living room and slowly die," Stew says.

All of them stand still staring at the floor.

"I tell you what. In the morning I will go and get some medicine for him from the pharmacy in town," Stew says.

Ghost's fingers start twitching rapidly for a couple of seconds with slight moans following. Harrison looks away from the sight of him.

"I will go for you," Harrison announces. "People know who you are in town and will be wondering why you are so banged up. We don't want that type of attention."

"I will go with you," JT says.

"Sounds like a plan to me," Stew replies. "The pharmacy is a small little building as soon as you get into the city. It is called Purhara Pharmacy."

"Alright. I think we can remember that. Thanks," Harrison responds.

Stew heads down the hallway towards his room. "See y'all in the morning. And please don't let the kid die in my living room."

Tommy grabs a torn purple blanket and lays underneath it, closing his eyes tightly. Jaylen and Joseph

321

scoot their white dingy blankets away from Ghost, who has changed the towel from beige to red because of all the blood gushing from his face.

Their eyes make contact with Harrison's and JT's with an awkward glance.

Harrison and JT close the door slowly trying to prevent the squeak from being loud. Rising behind the mountains, the burnt orange sun peeks behind them. The chill in the air feels as if it is battling with the warmth of the sun. Harrison embraces the rays emitting from it. JT seems as if he is doing the same

Approaching a huge pier connecting to the small city full of mid-sized buildings right next to each other, Harrison and JT stop to marvel at the white seagulls lining up on the pier. Hundreds of them sit still twitching as the sun's rays land on their bodies.

"Not to be weird or anything. But this is kind of beautiful," JT says smiling and watching the birds flap their wings and scratch themselves.

Harrison closes his eyes to enjoy the warm rays shining on his face. "I agree. And after last night and the last couple of days, I think we needed to see this sight."

Walking past the pier into the city, the seagulls' flap away in the air towards the mountains. People walk alongside them as they approach the pharmacy. Entering, a tiny bell rings twice, signaling to the bald guy behind the counter with a long white jacket on.

"Welcome to Purhara Pharmacy," the man behind the counter says while reading a magazine.

As Harrison starts to respond, a loud screeching noise grabs their attention.

Harrison and JT try to look through the doors behind them to see what the noise is. Piercing through the bottom of the doors with glass, they can only see the bottom of two long creamy school buses. Loud chatter erupts from kids getting off the buses, breaking the peaceful silence in the streets.

The man behind the counter peeks behind the thin wavy shades. He shakes his slick bald head. Snapping back to reading his magazine he sucks his lips in disgust. "I can't stand when the other nations bring their kids here for field trips."

Harrison approaches the counter trying to tune out the noise in the streets. "Excuse me. Where are your pain medications and band-aids at?"

"Aisle five, right over there," the man says pointing while still reading the magazine.

"Thank you," Harrison replies walking to the aisle.

JT picks up two boxes of band-aids as Harrison grabs the biggest bottle of pain medicine there. Taking the items up to the counter, the ceiling lights bounce a strong thick glare off of his bald head.

Harrison pays and takes the bag. Exiting the store, Harrison gazes at the stuff in the thin plastic bag in the crowded street full of kids. Suddenly, someone bumps into Harrison making him drop the bag. Harrison bends down to pick it up and is met with a soft skinned hand grabbing the other side. Lifting the bag up together, Harrison glances in front of him, as if he has seen a ghost.

"Harrison?" Victoria says.

CHAPTER 30

Unexpected Turns

Her eyes sparkle in the morning sun. The twinkle in her eyes sends chills down Harrison's spine just like that night at the skating rink. She looks confused as she glances back at her two friends.

"Harrison. What are you and JT doing here? I wouldn't have imagined in a million years that we would see you," Victoria says running her hand through her long shiny hair.

Rubbing the side of his face, JT looks at Harrison as if waiting for him to say something. Harrison waits a moment, as he is surprised to see her also.

"We...ummm, are here for the Academy. They sent us on an a....ummm educational mission," Harrison replies.

People crowd them as the rest of the people get off the bus. Pushing up against him, Harrison and JT scoot closer to hear Victoria.

"Wow. That is pretty cool," Victoria says.

All of a sudden, a screaming voice erupts from the crowd.

"*HARRISON...HARRISON.*"

Gazing around the crowd of people, he doesn't spot the person screaming his name. Suddenly, someone tackles him grabbing him tightly. Gavin smiles from ear to ear as he continues to tighten his grip.

"Gavin, it's good to see you," Harrison says while watching Victoria out of the corner of his eye. "How have you been lately?"

Gavin lets go of his tight hold.

"I have been pretty good," Gavin replies. "Just training so I can get ready to attend the academy like you."

Harrison places his hand on his shoulder, smiling slightly.

"What are you guys doing here?" Harrison asks.

Gavin punches Harrison softly in his stomach. "Shows how much you pay attention to the letters I write to you. I wrote you a couple of months ago and told you that I was excited about our field trip here."

Grabbing his stomach, Harrison laughs under his breath. "I remember now after you say it."

Victoria's friends walk off. Victoria stands there staring at Harrison.

"We both have got to get going. If they don't see us in there, we will get in trouble," Victoria announces.

She smiles at him. Harrison loses his breath as he gazes at her beautiful smile.

"Yeah. Sure," Harrison says. "It was great seeing you two. Maybe we will get to see each other again before we all leave and head back."

Victoria puts her hand on Gavin's back, guiding him slowly with her.

"Next time we see each other, you really are going to be hurting," Gavin says lifting his fist up in the air.

Entering into the building, Harrison and Victoria lock eyes with a tender smile.

"Cute," JT says sarcastically. "Are you ready to go now? While you are smiling at one another, we do have a guy lying in a bloody mess waiting for us. But go ahead, we can stay a little longer so you can go in there and smile some more."

Harrison punches him in the stomach as JT blocks it and slides back.

"Shut up," Harrison responds walking away.

Stew sits on his porch rocking in an old wooden rocker that is screeching as if in pain. Harrison and JT stop at the steps.

"He is trying to wake up. Glad you guys got here. I am sure he is in some pain," Stew says with his nose pointing to the side.

JT rushes in the door with the bag of supplies. Harrison walks behind him. Stew stops Harrison from entering the house. The door shuts in front of him violently, bouncing off the frame.

"Son. Listen to me for a moment," Stew says with his arm stretched out preventing him from going in.

"He looks scared. He looks about the same age as you," Stew says. "I understand he and his friends tried to take you guys out, but I want you to know that sometimes people make bad decisions. We all can fall into the wrong company."

Harrison listens intently.

"Having the wrong people in your life can corrupt your character. That had to happen to this young kid," Stew says. "Show him what character really looks like. Show him that you are willing to trust him. It could change him and ultimately help him."

Nodding his head gently, Harrison walks inside. Ghost is sitting in a chair with his head dangling as Jaylen and Joseph bandage the wounds on his leg.

Slowly lifting his head, Ghost looks directly into Harrison's eyes as he enters the living room. The swelling in his face makes all the freckles on his face form together.

Tommy sits on the floor in the corner of the room, leaning against the old, worn, white wall.

Harrison walks towards Tommy, but suddenly he feels Ghost grab his thigh softly. "I...wan...I...want to talk...to you...alone."

Harrison nods in agreement. "Can all of you give us a moment please?"

Jaylen and Joseph get up and walk toward the kitchen. Tommy slides up the wall.

After everyone leaves, Harrison squats down on eye level with him. "What do you want?"

Ghost lifts his head slowly again, shaking as he tries to hold it up. "I... want to make.... a deal?"

"What type of deal can you make us?" Harrison says.

"I... can take...you to the Ark. We found it...and it had some things of your dad and his crew... around it," Ghost responds dropping his head after he speaks.

Harrison stops breathing for a second. Trying to breath seems impossible at the moment.

"What...what do you want from me?"

Lifting his head slowly again, Ghost's swollen eyes peer into Harrison's.

"I want to be set free so I can meet back up with my dad and brother. I will take you there if you can help me get back to them and not tell them that I joined this masked group."

Harrison takes a step back to get a better look at him. "You have a deal."

The steam stiffens the air from the shower as if it was trying to overtake every ounce of the air in the bathroom. Taking deep breaths, Harrison's lungs feel hefty like he was breathing in giant stones instead of the air in the bathroom.

Drying his hair with an old shrill pine green colored towel that Stew gave him, he squints as water from the tips of his hair drips into his eyes. He shakes his head quickly making water splash on the tiny oval mirror overtop a small rusty pearl white sink. The water running down it allows Harrison to see small streaks of his face.

Loud banging on the other side of the door makes Harrison opens his eyes.

"Son...you alright in there?" Stew says.

Harrison hurries and puts his clothes on, wiping his hair again quickly with the towel.

"Yeah...everything is fine. Just getting dressed," Harrison replies as he opens the door.

Staring into the swollen black and yellow eyes of Stew, he places the wet towel around his neck.

"You always make that much racket when you are changing?" Stew asks.

Grinning back at him, Harrison lowers his head and walks past him slowly.

"I don't know. Never really paid attention," Harrison says with a giggle.

"Well if you broke anything in there, you will be paying for something," Stew says as Harrison walks out of the hallway.

Harrison's smile grows wider as he enters the living room. Glancing around, he surveys everybody else packing their bags with their dirty clothes from the journey. Sleeping and still tied up, Ghost snores stridently with each breath he takes.

Harrison watches him struggle to breathe, with a concerned look on his face. Zipping his bag forcefully, Tommy glares Harrison's way making eye contact with him as he watches Ghost sleep.

"I wonder if he was always a snorer. Or did that just start recently?" JT zips up his bag and flings it on his back.

Harrison stares at JT, shaking his head in disbelief.

"What?" JT asks with a slight attitude. "I mean it is a fair question, isn't it? Don't tell me you didn't think it also Harrison. We all know he sounds that way because of the beating he took."

JT walks past Tommy who just blinks with a blank expression and points at Ghost. "Just look at him. He can barely breathe right while he sleeps, Harrison. How the heck is he supposed to lead us to the Ark in the Purhara Mountains like this?"

Sluggishly opening his eyes, Ghost looks around with a swollen face weighing his head down. Harrison gazes at him.

Suddenly, a deep cough erupts from Ghost splattering blood all over JT's pants and bottom part of his shirt. Turning quickly to evade it, JT faces Tommy with blood painted on his clothes.

"Just great," JT looks at Tommy. "I blame this on you. If you didn't beat his face in, then my last set of clean clothes that I have wouldn't be stained with his blood."

Tommy responds by just blinking at JT. Shaking his head JT walks out of the room stomping his feet.

Harrison walks in front of Ghost as he tries to lift his head to look up to him.

"Joseph. Untie him please." Harrison says.

Joseph rips the tape off his wrist. He falls to his knees in front of Harrison.

"Not going to help me up you Destine scum?" Ghost says. "Do you like me kneeling before you?"

All of a sudden, Tommy punches Ghost in the face making his face bounce off the floor.

"If you want my opinion, I like you better like this," Tommy says. "Let's get him up so we can go."

Harrison and Joseph stand on each side of him, lifting him up slowly.

"What's that all about?" Jaylen says.

Moving closer to Jaylen, Tommy looks around the room.

"If Stew heard him call Harrison a Destine, we would be found out," Tommy whispers to Jaylen.

At that moment, Stew walks into the living room.

"What are you guys doing with him?" Stew says in confusion. "He can barely walk."

Harrison's heart beats quickly as he doesn't know how to answer.

Crap. We can't let him know that he is leading us to the Ark. We will be found out that way.

"We are taking him to his parents who are at the Purhara mountains," Tommy answers. "He told us that they would be there, so we told him that if he could lead us to them then we would take him there. It's the least we could do."

Stew smiles at them as he takes small steps towards them.

"Sounds like a great idea," Stew replies. "I tell you what. He can't walk really well so I will drive you all to the mountains."

Harrison's heart sinks. "No, you don't have to. You don't need to go out of your way."

"I know I don't have to son, but it's the least I can do. I want to make sure he gets to his parents," Stew says walking to the kitchen.

Harrison hears keys rattle loudly from in there.

"Plus, I needed to head that way and get some hay. I will get my pitchfork so I can load it up. You guys meet me at my truck. I will be there in a minute."

Ghost smiles slightly as Harrison and the others droop their heads lightly.

"Sounds like a deal," Ghost announces.

Tommy shakes his head, walking out of the room in disgust. Harrison and Joseph walk gently holding Ghost up. Jaylen lifts Harrison and Joseph's bags up slinging them on to his back with him following behind them.

"You guys heard Tommy. Let's get going," Ghost says with a sarcastic tone.

JT helps grab the bags from Jaylen as Harrison and Joseph lift Ghost on the back of the truck bed. Harrison brushes small pieces of broken and crinkled hay off as Ghost gingerly sits on the rusted burgundy truck bed. Stew, holding his pitchfork, throws it next to Ghost.

"Make sure nothing happens to my pitchfork back there," Stew says, opening the door on the truck. "Two people need to sit back there with him since there are only four seats in here," Stew sits down and closes the door.

"I will sit back here with him," Harrison jumps up in the bed of the truck.

Tommy takes small strides towards the back as JT places his hand on his chest, scooting him back softly. JT jumps in on the other side of Ghost.

"I got back here, you can sit in the truck," JT says. "Go ahead."

JT waves his hand motioning Tommy to get in the truck.

"C' mon boys looks like we are about to get a nice storm by the look of those clouds, so let's hurry up," Stew announces loudly knocking the dashboard.

Dust bounces in the air from the dashboard making Tommy sneeze as he sits in the front passenger seat.

Turning the key, the truck shakes from side to side as if an earthquake just happened. All of them grab hold tight and hang on as everyone bounces except Stew. Stew takes his hat off, placing it on his dashboard. "Time to roll boys."

Ghost grimaces with each bounce of the truck. He moans and grunts on each bump.

"It's going to be alright," Harrison holds tightly onto the truck.

A huge bump makes them come up off their butts. Slamming down quickly, Ghost grunts in pain, grabbing his leg.

"Keep telling yourself that. You going to need to," Ghost responds.

Harrison and JT gaze at one another as JT shakes his head with a small smirk. Harrison glares to his right and sees the giant gray clouds stopping the sun from shining on the Purhara city in the distance.

Driving around on the outskirts made the Purhara Mountains seem larger than any other mountains he had ever seen. The city rests underneath the giant mountains.

Harrison closes his eyes. Calmness eases his muscles as he takes deep breaths.

He opens his eyes seeing the clear blue water on the other side of the city glisten by the sun that was starting to get overtaken by puffy, dark gray clouds.

A single small raindrop crashes on Harrison's forehead. Trickling down his nose, Harrison wipes it off as it tickles the tip of his nose.

Unexpectedly, an energy blast slams underneath the truck lifting the back of it in the air. Harrison and JT grab a hold of Ghost as they stare up into the clouds. The truck bounces as the back wheels bang back onto the narrow dirt road. Dust flies into Harrison's eyes. Harrison and JT cough continually as the truck slows down.

Harrison digs his fingers on the side of his eyes and flings the small bit of dust and dirt out.

"What the heck," Stew says softly hitting the steering wheel.

Harrison stands grabbing the top of the truck and gazes straight ahead. About ten people dressed in all black and wearing masks stand there.

Harrison hits the top of the truck three times. "Keep some distance."

The truck stops. Thick black smoke rises out of the rusted muffler.

"Trying to get somewhere?" the one in the front of the group says.

Stew sticks his head out of his window. "I am going to ask you nicely to move."

Scratching the back of his head, the one in the front takes a couple steps toward the truck.

"You see...we can't do that because you have one of ours, and we are going to need him back," he says, taking a couple more steps closer. "So just go ahead and hand him over. We already gave you a warning. Next time I will hit the whole truck."

Ghost starts rolling around in the back of the truck.

"I am back here," Ghost screams as loud as he can.

JT quickly covers his mouth. Muffled squeaks try to squeeze through JT's fingertips.

"Shut up. What type of friends are they if they almost killed you with that blast? I mean really what type of friends do you have?" JT says, pressing his hand harder over his mouth. Harrison and JT glance at one another quickly. "You know what...never mind, don't answer that, my friends have almost got me killed multiple times."

Tommy starts to open the door. Quickly, Stew grabs his arm holding him in the truck.

"You don't need to go out there. I know another way to the entrance of the mountains," Stew puts the truck in reverse.

Slowly he drives backward as the group walk toward them.

337

"We are taking him to his family. He isn't with you knuckleheads anymore," Stew announces out the window as he turns around.

"We are his family," he screams back at Stew.

Suddenly, he forms a bright orange energy ball and slings it at the truck.

"Hold on," Harrison screams.

Harrison sends energy to his feet sticking him firmly to the bed of the truck. He slaps the orange energy ball with his backhand sending it flying to the road and exploding. Harrison fires two energy attacks back at them.

The truck starts swerving from the explosion. The person in the front blocks Harrison's energy blast. The other energy blast slams into the chest of one of the ones in the back, knocking him on the ground.

"Take this you Destine scums," he says.

All of them shoot energy attacks at the truck.

"Brace yourselves, everyone," Harrison cries out.

Two of them hit the back of the truck lifting the truck back in the air. As the truck flies up in the air the other energy blasts smash into the bottom of it making it turn in midair. All of a sudden, Harrison, Ghost and JT soar out of the truck bed.

Ghost and JT land next to each other. The truck crashes on to its side and slides for several feet. Black smoke rises from the hood of the truck as moans from inside of it escape through the broken glass shattered everywhere.

Harrison lands, sliding and spinning on the ground on the other side of the road from Ghost and JT. Lifting up slowly, Harrison sees JT rise gently.

Pushing himself up, he feels aches throughout his whole body. The group walks over towards JT and Ghost. The one in the front kicks JT as he tries to get up. JT hits the ground and moans in pain.

"No. Leave him alone," Harrison yells.

He looks over at Harrison, staring at him through his mask for a couple of moments as JT holds his stomach with both hands. He grabs JT by his hair and pulls him up. JT flings his arms towards his face trying to grab him. He punches JT three times in the stomach.

Harrison arises. As he stands, a blue energy ball knocks him back down. Harrison falls on his back. He sits up with a burning pain in his chest from the blast.

"You took our friend and played with him a little we see, so we will take your friend and play with him also," he announces to Harrison. "You can meet us in the mountain. You can get him back from us there, Harrison."

The others pick up Ghost as a giant black truck pulls up. They fling Ghost and JT on the back of it.

"See you in a little, Grady," he waves as the truck pulls off.

Harrison drops his head and turns over as the rain pours from the dark clouds.

CHAPTER
31

The Purhara Mountains

Harrison stands to his feet. He wobbles from side to side as he moves to the overturned truck. The driver's side is at the bottom with the passenger's side sticking up in the air. Tommy climbs out of the broken window on his side. He falls on his face moaning in pain. Jaylen climbs out from the back of the truck and into the crushed truck bed. Joseph follows behind Jaylen, dropping into the truck bed.

"Are you guys okay?" Harrison says helping Jaylen step down on the ground.

As he steps down, he trips on Stew's pitchfork right next to the truck.

Harrison and Tommy walk to the front of the truck. The thick black smoke rushes out of the engine making Stew hardly visible behind the cracked windshield.

"We have to get him out," Harrison says.

"Scoot back, Stew," Tommy yells.

Tommy lifts his hand up with his palm facing the truck. He shoots a small energy ball at the windshield blasting it to pieces. Small pieces of glass hover through the smoke at them. Stew slides out from the front of the truck.

Harrison and Tommy lift him up as Jaylen and Joseph come over to them.

"You okay, Stew?" Jaylen asks.

"Yeah. I am okay," Stew replies.

Joseph hands him his pitchfork.

"We have to hurry and go get JT. They took him to the mountains," Harrison says. "How do we get there Stew?"

Stew points down the road they were traveling. "The quickest way is to take the road we were on in the beginning. It leads us to the entrance. It will take us about an hour if we walk."

Harrison takes a couple of steps. "We better get going."

Harrison marches a couple of steps but notices that he doesn't hear the others following. Looking over his left shoulder, the others stand there with a blank stare.

"C' mon we got to hurry up, guys. We can't waste any more time. We have to go and get JT back from them." Harrison says taking a couple more steps.

"Harrison. We want to go get JT back more than anything too, believe me. But we don't know how many people they have waiting for us up there. It could be too dangerous for just us," Jaylen announces.

Harrison stops and puts his head down.

"Yeah man, I mean this just seems too risky. I think we are over our heads with this. We weren't expecting all of this to happen," Joseph says.

Turning around quickly, Harrison still hangs his head towards the ground.

"He was captured because of me. No matter what, I have to get him back. This is my fault," Harrison says lifting his head.

Tears mix in the rain running down Harrison's face. Tommy walks over and lays his hand on his right shoulder.

"We will go and get him, whatever it takes, we will get him back," Tommy says. "I don't care how many of them there are."

Stew limps over to Harrison and Tommy.

"I am no good to help you all. I am going to get some help and get my truck towed. But please be careful boys," Stew says.

Jaylen and Joseph walk over joining all of them.

"Thanks, for everything Stew," Harrison says. "Let's get going guys."

Stew taps Jaylen's back as he walks with them.

"Here, you all might need this more than me. Just take it and bring it back to me when you all get back."

Stew hands his pitchfork to them. Jaylen grabs it.

They walk toward the mountains rising in front of them in the near distance. Each step splashes mud on Harrison's pants. The only thing making noise is the rain falling from the sky. Thunder erupts every couple of seconds followed by various streaks of lightning behind the mountains.

Harrison grabs his bag from Joseph, unzipping it. Yanking the compass out, it drools with its eyes closed tightly. Harrison shakes it violently making the drool sling from its mouth and its eyes open quickly.

"Whoa. What's going on?" the compass shouts, confused.

"We are right here near the Purhara Mountains. But I need to know which way to take to get inside, Harrison asks coming up to a part in the road that leads to two separate parts of the mountain.

"Show me exactly where we are," the compass replies.

Harrison faces the compass towards the roads splitting to two different parts of the mountain. He points the compass at the dark silver mountains stained with wetness from the rain.

"I can sense the Ark very strongly. It is really close. We need to take the trail on the left. The trail called the Trail of Tears," the compass responds.

Harrison lowers the compass.

"Why is it called that?" Josephs asks.

"Because this is the trail the Supreme Elder's brother took into the mountain when he returned. They said he cried on his journey back here because the girl he loved was afraid of him," the compass reveals.

Harrison throws the compass back into the bag and zips it up.

They travel down the trail getting closer to the entrance of the monstrous mountain. A vast opening is visible at the bottom of it.

"There is the entrance," Tommy points.

Unexpectedly, energy blasts start smashing all around them exploding the mud everywhere.

"Watch out," Harrison screams.

Sprinting to the mountain the energy blasts keep slamming near their feet. Harrison dives in the mountain entrance. Rolling on his side he stops on his back as the others land beside him.

They rise to their feet rapidly.

"They weren't trying to hit us. They were aiming the blasts at our feet," Tommy says.

"Why?" Joseph asks trying to catch his breath.

"They wanted to make sure we came into the mountain," Harrison surveys the mountain.

Torches on both sides of the walls light up the hallway that leads to a set of stairs at the end of the hallway. All of a sudden, a group of ten men dressed in all black with masks on, walk down the stairs.

"Glad you made it here, Grady," the one in the front says. "Now just follow us. Our master would like to meet you."

"We aren't going anywhere," Tommy throws an energy ball at them.

Exploding in front of them, they scatter from the stairs. Meeting mid-point in the hallway they all throw punches at one another. Harrison is circled by three of them throwing various punches and kicks at him.

The one in front of him heaves a strong right hook. Harrison grabs it and throws him to into the man behind him. The other one kicks twice as Harrison blocks both. Harrison fakes him with his left leg. Falling for the fake kick, Harrison jumps up into the air spinning and lands his foot across his face.

Joseph is backed against the wall as one of them keeps throwing punches at his gut. Harrison shoots an energy ball nailing him in the back. He slams against the wall next to Joseph. Jaylen knocks one out with the bottom of the pitchfork.

The last two run towards Tommy. Tommy runs and flips in-between both of them. As he lands, he charges up his energy. They run toward him again.

"Supersonic Omega Blast," Tommy screams.

He slams it into the one in the front knocking him and the one behind him to the ground.

Laying on the ground, flinching, the group moan in pain. Harrison and the others start to walk up the stairs which seem to go all the way to the top of the mountain. Each dark gray stone feels different with each step. The steps begin to circle the higher they get. Halfway up the steps, loud chanting rings through it.

"Slow down," Tommy says.

Harrison, Joseph, and Jaylen stop and listen to Tommy.

"We need to be really careful when we get to the top. Whatever we do, try not to separate. We will get taken out faster if we are by ourselves," Harrison says.

Each of them nods their heads in agreement. The chanting gets louder with each step. Harrison struggles to understand what they are saying. Approaching the end, Harrison and the others crouch low, peeking over the last step. There are about twenty people all dressed in black and wearing the same masks.

"Okay, on the count of three we stand and throw energy balls at them," Harrison says.

"One...two...three," Harrison forms an energy ball and stands quickly while the others do the same thing.

Harrison gasps at the sight he rises to. Behind the twenty, stands hundreds of people dressed in all black and wearing masks. Harrison and the others continue to hold the energy balls in their hands, stunned at what they see.

The hundreds of masked people continue to chant, standing completely still and staring right at them.

Harrison senses his heart beat faster than it ever has. The pounding in his chest proves it. Harrison tries to swallow but can't seem to. The eerie chants fill the large room bouncing off the gloomy walls.

"MAR... THAR."

"MAR... THAR."

Harrison tightens his fist.

"Harrison. Don't do it," Joseph whispers.

Abruptly, Harrison launches his energy ball into the group of twenty standing the closest to him. Running at them full speed, the explosion from his blast separates the small group. Harrison shoots through the air with a flying punch.

He nails the one in the front in the face. He continues to throw kicks and punches at the others. Tommy, Jaylen, and Joseph follow in behind him and join in on the fight. The rest of the people chanting stand completely still.

"MAR... THAR."

"MAR... THAR."

Tommy punches one in the face making him fall to the ground. Two come beside him. He forms two energy balls in both hands. Squatting down he places both of them on each one's hip and blasts them.

Joseph hits one in the head with the end of the pitchfork, knocking them on the floor. All of a sudden, one of them kicks the pitchfork out of his hand. Flying through the air, it lands too far away for him to get it.

The masked person throws two punches at Joseph. The first one hits him in the chest while he catches the second one. Creating an energy ball, he shoots him in the chest sending him flying towards other masked people.

Harrison and Jaylen fight side by side punching and kicking through multiple masked people. Jaylen jumps through the air and kicks the last one towards Harrison. Harrison forms an energy ball in both hands and slams it into his chest sending him soaring in the air.

All four of them watch the last one bounce off the ground.

Suddenly, silence fills the room. The loud chanting stops. They get blank stares from the hundreds of masked people near them. Harrison and the others try to catch their breath with deep inhaling and exhaling as they hear slow clapping coming from one person. Harrison looks for the person clapping but can't spot him.

Finally, from behind the mass of people in front of Harrison, the black-robed guy walks through, slowly clapping. His deep raspy voice rattles Harrison's ears just like the first time he heard it.

"I wouldn't expect anything less from a Grady," the black robed guy says walking closer to them.

Harrison, Tommy, Joseph, and Jaylen get closer together with each step he takes.

"Taking out what, ten guys down there and now about twenty up here. Impressive."

He finally stands right in front of them, just a couple feet away. Harrison tries to see his face, but it is completely dark underneath his hood.

"Where is our friend JT?" Harrison says, angrily.

"You don't get to talk to me yet. Don't ask another question," he responds pacing back and forth.

Harrison and the others just watch.

"What you are really up here looking for, the Ark, right? I mean that is why you and your little friends left the academy right?"

Harrison remains silent.

"See, this is where you talk. I just asked you a question," he says.

Harrison just stares back without blinking.

"Answer me!" he yells.

Gasps from some of the masked people behind him fill the air.

"Yes," Harrison says reluctantly.

"And why are you searching for the Ark?" he asks.

"I am-" Harrison stops and stares at him.

"Did you forget how to speak mid-sentence? Answer me," he replies.

"I am looking for my dad. I learned that the Silent Mission was all about him and the Silver Falcons looking for it. So, I was hoping it would help lead me to him or at least give me some clues," Harrison responds.

The man stops pacing and faces Harrison.

"So, you went through all this work and effort to just find it and hope that it would give you clues of your dad's whereabouts? That leaves me speechless," he says.

"Well, it just so happens that the Ark is right over there. Follow me, I will take you to it," he walks back towards the large mass of people.

Harrison and the others stand there. Seeing that they aren't moving, he nods his head. Suddenly, a group of fifteen people come and push them forward. Following behind him, the mass of people split, letting them walk through.

On the other side, a giant gold box with silver at the bottom glistens. Two silver eagles spreading their wings sit on top of it. The man stands next to it. "I want to make you a deal. A deal I know you can't refuse."

"What's the deal?" Harrison asks.

"I want you to open the Ark. If you open it, I will give you your friend back, tell you where your dad is, and let you and your friends leave," he replies.

All of a sudden, Ghost and another person bring JT over to them, tied up. They drop him to his knees facing them.

"He will die if he touches that, are you crazy," Joseph says.

"He won't. He is the only one that can open it," he says.

"What are you talking about?" Harrison says.

"You are the only one that can open it because you are the chosen one. The one who the First Destine Elder foresaw," he says.

DAVID BARCO

CHAPTER
3 2

Truth Told

Harrison stands there quietly for a couple of moments trying to figure out what he is talking about.

"What? That sounds crazy," Jaylen says interrupting the awkward silence.

He steps closer to Harrison who just stares back at him.

"As crazy as it may sound, it's true. Ask the Drake boy next to you," he says, pointing at Tommy. "He knows. He has known for a while. He was told a long time ago. That is why he was trained at such a young age. He was assigned to protect the chosen one. Tell them."

Tommy takes a deep breath, sighing slowly.

"He is right. Harrison is the chosen one prophesized about," Tommy says.

"So, since we all are on the same page, why don't you come open it for me," he says.

Harrison gazes at him without speaking.

"C' mon....don't play shy. Come open this and I will keep my part of the deal. But if you refuse, well let's just say this evening will get a whole lot worse than what it has to," he says.

"I'm not doing it. I don't know how or why you want to use it, but I am not going to help you," Harrison responds.

"Okay. Have it your way. I was trying to be reasonable, but I will go back to what my original plan was months ago," he says.

"Line them up."

People behind them push them to their knees next to JT. The black robed guy stands over them as the golden Ark sits behind him. Its majestic gold radiates soft shimmers of light.

The icy, dense air bounces off of the silver eagles that stare in opposite directions. Their wings stretch in magnificent grandeur as if they are about to fly off of it.

"You see Harrison, now I am going to make you pay for all the trouble you have caused me since the beginning. I was just going to kill you and just take your body and press it against the Ark. That is why I sent the acceptance letter to you. It was supposed to kill you and then I was going to take your body, but we see that didn't work because you survived the blast," he says.

"Oh. I forgot, bring out the other people we have. I have a surprise for you Harrison," he says.

Unexpectedly, another black robed person with their hood on walks out with Victoria and Gavin. They drop them on their knees alongside them. The person that brought them out stands next to him.

"What? Why did you take them? They have nothing to do with this," Harrison shouts.

"Oh, but they do. You see, they are important in your life so that means they have everything to do with it," he says.

"Who are you?"

Suddenly, he grabs his hood and pulls it back showing his face.

Harrison feels his heart drop.

Sebastian Darby smiles at him bouncing on his toes and rolling his thumbs around each other.

"Well to answer your other question, Harrison. I saw Victoria, is that your name?"

He points at her as tears roll down her face. "Yeah, I think that is her name, I saw her with you at the Rose Garden when you were at the hospital. But I had a little help remembering who she was," he says pointing at the person next to him.

All of a sudden, the person next to him pulls back the hood covering their face.

Harrison drops his head in disbelief.

"She helped me out, a lot," Sebastian says kissing Rena Rush.

"Aww. Thanks, sweetie," she says. "I saw her with him in the street here in town and I just couldn't believe it. So, I took them just in case we needed them for a moment like this."

Sebastian smiles at her while shaking his head.

"See that is why I trusted her with keeping up with you Harrison. She was supposed to get your dead body from the hospital after the letter incident. You see I sent the letter to you. I was going to take your dead body and use it to open the Ark, but you survived. So, I told her to just kill you and bring you to me, but your mom wouldn't leave the room, so that messed that up," Sebastian says, clearly aggravated. "So, I got her on at the school so she could watch you for me. That's how we knew you were going to be here this week."

Harrison places his hands on the ground squeezing the little bit of dirt that is on the stone floor.

"Don't feel so upset, kid. I did give you some information about your father. I didn't have to give you those notes in your dorm. I thought that was really nice of me. Made you not trust your uncle as much but hey helped me out," Sebastian says. "But anyways back to what I was about to do," Sebastian says, wiping the smile off his face.

"You have caused me some serious trouble in your little search for your daddy. You have hurt many of my men, including one of my first followers, Ghost," he says, pointing at Ghost.

"Also, you killed one of my favorite pets, Ripper. And for that, you are going to pay."

Harrison lifts his head up as tears start to form.

"Why would you do all of this? You were the next in line to lead the Destine nation? Why try to betray the Destines?" Harrison says with tears dripping down his face.

"If only your precious daddy could see you now. I am sure he would be disappointed in what he saw, I will be honest with you, kid. I never liked your dad. Shoot, not even your uncle. Actually, I had the idea to drop your dead body off to your father after I used it," Sebastian says.

Harrison interrupts him.

"Wait, my dad is alive?" Harrison wipes his tears away.

"I will tell you that much. He is alive and I can't stand the guy. I hope the next time I see him I get to kill him," Sebastian says.

"But, back to it, you have to pay. You have caused me enough trouble and I am going to show my loyal followers that I am not one to be reckoned with like the other guys in the group," Sebastian says. "Hand me that pitchfork over there."

Someone picks up the pitchfork, marches it over, and hands it to Sebastian. He examines it by constantly turning it in his hand.

"Who are you guys? And what do you want with the Ark?" Harrison says.

Sebastian jerks him up aggressively by his shirt. He pulls him around showing him to all the people around the room.

"He wants to know who we are. Tell him who we are," Sebastian yells.

"WE ARE ONE."

"WE ARE ONE."

He punches Harrison in the stomach. Harrison feels his fist lift his body off the ground. Coughs of spit blast out of his mouth.

"Leave him alone," Gavin screams.

Sebastian stares at Gavin with an evil scowl.

"Gavin, please be quiet," Victoria says sobbing.

Sebastian walks over and picks Gavin up the same way he did Harrison.

"To answer your question, Harrison, we are the G.O.M. We are one. The reason I want the Ark isn't because of what it looks like or it's stupid power. No, we have bigger plans. The Destines and the other nations worship the Supreme Elder. But I think he was a traitor to his brother and weak compared to him. You see inside here is the Supreme Elder's bones. I am going to take his bones," Sebastian says, facing Gavin towards them on their knees.

"For what?" JT asks.

Sebastian smiles at JT with excitement.

"You see, Master Marthar, the Supreme Elder's brother left the energy from his Power Flow in the rare black gems. Once we pour the black gem on his brother's bones, we can resurrect Master Marthar. And we then can take down the last three nations and become one. We will right all the wrong that the Supreme Elder caused," Sebastian reveals.

Gavin tries to pull away from Sebastian's grip. Hastily, Sebastian punches him in the back.

Gavin hollers in pain. Harrison lifts up, but Rena pulls him back down. Other people step behind Jaylen, Joseph, Tommy, JT, and Victoria.

"Stop this!" Harrison screams.

Sebastian knees Gavin's side continuously and throws him the ground, kicking him right in front of Harrison, multiple times.

"Stop what?" Sebastian asks staring at Harrison, while still kicking Gavin.

Harrison squints in anger as Gavin screeches in pain. Sebastian stops, squatting down to his level.

"I told you that you are going to pay. There are consequences to the decisions we make, kid, and I am going to show you that," he says, gently slapping Harrison on his face.

Standing up quickly, he picks back up the pitchfork, walks over to Joseph, and stares down at him. "You walked in with this pitchfork. Ghost over there looks like he was stabbed with a pitchfork. Did you stab him?"

Ghost interrupts before Joseph can answer. "I can tell you who did everything."

Sebastian raises his hand to Ghost, signaling him to stop. "Shhhhh. I want to hear it from them. It's a little bit more fun that way."

Joseph looks up at him. "It's not mine. We met a farmer. It belongs to him," Joseph says.

Sebastian paces a couple steps.

"Okay. How about you?" Sebastian says, gazing down at JT. "I heard that you have Ghost's blood on your clothes. He took a pretty bad beating from one of you, I was told. It must have been you since you have his blood on you. And whoever did that to him is going to pay."

JT looks Tommy's way for a second. Tommy remains still, on his knees, watching Sebastian.

"I did it. I beat him so he wouldn't talk," JT says.

Harrison lifts up on his hands and knees.

"Well now, you must pay," Sebastian yells.

"It was me. He is lying to cover for me. I beat him so he wouldn't talk. They didn't want to. He was against it. It was me," Tommy announces.

Sebastian walks over and stands in front of him.

"Norman Drake's son. You really thought you were going to be able to protect him? From me? From us?" Sebastian says angrily. "See this is why the Destines are so stupid and weak. The Elder and the Ragnar Council truly believed that they could train you and you would be able to protect him. Well, you just helped me prove how wrong they were."

Unexpectedly, he lifts the pitchfork in the air and runs it into Tommy's chest. The pitchfork drives through him and sticks out of his back. Tommy's mouth drops in pain as he tries to grab the pitchfork.

Sebastian pushes it harder into him. Tommy gasps for air as blood runs from his mouth and hits the floor. Sebastian yanks it out of him. Tommy drops lifeless on his side.

"Noooooooooooooooo," Harrison yells trying to stand. Rena pushes him back down. JT stares at him with a scared expression. Jaylen and Joseph lower their heads with tears running down their faces.

Sebastian drops the pitchfork in front of Tommy's body. He closes his eyes, raising his hand straight up in the air. His followers chant emphatically.

"MAR... THAR."

"MAR... THAR."

They repeat it continuously.

Sebastian walks in front of Harrison. Rena backs off smiling at Sebastian.

"Feel how out of control you really are? No one can protect you from me. So why don't you just stand up and go open the Ark for me," Sebastian whispers down to Harrison.

Harrison rises slowly, grabbing his right wrist with his right palm facing up.

Sebastian giggles. "Really? Okay, try to hit me with those little attacks that Drake taught you. I want to see how pathetic it is."

Harrison squats slightly as he forces the energy from his Power Flow into his palm. Green energy circles around him causing the dust on the floor to blow around. Harrison screams as green electricity zaps from his hand. Sebastian and everyone kneeling stare in amazement.

"You want me to show you. I will show you what I learned from Drake. From his son," Harrison yells.

He screams louder as wind from him powering up gusts Sebastian next to the Ark and the others sliding on their backs. Suddenly, a giant green energy ball the size of a watermelon forms, hovering above his hand.

"What the heck is that?" Sebastian says.

"POWER LIGHT EXPLOSION," Harrison screams.

Harrison steps right in front of Sebastian, launching it at him. The giant green energy attack flies at him. He turns quickly to the side escaping the attack. It soars and crashes into the wall blowing the top part of the mountain up.

A giant chunk falls, crashing into the Purhara City. They all can hear the sound of destruction outside.

Harrison feels the floor start to shake. More parts of the mountain begin to crumble and tumble down. Sebastian's followers fall with parts of it as some run for safety past them. Finally, a giant part of the room crumbles and falls right behind Sebastian leaving him and the Ark on the edge of the opening.

Harrison runs at him throwing a punch, trying to punch him off the mountain. Sebastian grabs his hand, launching a punch of his own. Harrison pushes it down and hits him in the face with the other one.

Sebastian grabs Harrison's neck and hangs him towards the opening. Sebastian's back is facing the inside of the mountain as Harrison tries to keep his footing on the edge.

"I am going to drop you and pick up your dead body and open the Ark myself," Sebastian says, about to push him.

All of a sudden, Harrison sees the pitchfork burst through Sebastian's chest. Sebastian's eyes widen in pain as he starts to lose his grip on Harrison. Behind Sebastian stands Gavin, pushing the pitchfork in him harder. He pulls it out. Sebastian let's go of Harrison and falls off.

"Gavin," Harrison says confused.

Suddenly, the edge they are standing on starts leaning. The Ark slides towards them.

"Watch out," Harrison yells.

He pushes Gavin out the way as the Ark slams into Harrison. He grabs a hold of it. Green energy blasts in all different directions as he holds on for dear life. Harrison slides off with the Ark towards the ground. Slamming into the ground, Harrison sees everything go black.

CHAPTER
33

Things Looking Up

Opening his eyes, Harrison sees parts of the mountain surrounding him. Sebastian's followers lay around him, lifeless. Harrison's eyes shut and open every couple of minutes. Harrison notices the Ark next to him cracked and opened slightly. Lifting his head up, some of the Red Hawks walk towards him.

"We found him."

"I think he is still alive."

Harrison's head falls back.

Cool air blows his hair into his face from the cracked window, itching his forehead. Harrison blinks rapidly and is surprised. He is laying in the hospital back in his hometown. His mom lays next to him asleep in the chair holding his hand tightly. Moving gently, he wakes his mom up.

"Harrison, baby, take it easy," she says putting her other hand on his hand.

"Where is everyone?" Harrison asks trying to sit up.

"Honey, take it easy," she says. "Someone has been waiting here to talk to you about everything."

All of a sudden, the door opens and the Destine Elder walks in.

"Harrison. It's good to see you are finally awake. You sleep well?" he asks with a warm smile.

"Elder Dirk, are my friends okay?" Harrison says concerned.

Putting his hand on Harrison's chest, he eases him back down to the bed. "Would you mind excusing us, Ms. Grady?"

"Yes, Your Honor," she replies.

Getting up, she kisses Harrison's forehead, grinning with a tear running down her face.

"I am so glad you are okay," she says, walking out.

The Elder stands in front of the window and takes his hat off holding it against his chest. The breeze rushes through his thin hair making small strands in the front blow.

"Your friends are okay. The Red Hawks arrived the same time you fell with the Ark. They were able to get them and take them back safe and sound." Elder Dirk stares out the window.

"How did they know where to find us," Harrison asks.

"Tommy contacted the Red Hawks when he figured you all were about to run into trouble," he replies, glancing at Harrison.

Harrison closes his eyes trying to hold back the tears. "Were you able to bring back-"

"Yes, we were able to bring back Tommy's body. His family has it and is making preparations for his funeral."

He begins to sob. "It's all my fault."

"A lot of things played into Tommy's unfortunate death. You should not bear all the blame," he says looking back out the window.

"I was blind to the fact that Sebastian was part of that group. I should have been more observant," he says.

"I want to share something with you that I probably should have before," he pulls up a chair and sits beside him, laying his hat on his lap.

"We believe your father is still alive and we have pretty good evidence to prove that. He has gone rogue we believe, and we haven't figured out why yet. We haven't even old your mother this. I think personally, he knew something about this group forming years ago and wanted to take them out."

Harrison sits up slowly. "Yeah but my mom has the note that you slid underneath the door for him the night he left. You told him to leave early and to remain quiet."

"I did not write that note. I didn't even send your dad on the silent mission."

"What...what do you mean?"

"Your dad covered it up. I believe the Silver Falcons went on a mission that he had planned. He used me as a decoy to throw your mom off. I respect your dad too much to make him look like he was disobeying me and the Destine nation, so I took responsibility and covered it up," he stands up.

"You know for sure he is alive?" Harrison asks.

Turning back towards him, the Elder smiles softly at him.

"I do. And I want to help you out. You don't need to go rogue anymore either. We can bring your dad back, together."

He extends his hand. Harrison looks at it for a couple of seconds. He lifts his hand from under the covers and shakes his hand as firm as he can.

"We will talk about everything else when you get back to the academy after the summer break. But till then, rest up."

"Thanks. Sounds great," Harrison replies.

Harrison closes his eyes and goes back to sleep when the door shuts.

Harrison sits in the front seat of his mom's car feeling every bruise on each bump of the road. His neighborhood looks different.

"You know I didn't get to ask The Elder some of questions I had. I want to know-"

His mom interrupts him. "Harrison. You will have time to ask him in a couple of months. As of now, since you are home you aren't going to worry about anything like that. You understand me?"

"Yes, Ma'am."

They pull up to their house. JT, Joseph, Jaylen, Victoria, and Gavin are standing in the front yard waiting for them. Harrison sits up smiling as big as he can. Parking in the driveway, he bursts open the door and runs to them. They all embrace him, all trying to hug him tightly.

"I am so glad you guys are okay," Harrison says.

"We say the same thing about you," JT says pulling him close.

His mom walks past them. "I will go make some tea and we can sit inside and enjoy it."

Gavin latches onto him. Harrison hugs him tightly.

"Gavin. Thank you so much. I can't thank you enough for saving me," he says.

"Hey. What are neighbors for?" Gavin replies.

Laughter bursts out of each of them. Harrison walks over to Victoria. She pulls him close and cries.

"I am so sorry that you had to be part of this. I wish I would have listened to you in the fall," Harrison whispers in her ear.

She kisses him on the cheek. "I am just glad you're okay."

Harrison's mom slings the door open. "C' mon guys. I got the tea ready." They all march into the house. Harrison gets his bags off the floor where his mom dropped them and takes them to his room. His room looks the same. Dropping his bags on the floor he walks over to his nightstand.

His family picture from when he was two is still facing down. Slowly he picks it up staring at him and his dad. He rubs the glass on the picture smiling back at it.

"Harrison, hurry up and get in here. Your family is waiting," his mom yells.

"Okay," Harrison responds back.

He places the picture back on the nightstand, with his father looking up at him.

"You are right. My family is waiting," Harrison whispers to himself. Harrison exits his room, shutting the door behind him.

DAVID BARCO

David Barco was born and raised in Fayetteville, NC. He was a teacher and basketball coach at a high school in Fayetteville, NC for four years. In 2016 he was voted Best Teacher and Best School Coach in *The Fayetteville Observer Reader's Choice Awards.* He currently lives in Van Wert, Ohio and is a Student Director. He is married to his wife Danielle and they have a daughter named Peyton. DESTINES: THE ARK OF POWER is his debut novel.

DAVID BARCO

Follow him on Social Media:

Facebook: @AuthorDavidBarco
Instagram: @AuthorDavidBarco
Twitter: @davidbarco90

Author photo taken by Trey Snipes of *Snipes Media*. Follow him on Instagram @snipesmedia

If you enjoyed the first installment in Harrison's story, then please go leave a review on Amazon.

Make sure to share this book to your friends and family.

Harrison's story will continue in:

Destines: The Temple of Destiny

57944591R00227

Made in the USA
Middletown, DE
03 August 2019